The Last Sunday

The Last Sunday

Terry E. Hill

www.urbanbooks.net

Urban Books, LLC
97 N18th Street
Wyandanch, NY 11798

ISBN 13: 978-1-60162-395-9
ISBN 10: 1-60162-395-X

First Trade Paperback Printing November 2013
Printed in the United States of America

10 9 8 7 6 5 4 3 2 1

This is a work of fiction. Any references or similarities to actual events, real people, living or dead, or to real locales are intended to give the novel a sense of reality. Any similarity in other names, characters, places, and incidents is entirely coincidental.

Distributed by Kensington Publishing Corp.
Submit Wholesale Orders to:
Kensington Publishing Corp.
C/O Penguin Group (USA) Inc.
Attention: Order Processing
405 Murray Hill Parkway
East Rutherford, NJ 07073-2316
Phone: 1-800-526-0275
Fax: 1-800-227-9604

The Last Sunday

by

Terry E. Hill

Chapter 1

Danny St. John collapsed into Gideon Truman's waiting arms in the entry hall of Gideon's home in Hollywood Hills. It was 2:00 a.m. Danny coughed weakly. Gideon hoisted his arm around Danny's shoulder and carried him, limping, into the living room. The room was dark and still. The only sound was Danny gasping for breath. Gideon felt moisture on his bare arm as he laid the injured young man on the sofa.

"You're bleeding!" Gideon said in a panic. "What happened to you?"

The value Danny had assigned to his silence about his relationship with Hezekiah had been two million dollars. The money would buy his escape from the fear of being discovered by the media and, more so, of being hunted by Samantha Cleaveland. In his grief over Hezekiah's death, he reasoned this was the only way he could ever be safe. Danny knew Samantha would stop at nothing to remain the head of the ministry.

I know she killed him, and if she finds out who I am, she'll do the same to me. I have to get out of this city, were the thoughts that had rushed through his mind each night since Hezekiah's death. *Make the woman who destroyed my life pay for me to leave the country and disappear. God, please forgive me.*

"Who is this? How did you get this number?" Samantha had asked on the night Danny made the call that almost cost him his life.

"I'll ask the questions," had come his breathy response. "Is this Samantha Cleaveland?"

Samantha removed the phone from her ear and pressed the DISCONNECT button. The phone rang again before she could return it to her purse.

Unidentified Caller glowed on the screen. Samantha dropped the phone in her purse. After the third ring there was a pause, and then the ringing started again.

Samantha snatched the phone from her purse and asked, "Who is this?"

"Hang up on me again and you'll regret it," came the reply. "Now, answer my question. Is this Samantha Cleaveland?"

"Yes, it is," she said calmly. "What do you want?"

"I know about Danny," the voice said, waiting for a reaction.

"Who is Danny?" she asked impatiently.

"You know exactly who he is."

"Look, whoever you are, I don't have time for this. Either get to the point or I'm hanging up and calling the police," she said.

"Such impatience for a pastor," he said sarcastically.

"I'm hanging up. Don't call me again, or I will call the police."

"If you hang up this phone," the voice said aggressively, "I'll be forced to turn over evidence to the media that proves that before your husband died, he was involved with a man."

Samantha leaned forward in her seat. "What evidence?" she asked. "That is preposterous. My husband wasn't gay."

"To start with, I've got a stack of e-mails full of language so graphic, it would make even you blush. There's some in there that even suggest you knew about it."

"You're lying."

"Don't call me a liar again, or this time next week you and Hezekiah will be on the cover of every tabloid in the country," the voice said angrily.

"How dare you try to blackmail me! I've just buried my husband. What kind of monster are you?"

"You can save the grieving widow routine for your Sunday morning sermon. I know you were glad to get rid of him. He almost cost you millions. I wouldn't be surprised if you had something to do with his death yourself."

Samantha froze after hearing those last words. With lightning speed and cold logic, she weighed the cost of either notion circulating in public and decided she could not risk even the rumors being discussed.

"What do you want from me?"

"Now, that's what I like. A woman who knows when she's been beaten."

"There's no need to be sarcastic," Samantha said coolly.

"You're not in a position to preach to me. In this relationship I'm the preacher. You do what I say. Got it?"

Samantha said nothing.

"I want one million dollars cash. You have seventy-two hours to make it happen. That gives you until Saturday to come up with the money."

"A million dollars? You're out of your mind," she said.

"I am? Then I guess I should hang up and let Gideon Truman decide if I'm crazy or not."

"No, wait," Samantha said quickly. "Don't hang up. I don't have that kind of money."

"Bullshit," the caller said. "You collect twice that much every Sunday morning. Why don't you take up a special offering this Sunday? Tell them it's so you can continue to do God's work."

"There is no way I can come up with that much cash on such short notice."

"Every time you lie to me, the price goes up five hundred thousand dollars. It's now at one and a half million."

"You can't prove any of this. My husband was not gay," Samantha said emphatically.

"Two million," the voice said calmly.

Samantha paused to regain her composure. "What will you give me in return?" she finally asked.

"My word that you will never hear from me again," the voice said sincerely.

Samantha scoffed. "The word of a blackmailer."

"I prefer to think of myself as a keeper of secrets."

"I'll need more time," Samantha said hesitantly.

"You don't have more time. I will call you in two days with instructions. If you contact the police, I will immediately send copies of every e-mail in my possession to all the major news outlets in the country. I know that sounds like a cliché, but I had to say it, anyway," the voice said and disconnected the line.

Now Danny lay bleeding on the couch as Gideon rushed to the bathroom for a towel. When he returned and flicked on the living room light, he saw the full extent of Danny's injuries. Blood surrounded a hole in the sleeve of the dark blue jacket he wore. His eyes were puffy, and there were fresh scratches on one side of his face.

"I have to get you to the hospital," Gideon said as he dabbed the blood on Danny's arm with the wet towel.

"No!" was the first breathless word Danny spoke since he had entered the house.

"You're hurt. It looks like you've been shot."

"It's only a flesh wound," Danny said, grasping his arm. "I'll be fine. The bullet just grazed me."

"Bullet!" Gideon exclaimed. "You were shot!"

"No. Shot at. They thought they killed me, but he missed. I pretended to be dead until they left."

"Who did this to you? Were you robbed?"

"No," Danny said, avoiding Gideon's worried gaze.

"Then what happened?"

Danny rested his head on the cushion and said nothing.

"Danny, you have to tell me what happened. We have to call the police. This is serious. You could have been killed."

Danny looked up into Gideon's caring eyes. In them he saw the same concern and love he had seen when he looked at Hezekiah. He could feel the exchange of pain pass between them as if they were one body and one soul. It both frightened and comforted him. No one before Hezekiah had ever made him feel so safe. No one had ever made him feel connected. Now Gideon, a man he had met as a direct result of Hezekiah's death, sat on the sofa next to him, tending to his injured arm and comforting his wounded soul after a narrow escape from death.

"Danny," Gideon urged, "you have to tell me what happened. Are you in any type of trouble?"

Danny detected the hint of suspicion that hung on the end of his question.

"Do you know who did this to you?"

"Yes," Danny answered reluctantly. "I know who it was."

Gideon pried his eyes away from Danny's tormented face to give him room to respond. "Tell me who did this to you, Danny. Was it Samantha?" he asked softly.

Moments passed as the answer weighed on Danny's lips. The flow of blood slowly subsided as Gideon continued to apply pressure on the gash. Only the skin had been broken. The towel felt cold and wet in his hand. The tips of his fingers were now covered with Danny's blood.

"Was it Samantha?" he repeated.

Danny looked again at Gideon's face and softly replied, "Yes. They left me for dead."

Gideon then bolted from the sofa and darted across the room to a telephone on a small desk near the window. Los Angeles slept at their feet. In the dead of night the skyline sparkled like a thousand stars.

"No!" Danny shouted weakly behind him. "You can't." Danny made his way to Gideon's side and grabbed his hand. "Stay out of this, Gideon. I don't want you to get involved."

"*Involved?*" Gideon said through anguished breaths. "I'm already involved. I love you, and I'm not going to let that woman get away with this."

Still clutching Gideon's hand that held the phone, Danny froze when he heard the words. He looked sadly into Gideon's eyes and replied, "*Love?*"

Gideon looked embarrassed. He hadn't intended to make such a revelation so soon. Especially not under these circumstances. But now that the words had been spoken, he pressed on. "That's right. You heard me correctly. I love you, Danny St. John, and I'm not going to let anyone hurt you again."

Danny quickly recovered from the shock and brushed the declaration of love from the air between them. "You can't call the police, Gideon," he said, bracing himself for his own confession.

"Why not? She tried to kill you. It's attempted murder. She probably used the same gun she used on Hezekiah. She has to be stopped."

"Listen to me, Gideon. It's all very complicated. And I don't really know how to explain it to you."

Gideon returned the telephone to the cradle. And calmly he said, "Just tell me what happened."

"Do you promise not to judge me until I've told you everything?"

"Yes, I promise," Gideon said with a hesitant voice.

"Come back to the sofa and I'll tell you everything," Danny said, guiding him by the hand.

The two men sat at opposite ends of the sofa, and Danny dramatically began his tale with, “I tried to blackmail her.”

“Blackmail!” Gideon jerked forward and shouted.

“You promised not to judge me until I told you everything.”

Gideon leaned back on the sofa with both eyes locked on Danny as he continued.

“I know it was wrong. I’m not sure what I was thinking. I was afraid. I was confused and . . .” His words trailed off as he tried to make sense of the nightmare he now found himself in. “I thought if I could get enough money, I would be able to just disappear. You don’t know what it’s been like for me since Hezekiah’s death. Not only am I missing him more than you could ever imagine, but I’m also afraid for my life. I hadn’t slept a full night until I moved in here with you. I look over my shoulder every time I leave the house. I can’t walk down the street or go to work without thinking the same person she got to kill Hezekiah is following me.”

“But blackmail? How could you have thought you could get away with something like that?”

Danny looked at him sharply.

“I’m sorry,” Gideon said, leaning back again. “Go on.”

“One day, about a year ago, Hezekiah lost his cell phone, and he used mine to call her. I don’t know why I saved her number in my contacts, but it’s been there ever since he made that call. I guess even back then I was afraid of her finding out who I was, and thought if something every happened to me, maybe someone would check my contacts. I even put in the note section, ‘Question in the event of my untimely death.’ Anyway, I finally got up the nerve to call her and ask for the money.”

“How much?” Gideon asked like the inquisitive reporter he was. His tone was now neutral and professional, but passion and fear percolated just beneath the calm surface.

"Two million dollars," Danny said with unmistakable embarrassment. "I know it's crazy, but somehow I'd convinced myself that she owed it to me. She took Hezekiah from me. She ruined my life and relegated me to a paranoid state that at times was almost unbearable. I didn't know what else to do. I know I wasn't thinking clearly, but at the time it seemed like my only option.

"Convincing her that I was serious was easier than I thought. She tried to blow me off at first, but before I knew it, she was agreeing to give me the money. By then there was no turning back. I called her again two days later and told her to meet me at midnight in an empty parking lot in Griffith Park, just off Western Avenue, and she agreed. I told her to come alone. I should have known she would bring someone with her."

Danny then recounted the events in the park as if he were narrating a movie.

"It was just past midnight when I approached her car in the parking lot. She looked so calm, almost smug, sitting in a disgustingly white Bentley. I tapped on the car window. She looked up at me, and I instantly felt like she could see right through me. It was a very frightening feeling. I motioned for her to roll down the window. 'Hello, Samantha,' I said and bent down to the open window. 'It's nice to finally meet you. I'm Danny St. John.'

"Samantha looked me in the eye and said, 'I should have guessed it would be you, Danny. So you're the man who was sleeping with my husband.'

"'Yes. I'm also the man who loved him. Is that the money?' I said and pointed past her to a bag on the passenger seat. 'May I have it please?' I remember she kept trying to look over my shoulder, but I was standing too close to the car for her to see around me.

"Then she reached for the bag and said, 'They don't come much lower than you, do they, Danny?' I began to suspect she was just stalling for time. 'Sleeping with a married man and then blackmailing his widow,' she said with a slight snarl.

"I laughed nervously and said, 'This coming from a woman who killed her husband. You're in no position to judge me. Now, give me the money, and you'll never hear from me again.'

"We looked at each other intently. Seeing her in person, I immediately understood why Hezekiah had fallen in love with her. You met her. Even in the dark park I could tell she was one of the most beautiful women I'd ever seen. I saw pure, raw passion burning in her eyes. But I also saw evil, and a woman who would stop at nothing to get what she wanted, whether it was love, money, or power. An interesting thing happened to me at that point. In the dark there didn't seem to be any need for defenses. I spoke to her almost as if I were looking into a mirror.

"'Was this your plan all along?' she asked, looking me directly in the eyes. 'Was it always about the money, Danny?'

"For some reason I wasn't offended. I almost felt she had a right to know the truth, so I told her, 'This might be difficult for someone like you to understand, but it was never about money. I loved Hezekiah. Did you ever love him?'

"'In my own way,' she said with a nod of concession.

"I didn't even think before asking her, 'Then why did you kill him?' The words just came out. She paused for a moment. I could tell she was feeling the same way as me. There was something eerie between us, almost intimate.

"That's when she said, 'It's the law of the universe, Danny. In order to get something you want, you have to give up something you love.'"

Gideon let out a slight gasp when he heard Danny say the words, but he said nothing.

Danny continued his incredible story.

"'Then I guess that law worked well for you,' I said, looking her in the eye. When I said the last word, I felt a hand on my shoulder. I jerked around and found myself standing nose to nose with this massive man in a suit.

"Samantha shouted out loud, 'He's got a gun, David. Shoot him! Shoot him!'

"The man pushed me into the side of the car. We wrestled and fell to the ground. We rolled on the pavement. Our arms and legs were flying in every direction. Samantha unlocked the car door and jumped out and screamed, 'Shoot him, David! He tried to kill me. Shoot him now!'

"Suddenly a shot rang out, and I stopped wrestling with the man. I went limp on top of him, and after a moment so did he. I could hear Samantha walking toward us. I opened my eyes slightly and saw her reach down and snatch the gun away from the guy's hand. She took three steps backward, all while aiming the gun with both hands at us on the ground. His chest was heaving, but I didn't move.

"'David,' she said, still pointing the gun at us. 'David, are you okay?'

"Suddenly the guy moved under me and pushed me off his chest.

"'Get up, David,' Samantha said, directing the gun at me. 'Is he dead?'

"'I think so,' the guy said. 'He's not breathing.'

"'Good.' She said it as if they had just avoided a car accident.

"Then the man said, 'What are you talking about? I just killed a man.'

"'It was self-defense. If you hadn't been here, he would have killed me.' I couldn't believe my ears. She was claiming that I had tried to kill her. I swear to you, Gideon, I didn't have a gun and that was never my intent. I just wanted the money so I could disappear from the face of the earth."

"I believe you," Gideon said softly.

Danny continued, feeling a modicum of relief that Gideon believed he had had no intention of harming Samantha. "The man reached into his pocket for his cell phone and began to dial. Samantha grabbed his arm and said, 'What are you doing?'

"'I'm calling the police,' he yelled. 'We just killed a man. I'm calling the police.'

"'David, wait a minute,' she said. 'Let me at least check to see if he's dead. He may still be alive.'

"Samantha walked to me. She knelt down and first checked my coat pockets and then the pockets of my pants. I held my breath the entire time she was searching me. She stood up and faced the guy and said, 'He doesn't have a gun.'

"'What?' the man screamed.

"'You just killed an unarmed man,' she said coldly.

"'Oh shit!' the guy said. 'Oh shit! Oh God, Samantha, you said he had a gun! You said he was going to kill you.'

"'It looked like he had a gun in his pocket. I thought he had a gun,' Samantha said curtly.

"The guy, David, began to pace back and forth next to what they thought was my dead body. 'What have I done?' he said. 'Look what you made me do!'

"I saw Samantha throw the gun into her car. David was beginning to panic. She grabbed him by his shoulders and said, 'David, stop,' trying to calm him down. 'Listen to me. We have to leave. No one knows we were here. We need to just leave now and never speak of this to anyone. Do you understand me?'

"'Leave?' He was almost hysterical. 'Just leave him here? Are you sure?'

"'Yes, I'm sure. Everything will be fine. I want you to go home to Scarlett and not say a word about this to anyone.'"

Gideon bolted upright. "Scarlett?" he said. "She's a member of the church's board of trustees. That must've been her husband, David Shackelford."

Danny ignored him and continued. "Samantha kept shaking his shoulders. 'Do you understand me? Someone will find him here in the morning. They'll never be able to link any of this to either you or me as long as we both agree that it never happened. Okay?'

"'Are you sure no one will find out?' the guy asked.

"'I'm sure. Now, go to your car and wait for me at the bottom of the hill. I'll follow you as far as Wilshire Boulevard. Then I want you to drive straight home and put this out of you mind.'

"The guy said he understood. Samantha started to dust off his suit and said, 'Make sure you are at church tomorrow. I want to see you there with Scarlett on one side and Natalie on your lap. We have to act like everything is normal. Do you understand?'

"'Yes,' he said.

"'Good. Everything is going to be fine, David. I'll call you in the morning to check on you.'"

Danny paused for a moment and took a deep breath. Recalling the events had caused his body to tremble slightly. Then he continued.

"I heard the guy walk away. It was so dark that I couldn't see him after he was only a few feet away from me. I could still see her standing near the car, watching him. Suddenly I heard a thud in the distance. I think he fell down the side of the short cliff that led to the road below, where he parked his car. Eventually, I heard a car start in the distance. When Samantha heard the car, she walked back to where I lay on the ground. She lifted my wrist.

"That's when I heard her say, 'I assume Hezekiah gave this to you, so technically it belongs to me.' She took the Rolex you gave me off my wrist, removed my wallet, and said, 'Good-bye, Danny St. John. It was so nice to finally meet you.'

"She got into her car and drove away." Danny said, dropping his head on the cushion again. "They just left me there. What kind of person would do that? I can't stop shaking."Danny coughed again as the two sat in silence. He could now feel the throbbing in his arm.

"This is incredible. I can't believe you would try something so crazy," Gideon said softly.

"You know what she's capable of. You could have been killed."

"I was desperate, Gideon. I wasn't thinking clearly. I know it was wrong. I'm sorry."

"I'm not talking about the blackmail."

Danny looked at him with surprise.

"I understand how you could conclude that blackmailing her was your only option. Hell, I might have thought the same thing if it were me. You made a mistake. We all do. What I'm talking about is you underestimating just how dangerous she really is. The thought of losing you, Danny, is more that I can take. Please don't ever do anything crazy like that again. It took me my whole life to find you, and I don't know what I would do if I lost you."

Gideon pulled Danny's quivering body to his chest and held him tightly. Gideon began to sob in his ear. "Please don't ever do anything that stupid again, Danny. I can't bear the thought of not having you in my life."

Danny began to match his sobs breath for breath and tear for tear. The two men held each other close and cried for what they had almost lost. They cried for what they now had found in each other.

"She's going to pay for what she did to you, Danny St. John. I promise I'm going to make her pay."

Chapter 2

Hattie Williams looked at her reflection in the oval vanity mirror. Her eyes followed the road map of lines that had been paved by life in her almond skin. She could almost pinpoint the exact event that had preceded each distinct wrinkle. The creases in her brow had appeared shortly after her husband's death ten years earlier. The lines at the corner of each eye had come when she buried her mother. The hollows in her cheeks were the most recent indication that she had survived yet another tragedy. On a Sunday only three months ago, her beloved pastor, Hezekiah T. Cleaveland, had been gunned down in the pulpit of New Testament Cathedral.

Hattie ran the stiff bristles of a silver hairbrush through gray-streaked hair that cascaded over her shoulders. She never took her eyes off her face, fearing that if she looked away, she would miss the vision she knew was coming. Her few strands of black hair were awash in a sea of silky gray, which shimmered from the light of the full moon. Crickets could be heard chirping in the flower bed of pink and lavender foxgloves just outside her window.

She knew a message was only moments away. The light-headedness she always felt just before a vision came had caused her to wilt onto the stool at the vanity and had left her helpless, able only to wait for the scene to appear in the mirror. Sheer white curtains bristled slightly from the evening breeze, and the scent of lilac powder from a cloth-covered box on the vanity filled the room.

And then he appeared. Hattie's face in the mirror slowly gave way to the image of Hezekiah Cleaveland. He looked just as he had only months earlier, when he was full of life, love, and hope. Light seemed to pour from beneath the surface of his glowing brown skin. His eyes were clear and bright, even brighter than she remembered. He looked to her lovingly, as if he knew she was there. But there was a divide between them that prevented her from reaching out and touching his gentle face.

Hezekiah didn't speak, but she could hear every word in his heart, as if he were in the room. She felt every emotion. There was a peace that she had never felt from him when he was alive. His face was content, but beneath the surface she could also sense fear.

"What are you afraid of, Pastor?" she asked out loud.

But he did not respond. Instead, the feelings of fear and concern seemed to grow and overtake the peace and contentment.

"You're with the Lord now," she said gently. "No one can hurt you anymore."

Hezekiah's expression grew dire as her words evaporated into the moonlight. Now a pain so intense that she could feel it in her stomach poured from the mirror. Then she heard the words "Don't let her do it." Hezekiah's lips didn't move, but she knew his voice. Then she heard it again. "Don't let her do it."

"Do what, Pastor?" she asked the mirror. Hattie placed the silver brush on the vanity and leaned closer to the image. "Don't let who do what? I can't know what I'm not told." She reached out and placed her open palm on the mirror and touched Hezekiah's cheek. The glass surface was hot against her skin. She jerked away as if she had touched an open flame. Hezekiah looked more intently at her. A tear fell from his eye as he stared pleadingly.

"Don't let Samantha do it again," were the words from the mirror. "Please don't let her do it again."

At that point Hattie understood clearly. The guilt she had felt for not preventing his death washed over her like a flood. She had known Hezekiah was in danger months before he was killed, but she did nothing to prevent his death. She remembered the warning vision she had received in her kitchen window weeks before he was killed.

Until that sunny day four months earlier, Hattie had never seen so many warriors on the battlefield of one man's soul. She had seen deadly equestrians attacking Hezekiah as she sat helplessly before her kitchen window. A white horse whose rider was death had galloped at full speed toward Hezekiah. Another horseman had thrashed at his breastplate. Confusion, riding a black horse, had delivered crushing blows to his head, and death had leveled the final assault, which had left him lifeless in the dust, under the horse's hooves. Recalling the horrible images brought tears to Hattie's eyes.

"I couldn't interfere with the path you chose for yourself, Pastor," she said pleadingly to his tormented image in her mirror. "A man's life is between himself and God. It's not my place to interfere," she added, appealing to his unresponsive face.

The words came again. This time they were more intense. "Don't let her do it again."

Hattie began to sob out loud. "I prayed for you, Pastor," Hattie said through her tears. "You know I did my best to intercede, but that was the path you chose."

"Don't let her do it again," came even louder. Hezekiah's face did not change. Her pleas had no effect on his expression or the feelings that poured from the mirror.

"But what could I have done to stop her? What can I do now? I'm an old woman. All I have is my faith and my prayers," she said pleadingly. "That's all I have to give anyone, and I gave that freely to you from the first day I met you until the day you died."

Her words crashed onto the flat, shiny surface of the mirror and rushed back at her like a gust of wind, causing her tears to flow in a steady stream. "I'm so sorry, Pastor. I should have done something. I should have told you about the danger that was ahead, but . . . but I just didn't know how. Please forgive me, Pastor. I should have warned you."

Hattie felt tormented by Hezekiah's unyielding glare, which seemed to look straight through her. She cupped a hand over her quivering mouth and sobbed uncontrollably. But the forgiveness she sought was nowhere to be found in his pained expression or felt in his tortured spirit. He was oblivious to her pain and consumed by his own.

"Don't let her do it again," his voice insisted. "Don't let her hurt him."

Hattie froze when she heard the words. "Who, Pastor?" she begged. "Hurt who?" Her face was wet with tears as she leaned closer to the mirror. She reached her hand out again to the mirror but stopped short of touching it, remembering the fire she had felt during her last attempt to cross the divide. "Tell me who, Pastor," she desperately implored. "Who?"

When she said the words, the room grew still. She felt somehow suspended in time. The quivering curtains rested dead against the window seal. The chirping crickets could no longer be heard. Hezekiah's face became soft and expressionless. Hattie had sat frozen in front of the mirror for what seemed like an eternity when she finally heard his calm voice say, "Don't let her hurt Danny."

She could feel the fear that had flowed so powerfully from the mirror dissipate into the night as the words reverberated in her head. Once again peace came forward as the dominant emotion she felt from Hezekiah. The light from deep within him began to glow again, and his eyes were as bright as they had been when he first appeared. She knew he was free now. He had spoken his heart and revealed his love. Now he could rest in peace.

"It's all right, Pastor. I know you loved him, but more importantly, he knew it too," she said calmly as his image slowly faded from the mirror. "You can rest now."

The shimmering glass building had finally risen from the dust. The construction of the new church and media center was complete. It had taken three years, forty-five million dollars, and the lives of three men to build the shrine to the Cleavelands. The ten-story, twenty-five-thousand-seat sanctuary sparkled like a diamond on the lush green ten-acre compound in the heart of downtown Los Angeles. Three months had passed since Hezekiah's death. Samantha had insisted that construction continue the day after his murder and that the workers not stop until the last nail was hammered, the final Italian tile was laid, and the last glass panel was installed.

Cement trucks had churned along dirt roads while Hezekiah's cold body had lain in state in the mortuary. Scaffolding had been erected precariously along the sides of the steel skeleton, and workers had pounded, bolted, and soldered on all levels of the structure. On the morning after Hezekiah's death Samantha had received a call from Benny Winters, the general contractor for the construction project.

"Mrs. Cleaveland, this is Benny . . . ," he had said timidly. "Benny Winters. Ma'am, I don't know what to say. This is such a tragedy. Pastor Cleaveland was such a great man. He will be deeply missed."

"Thank you, Benny," Samantha had replied with a measured dose of grief.

"Everyone on the crew asked that I convey to you their deepest condolences."

"Please tell them, 'Thank you,' and to remember me in their prayers," she said, finding it tiresome to feign sorrow.

"Of course, I've halted construction in honor of Pastor Cleaveland, and I will wait until I receive further instructions from the board of trustees before we resume."

Samantha was standing in the window of her study at the Cleaveland estate on that Monday morning when Benny called. A burning cigarette in an ashtray on her desk released ribbons of smoke into the room. When she heard the words, her body became rigid.

"Who told you to stop construction?" she asked through clenched teeth.

"Well . . . no one, ma'am," Benny replied gently. "I assumed that under the circumstances the board of trustees would think it only appropriate."

At that moment in the conversation Samantha lost all ability to play the role of grieving widow convincingly.

"Mr. Winters," she said curtly, "you assumed incorrectly. First of all, stopping construction is neither your nor the board of trustees's decision. My husband and I raised the forty-five million dollars that is paying your salary and that of your crew. Therefore, in the absence of my husband, the decision becomes mine alone."

She took a threatening step toward the window, as if Benny were standing in front of her. "Secondly," she continued, no longer able to contain her contempt for the presumptuous blue-collar worker, "I want you to get your full crew onto that construction site within the hour."

Benny Winters couldn't believe what he was hearing. "But, Mrs. Cleaveland, it's standard industry practice in situations like this, when the primary client dies unexpectedly, to stop all work for at least two days. It's just common respect."

"I need you to respect me," she snapped. "Hezekiah is no longer your primary client, nor is the board of trustees. From the moment that bullet entered his head, I became your primary client. Do you understand?"

Benny was speechless. The cold way in which she spoke of her husband's death, which had happened only the day before, the contempt in her voice, and the callousness of her words left him both angry and afraid.

"I said, do you understand me, Mr. Winters?"

"Yes, m-ma'am," he finally stammered.

"Good. From now on do not make any decisions without consulting with me first." As she spoke, her anger slowly began to dissipate and the grieving widow returned. "Now, after I've buried my husband, I would like to meet with you to go over some changes to the designs. My secretary will contact you to let you know when."

"Ch-changes?" Benny sputtered. "What sort of . . ." As the words spilled from his lips, he imagined Samantha's eyebrows shooting up and her temper rising. He stopped short of completing the question and simply added, "Yes, ma'am."

"Good, Mr. Winters," she said. "I'm glad we have an understanding."

The construction went uninterrupted from that day forward for the next three months, and the world fell deeper in love with Samantha Cleaveland. Her face graced the covers of major newspapers and national magazines. The headline in the *New York Times* read, BRAVE WIDOW CONTINUES THE DREAM OF HER HUSBAND. The *Huffington Post*'s headline was, SAMANTHA CLEAVELAND, RELIGION'S JACKIE O. The front page of the *London Times* proclaimed, SAMANTHA CLEAVELAND, AMERICAN HEROINE.

Images of the beautiful woman flashed nightly on every major TV network. In the wake of her husband's death, she became one of the most beloved and photographed women in the country. The gleaming cathedral became a symbol of hope and fortitude for millions of people facing home foreclosures, the death of loved ones, and life-threatening illnesses.

"If Samantha Cleaveland can survive tragedy, then so can we," became the national mantra. After hearing of Samantha's decision to continue the construction uninterrupted, many said through tears, "She is such a brave woman."

And now the sun-drenched cathedral was complete. Cantilevered pews spilled from the top of the cavernous stadium down to the pulpit, affording all in attendance unobstructed views of Samantha Cleaveland. The slanted and jutting cathedral walls were constructed of five hundred thousand rectangular panes of glass, which had been woven together by threads of steel, forming a patchwork quilt of California sunlight, powder puff clouds, and pristine blue sky. Two fifty-foot-high waterfalls, constructed of pure white marble imported from quarries in Italy, flanked the pulpit and released sheets of water that flowed almost silently into pools at their base. The behemoth liquid works of art had added an additional two million dollars to the final cost of construction.

Two thirty-by-forty-foot JumboTron screens had been mounted at angles in the front corners of the room, offering front-row views of the beautiful Samantha Cleaveland even to those parishioners seated in the back rows during the Sunday morning services.

Glossy photographs of the cathedral appeared on the cover of that week's issues of *Newsweek, Time, Essence,* and *O,* two of the headlines reading, AMERICA'S MOST BEAUTIFUL CHURCH and THE CRYSTAL HOUSE BUILT BY PASTOR SAMANTHA

CLEAVELAND. The stories inside were dotted with pictures of a defiant and stunning Samantha standing in front of the cathedral.

"Did you ever consider not completing the construction of New Testament Cathedral after the tragic death of your husband, Pastor Hezekiah Cleaveland?" was one of the questions posed in *Newsweek*.

"Never," was Samantha's quoted response. "This was not only the vision of my late husband, but it was mine as well. His death was a tragedy, but I'm a woman of faith, and I never doubted for a second that this was exactly what God wanted me to do."

The first service to be held in the new sanctuary was scheduled for the coming Sunday morning. Parishioners from around the country and the world had RSVP'd for the privilege of sitting in one of the twenty-five thousand seats at the inaugural service. A special section at the front of the sanctuary had been reserved for the hundreds of VIPs whose press secretaries, managers, publicists, and schedulers had called to announce they would be in attendance. The list of celebrities, professional athletes, local, national, and international politicians, and six- figure donors who would make an appearance assured that the world's media would be focused that day on Samantha Cleaveland and the house of worship she had built, despite her grief and the unimaginable tragedy she had endured.

Cynthia Pryce pressed the button on the remote control, causing the flat-screen television in her den to flicker and bounce from one image to the next. It was seven o'clock on a Tuesday evening, and many of the air waves were dedicated to the evening news. On every news station Cynthia was assaulted either by stories heralding the grand opening of New Testament Cathedral or by the smiling face, coiffed hair, and conture swathed Samantha Cleaveland. She was everywhere. CNN, FOX . . . all the networks and all the local news stations.

Cynthia Pryce pressed the remote harder every time Samantha's high-definition smiling head filled the screen. Her fingers ached from the death grip she had on the device.

"Tonight our guest is the incomparable Pastor Samantha—" said Anderson Cooper. Cynthia flinched and quickly pressed the remote.

"Everyone wants to know just how you were able to build this magnificent church even though you just lost your husband," said Tavis Smiley.

"Faith in—"

Cynthia pressed the remote hard again before being battered by Samantha's response.

"New Testament Cathedral has risen like a phoenix from the ashes in downtown Los Angeles," the blank-faced brunette anchor read from the teleprompter. "The first service at New Testament Cathedral's new forty-five-million-dollar sanctuary is only five days away."

Cynthia had grown weary of running from Samantha and allowed the reporter to fill her head and home with the latest on the woman she hated.

"This coming Sunday morning, only eight weeks after the horrific assassination of her husband, Pastor Hezekiah Cleaveland," the reporter continued, "Pastor Samantha Cleaveland will preach the first sermon in her new twenty-five-thousand-seat glass cathedral."

Cynthia could feel the muscles in her shoulders and neck tighten as the woman spoke.

"In addition to the millions of viewers around the world who are expected to watch the live broadcast, the guest list for the service includes such names as Magic

Johnson and his wife, Cookie, Oprah Winfrey and Gayle King, Tyler Perry, Kevin Costner, Janet Jackson, former president Bill Clinton, and former secretaries of state Hillary Clinton and Condoleezza Rice."

Cynthia's left eye began to twitch as the reporter droned on about the woman who had captured the hearts and minds of millions. She twisted nervously on the leather sofa and resisted the urge to change the channel once again.

The demise of Hezekiah and Samantha Cleaveland had become an obsession for Cynthia over the past two years. She derived a modicum of pride from knowing that she had leaked the story of Hezekiah's homosexual affair to the *Los Angeles Chronicle* reporter Lance Savage.

If that little reporter hadn't gotten himself killed, she thought as she stared blankly at the TV screen, the story of that disgusting affair would have been front page news, and I would be the first lady of New Testament Cathedral right now.

It was Cynthia who had printed dozens of e-mails that Hezekiah had sent to Danny St. John from the computer in his office. These communications chronicled the passionate and emotional details of the relationship between one of the most powerful ministers in the country and a young social worker in downtown Los Angeles.

Cynthia squirmed even more when she recalled the cold night months earlier, when she talked with Lance Savage in her Mercedes, behind the large mounds of dirt piled near the then metal skeleton of New Testament Cathedral.

"I knew I couldn't trust you. This is extortion," she had said to the balding reporter.

"Now hold on, Mrs. Pryce," Lance had said seductively. "I wouldn't call it extortion. It's more like quid pro quo. You do something for me and . . . well, I make you the first lady of New Testament Cathedral."

A few minutes with this cretin, Cynthia had thought as the little man massaged her knee, *is a small price to pay to get Hezekiah and Samantha out of the way permanently.*

She then looked Lance in the eye and said, "I'll do this on one condition."

Cynthia squirmed more on the leather sofa in her den as the humiliation she had endured that cold night played in her head like a movie.

Lance looked at her guardedly and asked, "What's the condition?"

"That as soon as we're done, you'll let me send the article to your editor."

She remembered how horrible Lance had sounded when he laughed and said, "When we're done, I'll probably be too tired to send the story myself. It's a deal."

He removed his jacket and loosened his tie while Cynthia watched his every move.

Cynthia remembered how he had leaned forward and kissed her hard on the lips. She could still taste the remnants of stale cigarettes on his lips. His breathing became intense as he kissed her neck and caressed her breasts. "Mrs. Pryce," he panted, "you are such a beautiful woman."

Cynthia could almost smell his cheap aftershave in her den as she recalled the horrible events of that night.

Lance fumbled awkwardly as he unbuttoned Cynthia's blouse. She felt his lips gently circling her exposed nipples. The sounds of a cold wind whirling at the base of the building and the hum of the freeway in the distance could be heard through the car's darkly tinted windows.

Cynthia lifted Lance's head to hers and kissed him passionately. Her panting matched his breath for breath. She skillfully undid his belt buckle and pants and firmly gripped his erect member.

"Fuck me," she moaned. "I want you to fuck me, Lance."

Lance fumbled with the levers on the side of the seat and pressed buttons until he found the one to recline the driver's seat. Their writhing bodies descended in unison into the depths of the vehicle as the seat glided into a fully prone position.

Lance lifted Cynthia's skirt, slid her panties down around her ankles, and squirmed to lower his trousers. He then climbed on top of her to explore her waiting mouth once again.

"Hurry," she said in a whisper. "Fuck me, and then we'll send the story to your editor together."

Lance moaned as he thrust his hips against hers. "I'm going to fuck you first, and then we'll both fuck the Cleavelands."

Cynthia lifted her knees toward the roof of the car and in the process turned on the windshield wipers. Lance entered her forcefully and pounded double time to the beat of the whooshing rubber blades.

Cynthia could almost feel him pounding into her flesh as she thought of the sacrifices she had made that night. She remembered holding him tightly and raising her hips to meet each thrust. The two writhed in passion, heightened by the euphoric prospect of the Cleavelands' demise. The car bounced uncontrollably until Lance reached a fevered climax and then collapsed, breathless, into her arms.

Cynthia was the first to speak. "It's time. Get your computer from the backseat."

Exhausted, Lance rolled back into the passenger seat. "Wow," he panted. "You don't waste any time, do you?"

"That was the agreement wasn't it? I fuck you, and you fuck Hezekiah. Are you planning to back out again?"

"No, no," he protested. "I'm a man of my word." With his trousers still around his ankles, Lance reached behind and retrieved the laptop. He turned on the computer, and the glowing screen lit up the car. As he waited for the article to appear, he said, “You’re quite a woman, Mrs. Pryce. New Testament is in for one hell of a ride.”

The headline of the article flashed on the screen: PASTOR HEZEKIAH T. CLEAVELAND INVOLVED IN SECRET HOMOSEXUAL AFFAIR.

“There it is,” Lance said. “This is what you’ve been waiting for.”

“That’s exactly what I’ve been waiting for,” Cynthia said with a smile. “Now, stop wasting time. Let’s send it.”

“Okay, Mrs. Pryce. Just press ENTER and you’ll be one step closer to being queen of New Testament Cathedral.”

Cynthia returned her seat to its upright position. With her clothes still disheveled, she pressed the key without saying a word.

After a message appeared on the screen, confirming the article had been sent, Cynthia looked at Lance and firmly said, “Now, pull your pants up and get out of my car.”

The events of that night were etched in her brain. As Cynthia sat in her den, now months later, staring at the oversize head of Samantha Cleaveland on her television, she had no remorse for using her body to expose the story that would have brought down the Cleaveland dynasty. Her only regret was that the contemptible reporter and Hezekiah hadn’t lived long enough to make her sacrifice worthwhile. “If that little bastard was still alive, I’d fuck him again, and anyone else, if that’s what it would take to get rid of Samantha Cleaveland,” she said aloud.

Chapter 3

Scarlett Shackelford stood in front of the stove in her kitchen. An apron splattered with yellow sunflowers was cinched tightly around her slender waist. Steam rising from the stove formed a glistening layer of moisture on her forehead and cheeks. A pot filled to the brim with freshly washed collard greens, crushed garlic, sliced onions, and chicken stock simmered on one burner, and a one-inch-thick rib-eye steak sizzled on another. Steam from a casserole dish of macaroni and cheese bubbling in the oven poured from a vent on the side.

The evening sun reflected off every surface in the bright and cheery kitchen. White-glazed tile countertops held stainless-steel appliances, a neatly lined row of cookbooks, and a ceramic rooster cookie jar that required beheading before it would yield its sugary treats.

The three dishes were all her husband's favorites. Scarlett was desperate to keep her man, and she knew that one way to any man's heart was through his stomach. It had been weeks since the fateful day that David had coldly announced to her that he was in love with Samantha Cleaveland. As she stood in front of the boiling pot, she could still see the loathing in David's eyes. As she stirred the greens and recalled the slap she had planted on his expressionless face, her hand stung.

"Can't we talk about this? I've told you I wasn't in love with Hezekiah. I love you," she had pleaded on that day, only three feet from where she now stood. "Why can't you just accept that and allow us to move on?"

"This isn't about you for once, Scarlett," David had responded.

"I told you I lied to you for Natalie, not for myself."

"I don't believe that, and on some level I don't think you believe it, either," he said coldly. "You lied because you wanted to cover your tracks and preserve the ridiculous victim routine that you've used your entire life. You slept with Hezekiah because you wanted to. He didn't rape you. You were an adult. I don't buy for a minute your 'young and naive' excuse. You knew exactly what you were doing. You wanted him, and Samantha called your bluff and put you back in your place."

"How dare you? I was the victim. I walked away on my own because I didn't want anything from them," Scarlett replied indignantly.

"Correction, darling. You walked away because you knew you couldn't get the one thing you wanted—Hezekiah. Then the wounded little girl nonsense was the perfect cover for your being slapped back into reality by Samantha. It didn't matter that I or anyone else didn't know that Natalie was Hezekiah's daughter. The important thing was that you knew it, and you could feel like the victim back in your safe little cocoon of self-pity, and since then you've been alone there."

Scarlett raised her hand and slapped David hard on the cheek. His head turned from the blow, but his feet remained firmly planted.

"I guess now I'm supposed to slap you back. Is this a page from your battered wife script?" he said, rubbing his stinging cheek. "I'm afraid you'll have to remind me what my next line is. I don't seem to remember this scene."

Scarlett had been unprepared for his lack of emotion and his painfully pointed words on that day. His cold demeanor had been completely unexpected and had left her at a loss. His words swirled in her head, almost making her dizzy. Was she the perfect victim? Did the world, in fact, revolve around her and not Natalie? Was there some twisted desire to be abandoned and left alone with her scars and wounds? Was this the monster she'd created?

She slapped him again and waited for a response. But she was greeted only with a questioning stare.

"I hate you," she finally said in a whisper.

"You don't hate me, Scarlett. You hate the truth about yourself."

Scarlett looked puzzled. The words stung. For her entire life she felt she had sacrificed her happiness for others, and mostly for her daughter. But in the face of such a damning accusation, she slowly began to realize that in fact she had made all the sacrifices for herself. She needed to be the victim. It was all she knew. It was familiar and where she felt safe and, ironically, in control.

"You're a coward to leave me over this," she said, turning her back to him and walking to the sink. "I thought you were a better man than that."

"That's where you're wrong again," he said with a hint of irony. "I'm not leaving you because you're a liar. I'm not even leaving you because you're delusional."

Scarlett turned from the sink to face David. He had not moved from the threshold. Now the span of the room divided them. Steam from the coffeemaker on the marble island formed a light mist between them. "Then why?" she asked, her question tinged with a dare.

"I'm leaving you for Samantha Cleaveland."

The painful memory of that day caused her hand to shake as she turned the steak in the sizzling pan. She had lost track of time and hadn't realized the steak had burned on one side. The charred meat sent puffs of smoke into the kitchen.

David had not left her, and she had never asked him why. He had sat next to her on the pew at New Testament

Cathedral the following Sunday morning. Natalie had sat between them while Samantha looked down from the pulpit. He ate at the table with her and Natalie each night. He kept her car filled with gasoline, did the laundry, and paid the bills, just as he had before he learned that the little girl was the illegitimate child of his pastor.

Life seemed almost normal each day, until it was time to retire to bed. It was then that the chasm that had developed between the two became the most apparent. David, as he always had, would pull the covers over Natalie's shoulders as she drifted off to sleep, kiss her forehead, and whisper, "I love you, little princess." From there he would walk into the spare bedroom and close the door behind him. Scarlett would not see him again until the next morning at breakfast.

He hadn't touched her in weeks. His words were succinct and civil, but strictly utilitarian. "I'm on my way to the market. Do you need anything?" or "I will be home late for dinner tonight," was the typical length and depth of his communications to her.

Until Hezekiah's death Scarlett hadn't realized just how much she had loved him. The love she felt had been so heavily camouflaged by respect, admiration, and nostalgia that she herself hadn't recognized it for what it was.

Scarlett had been smart and beautiful her entire life, but she had never really known it. Her shyness had often been mistaken for conceitedness. Boys had found the attractive Southern girl captivating. Her naïveté and soft voice had garnered proposals of marriage long before she turned eighteen.

At nineteen she became Hezekiah Cleaveland's secretary. Scarlett was professional and efficient. Hezekiah was immediately attracted to the young beauty and pursued her from the start. She was flattered by the attention from the handsome minister but flatly refused his constant advances. She often cried after work and wondered what she had done to elicit such carnal responses from the man she admired.

After a year Scarlett could resist no longer. She gave in to the pastor and began a two-month affair. Hezekiah was the first man she had ever been with. He was gentle and attentive and never made her feel cheap. Scarlett soon learned she was pregnant. Hezekiah offered to put her up in an apartment until the baby was born. After that, he told her, she would have to give the baby up for adoption.

She was devastated. Not because she was pregnant, but because the man she had fallen in love with did not share her joy. Samantha soon learned of Scarlett's condition and immediately fired her. Scarlett then married a man who had pursued her since she was fifteen. It wasn't easy, but she convinced her new husband that the baby she was carrying was his.

For five years the couple lived a turbulent life filled with physical abuse and mistrust. Her new husband never believed the cute little girl was really his. In a violent argument he threw Scarlett and Natalie out on the street. Scarlett had never loved her husband, so the divorce came as a relief, but the pain of her secret lingered. She still held it close to her chest, like an unwanted family heirloom that she had been entrusted to protect.

Scarlett rejoined New Testament Cathedral after her marriage ended and soon became a trusted and valuable member of the church. Eventually, Hezekiah, who had never lost his deep affection for her, appointed Scarlett to the board of trustees.

She had harbored loathing for Samantha Cleaveland for years, and now it intensified. She had always suspected that Samantha would want to take over the church if Hezekiah ever died, and Scarlett vowed to do all within her power to prevent it if she ever tried.

Scarlett thought she had put all the love, pain, and rejection behind her, until she saw Hezekiah lying on the pulpit with blood pouring from his head and chest. The carnage released emotions she assumed had long passed. Now she realized that David was right. She had been in love with Hezekiah and grieved his death as a widow would. The feelings took her by surprise and left her a quivering, whimpering bundle of nerves, one who would burst into tears at the thought of him. The feelings were accompanied by a staggering dose of shame and embarrassment. Not over the fact that she had had an affair with a married man or that she had lied about Natalie. She was ashamed about the fact that she had not realized herself just how much she loved him and how much his rejection had shaped the fragile woman she had become.

Scarlett coughed from the billows of smoke that were again rising from the burning steak. Once again she had lost track of time. She quickly removed the charred meat from the pan and dropped it with a thud onto a waiting bundle of paper towels. She looked at the greens and discovered they were bubbling over the rim of the pot and spewing liquid onto the stove's surface. The beeping oven timer then caught her attention. It had run ten minutes past the time she had set. She immediately swung the oven door open and was greeted with another plume of smoke. The macaroni and cheese had bubbled over the sides of the casserole dish and had formed a pile of smoldering goo on the floor of the oven.

The meal was ruined in spite of her best efforts to please her husband. *Just like my marriage,* she thought as a tear fell from her eye. *Just like my life.*

The death of Pastor Cleaveland had served to reopen the wounds that had taken her years to heal. Feelings for Hezekiah had flooded back, as if she were nineteen again. Over the years, however, she had never stopped hating

Samantha, the woman who had treated her so cruelly. The woman she had once admired.

A bus filled with Japanese tourists drove onto the sacred grounds of New Testament Cathedral. Once the tourists set foot on the pavement, their digital cameras recorded images of the building and sounds of astonishment escaped their lips. They had traveled halfway around the world to see Disneyland and the new glass cathedral.

"It is magnificent!" one exclaimed in a distinct Hokkaido-ben dialect. "It is more beautiful than I imagined."

An army of groundskeepers, in green overalls emblazoned with the church's logo of a bejeweled gold crown with a cross running through the center, carefully maneuvered golf carts filled with fresh sod, blossoming perennials, shovels, and other supplies through the throngs of visitors, who had come from around the world to marvel at the building.

Reverend Percy Pryce stood at the fifth-floor window, looking down on the carnival below. His new office was twice the size of the one he had occupied in the old building. Two walls of intricately woven glass panes offered him unobstructed views of the walkway to the main entrance, a massive satellite dish pointing toward heaven, and the outdoor amphitheater, which could seat five thousand souls.

Percy found no joy in the beauty sprawled at his feet. Every click of a tourist's camera, every exclamation of "It's the most beautiful building in the world," and every plunge of a groundskeeper's shovel into the earth only served to remind him of the unthinkable act he and Associate Pastor Kenneth Davis had committed on the eve of Hezekiah's death.

The memory played like a horror movie in his mind, over which he had no control. He would never forget that Saturday evening when he and Kenneth had arrived at Lance Savage's little bungalow on the canals in Venice. It was a small, cluttered house with a permanent dampness in the air.

Lance had answered the door, wearing faded jogging shorts and a wrinkled T-shirt. "Hello, Kenneth," the *Los Angeles Chronicle* reporter had said, greeting them at the door. "You didn't say you were bringing Reverend Pryce with you. Is he here in an official capacity?"

"No, he's not," Kenneth had said as they entered the bungalow. "And neither am I. We're not here to speak on behalf of New Testament Cathedral or Hezekiah. We only represent ourselves."

"Have a seat, gentlemen. Can I get you a beer or something stronger?"

Percy recalled, as if it were only yesterday, the irritatingly casual tone in which the reporter had spoken to them.

"No thank you," Kenneth responded. "We don't plan on staying long."

Lance retrieved the beer he had already begun drinking and sat on a leather sofa next to Percy. Kenneth lowered his body into a chair in front of them and sat a briefcase filled with money on the floor at his feet.

Kenneth began calmly. "We would appreciate it if whatever we discuss does not leave this room. As far as anyone is concerned, this meeting never took place, and if you ever repeat anything we say, we will deny it."

"Fair enough," Lance said, setting the beer on a side table.

"First of all, we'd like for you to tell us exactly what it is that you know about this affair Hezekiah is allegedly involved in," Kenneth said.

"All right. It will soon be public information, anyway. Your pastor has been involved with a Mr. Danny St. John for the last year. They see each other no less than twice a week. Usually, they meet at Danny's apartment in the West Adams District, but they also have lunch together on occasion at various restaurants around the city. Danny is a social worker in downtown Los Angeles. He's twenty-nine, and quite a looker, I might add. Is there anything else you'd like to know?" Lance replied smugly.

"Yes," Percy said. "Everything you've just told us sounds relatively innocent. It doesn't prove the relationship was sexual."

"I agree," Kenneth said, chiming in. "There's no moral law against Hezekiah having a male friend. He's been to my home dozens of times, and we often dine together. That doesn't make us lovers."

Lance stood up and walked to a desk under a window overlooking the canals.

At that moment Percy recalled the sounds he had heard from a flock of ducks just outside the bungalow window. The story played on in Percy's mind as he stood at his office window, looking out at the church grounds.

Lance opened a drawer and retrieved a stack of papers held together by a metal clasp. He thumbed through the stack, pulled a sheet out, and handed it to Percy.

Percy read the e-mail silently.

My Dearest Danny,

Last night with you was wonderful. I love holding you in my arms and tasting your soft lips. Each time I kiss you feels as sweet as my first kiss. Feeling your body against mine gives me more pleasure than I ever thought possible. Caressing your soft skin makes me feel like the luckiest man in the world. I'm not a poet, and I know it. But I want you to know that I love you with all my heart.

I pray I can hold you in my arms forever.

Love you always,

Hez

Percy handed the e-mail to Kenneth, who in turn proceeded to read it silently.

"Would you like to see more?" Lance asked. "That's one of the tamer ones. There's a few in there that give you the size of each of their dicks and one in particular that goes into great detail about how much Danny likes it when Hezekiah sticks his finger up his ass when he's about to—"

Percy quickly held up his hand and said, "No, that won't be necessary."

"One thing I can assure you of is none of the more graphic details of their relationship will be in the article. I don't think the public is ready to hear how much Hezekiah loves to have his dick sucked in the shower," Lance said with a sly smile.

"This is so unseemly," Percy said in disgust. "I can't believe the *Los Angeles Chronicle* would stoop to gutter journalism like this. It's no better than the supermarket tabloids."

"Pathetic, isn't it?" Lance said sarcastically. "But it's a new day in journalism. The public craves shit like this, and if we want to stay in business, we've got to keep up with the times. No pun intended."

"I'm glad you think this is funny," Kenneth said angrily. "You don't seem to realize how many people will be hurt if this story is released. Hezekiah will be ruined. His wife and daughter will be devastated. The future of New Testament Cathedral will be placed in extreme jeopardy. Millions of people all over the country will lose faith in a man they deeply love, and many will possibly lose their faith in God as well."

"I'm sorry, gentlemen, but Hezekiah should have thought of all that before he got involved with a man," Lance said as he sat back down. "I'm a reporter, and I report the news. And this is definitely news."

Kenneth proceeded diplomatically. "You are obviously aware that the story would cause immeasurable damage to Hezekiah and New Testament Cathedral."

"I am," was Percy's recollection of the smug little reporter's response.

"Is there any way we can appeal to your conscience?" Kenneth asked passionately. "Surely you must feel some moral obligation to your fellow man. Hezekiah made a mistake, but who among us hasn't? I'm sure you've done things that you're not proud of. How would you like it if they were splashed all over the front pages?"

"I would hate that, but you fail to recognize a few significant differences between Hezekiah and myself. I don't claim any sort of moral authority. I'm not married. I'm not the head of a multimillion-dollar empire, and even more important, I am not on television twenty-four hours a day around the world, preaching about the evils of sin. Nobody gives a shit about who I'm fucking."

"Point taken," Kenneth conceded. "Then let's approach this from a different angle. Obviously, we want to put this entire ugly situation behind us as soon and as quietly as possible. To that end, we are prepared to pay you one hundred seventy-five thousand dollars to forget you ever heard the name Danny St. John."

It was at that point that Kenneth retrieved the briefcase from the floor and placed it on the coffee table. He opened it to reveal stacks of hundred-dollar bills bound by white paper strips.

Lance sat erect. "You've got to be kidding me," he said, laughing. "You think saving your boy's ass is worth only a hundred seventy-five thousand dollars?"

"That's all we are able to come up with," Kenneth replied.

Lance stood up and walked toward the door. "You and I both know that's not true. New Testament Cathedral brings in more than that just from the interest you earn on the money collected in the Sunday morning offering plate," he said. "Gentlemen, I think you've wasted enough of my time. I would appreciate it if you'd leave my home. I've got a story to finish."

Percy jumped from the sofa. "You parasite," he said, pointing his finger. "Now it's clear to me what this is all about. You're trying to get rich off the back of Hezekiah and New Testament Cathedral. That whole speech about 'the news' was a bunch of bullshit. You don't care about the news," he said angrily. "It's all about money."

"That's some strong language for a man of God," Lance said. "I'm impressed."

"Screw you," Percy continued. "If you have half a brain, you'll take the money and forget about this whole thing."

"It'll take a lot more than that for me to forget Danny St. John. Try half a million, and then maybe we can talk."

"You're out of your mind," Percy said, "if you think we're going to give you half a million dollars."

"I think that's a fair amount, Reverend Pryce, especially considering it was your wife who got you into this sordid mess," Lance replied as he opened the front door. "Now, if you don't mind."

Standing at the window of his office, Percy felt a stabbing sensation in his gut as he remembered the stunning revelation from the reporter. How could Cynthia have done this? he thought.

The scene played on in his mind. Stunned, Percy looked at Lance and then slammed the door shut. "What are you saying? My wife isn't involved in this."

Lance walked away from the door to a nearby telephone. "Are you trying to tell me you didn't know she is the one who leaked the story?"

Percy bolted across the room and grabbed Lance by the shoulders. "Cynthia had nothing to do with this. You're lying! Kenneth, don't listen to him. He's trying to get more money out of us," he shouted.

Kenneth bounded to his feet and said, "Let him go, Percy. At this point it doesn't matter who leaked the story." He then looked at Lance and said, "Half a million dollars is a lot of money. It'll take us some time to come up with it, but—"

"It matters to me," Percy interrupted. He then pushed the now shaking reporter against the wall, causing a picture to crash to the floor. "I'm not going to let this asshole extort that kind of money out of us."

"Reverend Pryce, you would be surprised at just what your wife was willing to do to ensure that you become the next pastor of New Testament Cathedral. But trust me, she knows her way around the backseat of a car."

Lance began to walk away, but Percy grabbed his neck. The two men struggled.

"Percy, stop it!" Kenneth said, grabbing Percy by the shoulders. "Let him go. Let's go."

But the scuffle only intensified. A lamp fell from a table. Stereo equipment and CDs lurched from shelves from the impact of slamming bodies. Lance struggled to get out of Percy's grip as Percy pushed him to the floor.

His head banged against the coffee table when he fell, causing the briefcase and all its contents to topple onto the floor. The reporter lay motionless with bundles of money strewn around his body.

"Oh God!" Kenneth said, kneeling next to Lance's body. "What have you done? He's not breathing."

Kenneth tried to revive Lance, while Percy panted over his shoulder.

"Wake up," Percy said through anguished breaths. "He tripped. Make him get up, Kenneth."

Kenneth shook Lance's shoulders, causing his head to flop from side to side. His arms hung limp and unresponsive, despite the additional abuse at the hands of such a large man.

"He's dead," Kenneth finally said. "You killed him."

"I barely touched him. You saw it. He tripped. Oh God. I don't believe this is happening. What are we going to do?"

Without responding, Kenneth carelessly dropped the mass of flesh and immediately began gathering the fallen money, throwing it into the briefcase.

"Quick," he finally said. "Get all the money. We have to get out of here."

"We can't just leave him here. We have to call the police."

"Are you crazy? You just killed a man! Let's just get out of here. Hopefully, no one saw us come in. They'll think he was killed by a burglar. Now, pull yourself together and help me pick up this money."

Kenneth surveyed the scene once the briefcase was filled. Much of the room's contents lay scattered on the floor along with the crumpled body. To his satisfaction, it looked like the classic robbery scene he had seen so often on prime-time crime shows.

"If we pass anyone on the street, don't make eye contact with them and try to look natural," Kenneth ordered.

Percy looked again at the devastation his hands had caused, and cried, "I don't believe this is happening."

Kenneth ran to the kitchen at the rear of the house and retrieved a dishtowel from the sink. He wrapped his hand in the towel and smashed a pane of glass in the back door.

With his hand still covered, he swung the door open and then stuffed the towel into his pocket.

The two men exited the apartment through the door they had entered. Cars raced down the busy street at speeds that permitted no more than cursory glances. No pedestrians were in sight as they drove away.

"This never happened, Percy," Kenneth said, looking directly ahead. "Do you understand? This never happened."

Percy was in shock and did not respond.

"You have to put this out of your head. We were never there."

"What if a neighbor saw us?"

"No one saw us," Kenneth replied impatiently. "We were never in Venice. Don't ever mention this to anyone. Understand?"

"I won't mention it. I understand. But I can't get his face out of my head. Why did he make me do it? I just snapped. I don't know what happened. He shouldn't have said those lies about Cynthia. She would never do anything so cruel. She loves Hezekiah and Samantha. This would have never happened if he had just taken the money."

Kenneth deposited his shaken passenger at the main entrance of the church. It was 5:10 p.m., and a tide of fleeing employees was streaming from the building.

"Are you going to be all right?" Kenneth asked as Percy exited the car. "Go directly to your office, get your things, and go home. And for God's sake, don't talk to anyone."

"I won't," Percy saidr. "But what about the story? If the editor doesn't hear from Lance, they'll run it."

"It's too late to worry about that now. It's out of our hands. We'll just have to brace ourselves for the worst."

Percy's brow was now damp as he stood at the window, recalling that fateful day. His hands shook nervously in his pockets. Now the throng of sightseers and the scurrying groundskeepers were a source of irritation for him.

Percy closed his eyes tightly and thought, *They wouldn't be so impressed if they knew how much this place really cost.*

Chapter 4

The television networks of the world were busily preparing themselves for the appearance of Pastor Samantha Cleaveland. It was 12:55 on Tuesday afternoon. Dozens of white, blue, and black vans, with their satellite antennas fully erect, their side doors open, and equipment lights blinking, were lined three deep in front of the steps of New Testament Cathedral. Technicians unfurled electrical cables and mounted cameras on tripods in spots that would give their audiences unobstructed views of the glass podium with twenty microphones attached. National and international news anchors scanned notepads and cleared their throats in preparation for the first press conference held by Samantha since the death of her husband. Throngs of photographers and reporters jockeyed for the best positions in the crowd to hear every word spoken and to capture images of the beautiful woman from every angle.

The press release, sent only two days earlier to thousands of news outlets, had invited the world's media to join Samantha on the steps as she announced the official completion of the new cathedral and media center.

"We are live in Los Angeles, California," said one anchor to her audience in the United Kingdom. "In just a few moments Pastor Samantha Cleaveland will come through those magnificently etched glass double doors and announce the official completion of what many are saying is one of the most beautiful churches in the world."

"Just three months earlier Pastor Samantha Cleaveland witnessed the assassination of her husband and the founder of New Testament Cathedral, Pastor Hezekiah Cleaveland," another reporter said to his camera, which sent the live feed to Australia. "Today this courageous woman is at the helm of one of the sixth wealthiest churches in America."

At exactly 1:00 p.m. two imposing men in black suits and sunglasses walked up the stairs to the main entrance and opened the twenty-foot-high glass double doors, revealing Samantha Cleaveland standing in the threshold. The crowd became frantic. A sea of Nikon, Canon, and Olympus cameras with telescopic lenses pointed in her direction and clicked frantically. Lights flashed, and voices from every direction called out, "Samantha, over here!" and "Pastor Cleaveland, could you turn this way please!"

Samantha gave the ravenous cameras all they craved and more. She allowed them ample time to bask in her presence. Her stunning black Chanel silk skirt and jacket, which had gold twist trim, a V-shaped neckline, and sparkling gold buttons engraved with the iconic CC, caused both the men and the women of the media to gasp when she first appeared from behind the doors. The classic lines of the impeccably constructed suit accentuated her full breasts, her perfect hourglass figure, and her long, elegant legs, which were supported by four-inch, red-soled black Prada pumps.

Samantha took measured, confident steps to the podium as the crowd continued to call for her to look in their direction.

"Good afternoon, ladies and gentlemen," she finally said over the calls of her name. "Thank you all for joining us on this momentous occasion." Her pearly smile dazzled the cameras, while her silky black hair danced gently in the summer breeze.

"Today marks the official day of completion of the construction of New Testament Cathedral. What you see behind me is the culmination of five years of sweat, blood, and tears of thousands of workers, innumerable donors, and prayer partners from around the world. Many said it couldn't be done. 'Build a forty-five-million-dollar glass cathedral in downtown Los Angeles?' some skeptics questioned. 'It can't be done.' Well, I'm standing here before you today as proof that with God on your side, you can do anything."

The cameras continued to capture every millisecond of Samantha as she spoke. "Not only have we completed this twenty-five-thousand-seat sanctuary, but behind you is the one-hundred-thousand-square-foot media center, where we will be producing Christian television programming and feature-length movies," she said. Raising her three-layer-deep diamond wrapped wrist, she added, "To your left, you see the campus of New Cathedral College, and to your right are the elementary, middle, and high schools, which will be franchised around the country."

Samantha went on to tell of the sacrifices she had had to make over the past five years as the crowd waited patiently for her to mention her dead husband.

"I've spent many sleepless nights wondering if I got in over my head on this project. Had I misunderstood God's plan for my life? Is this the best way to use the vast blessings God has given me? I'm proud to say this afternoon that no, I did not misunderstand God's plan, and yes, I truly believe this is the best use of the blessings God has given me."

Still no mention of her grief. "This Sunday will be the first time the saints will gather in this building for our morning worship service, which will be broadcast live around the world. And, of course, you are all invited."

A collective confusion slowly began to creep through the crowd of reporters as they silently wondered, Wasn't this whole thing Hezekiah Cleaveland's idea? Others in the crowd thought, but dared not say out loud, *What a bitch for taking credit for the work her husband did and not even mentioning the poor bastard.*

"This facility will serve as a beacon of light for wounded souls around the world," Samantha continued. "The message of God's love will be beamed from this complex twenty-four hours a day, seven days a week, and three hundred sixty-five days a year."

Samantha knew what they wanted to hear. She was aware they were all salivating in anticipation of her first tear, the first tremble in her voice, and the dramatic clutching of her breast as she relived the pain of her husband's murder. But she had already decided there would be no dramatic display of emotion on this day.

"So again I want to thank you all for coming out on this beautiful day," she said in conclusion, "and sharing in our joy and celebration of the completion of this magnificent complex. I encourage you all to explore the grounds. You have received press kits, which provide more information about the New Testament Cathedral ministry and a detailed description of the facilities. There are docents posted in the buildings who are there to answer any questions you have. God bless you all, and we'll see you on Sunday morning."

"Pastor Cleaveland!" everyone in the crowd yelled almost in unison. This was followed by a flurry of shouted questions.

"You lost your husband only three months ago. How have you been holding up since that day?"

"Do you think the church will be able to raise as much money as it did when your husband was at the helm?" shouted a man in the rear.

"Has there been any progress in the investigation of your husband's murder?" yelled a reporter who was waving a small recorder in her direction.

"Are you afraid for your own life?"

"What do you say to those who feel you took on too much too soon after your husband's death?"

The questions came in rapid fire, but Samantha only smiled broadly and waved to the reporters and flashing cameras. She took a step back from the microphones and continued to wave briefly before turning her back to the ravenous mob and gliding through the same entrance from which she had come. The two suited men slowly closed the glass doors behind her, leaving the crowd panting for more in the afternoon sun.

"Cynthia, are you home?" Percy called out as he entered the penthouse. "Baby, are you here?"

Percy went from room to room, looking for Cynthia. The kitchen was empty and looked like a showroom display that had never been used for cooking. The dining room, though perfect in every way, showed no signs of warm family meals or festive holiday dining. The bathrooms were cold and sterile, and the bedroom was dark, with no sign of life.

Finally, he opened the door to the den. Cynthia was sitting with her knees pressed to her chest, staring at the silent television screen. Don Lemon was reporting the latest breaking news. His lips were moving, but there was no sound.

"Cynthia, didn't you hear me calling you?"

She remained silent.

"Honey . . ." Percy said, slowly approaching the sofa where she sat.

"I'm sorry. I didn't hear you," she finally responded. "I was deep in thought."

Percy sat next to her on the sofa and asked cautiously, "What are you thinking about?"

"About us. About New Testament Cathedral. About . . ."

"Honey, I wish you would stop obsessing over this whole thing."

"I'm not obsessing. I just think the church would be in a much better position if you were pastor." Cynthia looked him directly in the eye and continued. "You should have seen her at the press conference today. She never even mentioned Hezekiah's name."

"I know," Percy said with a sigh. "I was there."

"Doesn't that tell you everything you need to know about her? Hezekiah poured his entire soul into that building. In a way, he even gave his life for it, and she didn't even have the decency to mention his name. She's a horrible woman, Percy."

"I think that's a bit harsh, Cynthia. There was so much activity out there. Questions were coming at her from every direction. Cameras were flashing. She may have just gotten flustered and forgot."

Cynthia looked at him sharply and laughed. "Samantha *flustered?* You've known her for years. When have you ever seen her flustered? Why do you continually make excuses for her horrible behavior? She's a monster, and you just won't admit it."

"Cynthia—"

"You know what I think, Percy?"

"No. What do you think?" he asked sarcastically.

"I think you make excuses for her and cover for her deplorable behavior because you are afraid to be pastor."

"That's ridiculous," he scoffed.

"Is it? This is really about the fact that you are a coward. You're hiding behind Samantha. If she weren't there, you know you would most likely be pastor, and that scares you to death."

"You're talking nonsense, and I don't want to participate in this conversation with you." Percy stood from the sofa and walked to the door. "I won't have this conversation with you again," he calmly said over his shoulder. "I'll be in the bedroom."

"Don't walk away from me when I'm talking to you."

"There's nothing more to discuss."

"This isn't over, Percy. I'm going to make you pastor even if it kills you."

Percy froze when he heard those words. "Don't say that, Cynthia."

"I mean it, Percy. I'm going to be man enough for both of us. I am going to make you the pastor of New Testament Cathedral, and I don't care who gets hurt in the process . . . even you."

Rage began to percolate from deep within Percy's gut. He turned sharply to face her where she still sat on the sofa. "I'm warning you, Cynthia. Stop this nonsense right now. Enough people have been hurt by you already. Haven't you done enough damage?"

"You don't know the half of what I'm capable of, Percy Pryce. But you will soon see."

With a sudden burst of anger, Percy charged toward the sofa. Cynthia did not flinch as the hulking man grabbed her arm and yanked her to her feet.

"What are you talking about? What are you planning, Cynthia?"

"None of your business. Just prepare yourself for center stage. And while you're at it, maybe . . . just maybe you could grow some balls."

Percy released his tight grip on her arm and unleashed a violent slap across Cynthia's left cheek. The blow sent her flying headfirst into the leather sofa. Her burnt-caramel hair splashed over her face.

Cynthia looked up at the panting man and calmly said, "What a big man. You can stand up to me, but you bend over and let her screw you."

The words caused Percy to lunge toward her crumpled body. He delivered another slap across her cheek. "Shut up. Shut up, or I'll . . ." He stopped short of leveling another violent blow.

"Or you'll what?" Cynthia demanded. "Kill me? Kill me like you killed Lance Savage?"

Percy froze when he heard the words. Startled, he looked at the screaming woman beneath him.

"Looks like I struck a nerve." She laughed. "I thought you had something to do with his death, and now the stupid expression on your face confirms it. You killed him, didn't you? And all to protect those ungrateful Cleavelands."

Percy rolled off Samantha and fell to the floor with a massive thud.

"Admit it," she said calmly, now looking down at him. "You killed him to stop the story about his disgusting affair from running."

Percy just sat there, silent and dazed. The leather, chrome, and glass room began to spin.

"You killed that reporter for nothing. Hezekiah was dead the next day. If you hadn't gotten involved, the story would have run. You ruined all my plans just because you were too afraid to be pastor."

Hearing the words caused Percy to weep. "Stop. Please stop."

"Your loyalty to those people caused you to take another man's life. Don't you see how insidious they are? How evil they are?"

"Please, I'm begging you to stop talking," he cried out, cradling his head in his hands.

"They made you do it. Can't you see that? If it wasn't for them, Lance Savage would still be alive. It's their fault, not yours."

Cynthia kneeled down next to the crumpled man. She pulled his head to her chest and lovingly stroked his hair while he cried uncontrollably into her bosom.

"Shhh, baby," she gently whispered into his ear. "It's not your fault. It's all right."

"I killed him," Percy blubbered. "I didn't mean to. It was an accident."

"I know that, baby, and God knows that too. *You* didn't kill him. *They* killed him. With their greed and immoral behavior. The Cleavelands killed him. It's not your fault. You just have to listen to me, baby, from now on. I know what's best for you. I know what's best for us. Trust me and everything will be just fine," she whispered as Percy wilted into the comfort of her gentle arms.

Chapter 5

A wall of television monitors in Samantha's office presented a steady stream of "triumphant widow" news feeds. She studied her images on the screens and each report intently.

Her new office was situated high above the main entrance of the church. Sunlight turned into an aquamarine mist as it filtered through the intricately woven ten-foot-high glass panes that formed the walls that encased her lofty tomb. From this new perch Samantha could see her kingdom and all its inhabitants, sprawled at her feet, but they could not see her.

Each national and international report covering the opening of New Testament Cathedral vied for Samantha's attention from the wall of television monitors opposite her acrylic desk.

She wore a black-and-white, cropped tweed Oscar de la Renta bolero jacket, a layered-front sheer blouse, and a printed sateen skirt. Shimmering black hair cascaded like water around her cheeks and framed the face that the world had come to love. Were the cameras rolling? Was there a room filled to capacity, the audience hanging on her every word? No, but Samantha Cleaveland was still perfect.

"Only days to the grand opening of what many are saying is the most beautiful church in the world," Diane Sawyer said while reporting on New Testament Cathedral during the news broadcast that had aired the evening before.

"Not only is she beautiful, but Samantha Cleaveland is one of the most courageous women I have ever met," gushed Don Lemon from another screen.

The images continued in rapid succession, all funneled to her office by a legion of technical minions buried somewhere deep within the bowels of the new media center at the opposite end of the campus. From her desk, Samantha pointed the remote to select the feed she wanted to hear. She controlled their sound and their words with the simple wave of her manicured hand.

"I'm sorry to disturb you, Pastor Cleaveland," said a disembodied voice from the phone on her desk. "David Shackelford is here to see you. I told him you didn't want to be disturbed, but he said it's urgent and you would want to speak with him."

Samantha slowly spun her white leather chair away from the wall of monitors to the window behind her desk. She gazed over the campus and thought, *I'm going to have to do something about him.*

"Send him in," she replied, making no attempt at hiding her exasperation. "And, Chantal, hold all my calls."

David Shackelford bolted into the room seconds later. His hulking frame and Ferragamo loafers hurled him across the expanse of the office toward Samantha, who was still seated behind the desk.

"I've been trying to reach you for two days. Why haven't you taken my calls?"

Samantha did not move. "I've been very busy, David," she responded coldly. "What is it that you want?"

David paused when greeted with her coldness. "I . . . I want you, Samantha," he stammered. "I need you. I've been going crazy without you."

"Don't be ridiculous, David. I've told you, you belong with Scarlett, not me. I don't have time for a relationship. Besides, how would it look for me to been seen with someone only months after Hezekiah died? He's barely cold in his grave."

"I don't give a fuck about what people think." David rushed around the desk and lifted Samantha by her shoulders. "I love you, Samantha. I need you."

"I don't like to be handled, David," she said, pushing him away. "Please take your hands off me."

"Please don't push me away, Samantha. I can't live without you. I'll do anything for you. You know that, don't you?"

The images of Samantha flashed on the television monitors as the two spoke. David tried again to reduce the distance between them.

"Please, Samantha," he whispered, nuzzling her neck. "Make love to me again. I love you."

Samantha could feel his hardening passion pressing against her stomach. She pushed him away again. "I don't love you, David," she said sharply. "I don't need you, and I don't want you in my life. Do you understand? Now, please leave my office, or I will have security escort you off the property."

David stumbled backward. "You don't mean that," was his wounded response. "I killed a man for you. Wasn't that enough to prove to you how much I love you?"

Samantha looked immediately to the telephone on her desk to make sure the red intercom light was not glowing.

She returned her cold gaze to his pleading face. "You didn't kill anyone for me. You killed that boy to save your own life."

"I killed him because you said he had a gun. I killed him because you told me to."

"You're insane. Go back to your wife and forget about us."

David began to tremble. Suddenly his legs felt as if they would not support his weight. "I don't think the police will see it the same as you," he managed to sputter.

Samantha froze. "The police? Don't be a fool, David," she barked. "You'll go to jail if you go to the police."

"I don't care!" he shouted. "What difference will it make if I don't have you?"

"David, you have Scarlett. She loves you. And the little girl. What would she do without you?"

"Fuck you, Samantha! The 'little girl' is more yours than mine. She's your husband's bastard child."

"Calm down, David. Someone might hear you."

"I don't care who hears me!" he screamed, with his hands flailing at his sides. "As a matter of fact, I want everyone to know how you used me. How you've ruined my life."

Samantha did not respond. Instead, she turned to the window to calculate her next move.

When she turned back to David, her expression had transformed to the calm, cool veneer of a woman on a mission.

"David, I can make you a very rich man," she finally said, looking him in the eye. "How much will it take for you to forget any of this ever happened?"

David became enraged. "You bitch. Is that what you think this is about?" he said. "I don't want your fucking money, Samantha. Don't you understand I only want you?"

A thousand scenes flashed in her mind as he spoke. Front page headline: PASTOR SAMANTHA CLEAVELAND ARRESTED FOR MURDER. This just in: "Samantha Cleaveland implicated in the assassination of her husband, Pastor Hezekiah Cleaveland," and emblazoned in bold yellow print on the front cover of the *Enquirer:* REVEREND SAMANTHA CLEAVELAND AT THE CENTER OF DEADLY LOVE TRIANGLE.

Samantha quickly wiped the images from her mind, moved to him, and cupped his quivering cheeks in her hands. He could feel the warmth of her breath as she neared. His pulse quickened when she touched his face.

"David, your life is not ruined."

"It is if I can't have you," his lips said and his eyes pleaded. "I need you, Samantha. I don't want to live without you."

"I didn't know I meant that much to you, David," she whispered.

"Why did you say those things to me?" he purred as she moved her lips closer to his. "Can't you see how much I love you? I'll do anything for you. I'd kill a thousand more men if you told me to."

"Would you really do that for me?"

"Yes . . . yes, I would, baby," he said as her intoxicating scent filled his nostrils. "I'll do anything you tell me to. Just make love to me."

Samantha gently pressed her lips to his. "I'm sorry, baby," she panted between passionate kisses. "I didn't mean to hurt you. Make love to me, David. I want to feel you inside me right now."

With one hand Samantha deftly unzipped David's tented slacks to expose his now pulsing member, and with the other she reached to press a security button under her desk that automatically bolted the door to her office. "Make love to me, David, here, on top of my cathedral."

Samantha slowly slid her silky hands along the length of his shaft, causing a hushed moan to escape his lips.

"I need you, David. I'm so glad you didn't listen to me," she whispered as she manipulated his flesh, which was like a hardening rod of clay. "I know I can be difficult sometimes. I was just afraid you would leave me first. I didn't want to be hurt again the way Hezekiah hurt me. That's why I said those horrible things to you."

David could hear only the pounding of his heart and the sound of blood rushing from his brain to his extremities. He pulled the bolero jacket from her shoulders, exposing arms so strong they built an empire, yet so soft they felt like the embrace of a gentle breeze.

"I need you inside me," she panted as she raised her leg to his waist.

Before David could respond, his pants fell to the floor and he felt himself enveloped in her warm, moist flesh. A whimpering gasp escaped his lips without warning.

"Fuck me, David," Samantha moaned as she slid up and down his trembling body.

David stood firm and locked his knees as Samantha consumed his body and his soul. News feeds continued to stream on the monitors behind them. The flashing images, scrolling news reports, and talking ciphers provided a media backdrop to the two writhing bodies. Samantha watched the wall of her images over David's shoulders as she moaned her undying devotion.

Without warning the climactic evidence of his passion violently bubbled to the surface. David leaned forward and braced himself on the glass desk as Samantha intensified her assault. His body shook and his knees trembled from supporting both their weight. With his eyes closed and his mouth clamped tight to prevent involuntary shrieks of ecstasy, David released a torrent of his love for Samantha. The two panted in unison until the rushes of passion subsided.

"You understand you belong to me now," Samantha said as David retrieved his pants from around his ankles and tucked in his shirt. "Do you understand what that means?"

David flashed a satisfied smile and said, "It's all I've ever wanted. Yes, I understand, baby."

"I'm not sure that you do. The world is different up here, David," she said, looking out over the grounds. "And now you're a part of it. You have to play by a different set of rules. Rules that may sometimes seem . . . contrary to what you've been taught. But there's no turning back now."

It was Jasmine Cleaveland's first night at home after spending twenty-eight days in a drug rehabilitation center in Arizona. The death of her father had caused her to sink deeper into a world of sex, alcohol, and drugs. When she arrived home, she was greeted at the door by Etta Washington, the live-in maid.

"Hello, Jasmine," Etta said from the threshold of the front door as the driver opened the rear door of the black Escalade. "Welcome home."

"Thank you," Jasmine replied with a smirk. "Is Mother home?"

"Yes, dear," Etta responded politely. "She's in the study. She would like to see you before you go to your room."

"Tell her I'm tired. I'll talk to her later."

At seventeen, Jasmine was the adolescent version of her mother. Her beautiful, flowing, satiny hair had been trained and pampered from a young age to never need artificial lengthening. Despite the fact that she had lived for years in the fast lane, her skin was flawless.

Her life had been what little girls' dreams were made of. She had known only the most elite private schools, had traveled around the world with tutors at the ready, and received a white convertible BMW 650 with a sable interior, wrapped with a red velvet bow, on her sixteenth birthday. Jasmine partied with her celebrity contemporaries, the children of movie stars, and trust-fund babies in New York, San Francisco, Milan, and Paris. There was neither day nor night in her world. There was no destination in the world that either a private jet or a first-class airline ticket would not take her and her friends to party and to shop. The world was her playground.

There would be days when neither Samantha nor Hezekiah knew where she was. And then a call would come.

"Mommy, it's me."

"Where are you, Jasmine?" would be her mother's distracted reply.

"I'm in the Hamptons, at a party," Jasmine explained on one particular occasion.

"You didn't tell me you were leaving the city. What party?"

"It's a release party for Beyoncé's new album."

"I need you home tomorrow afternoon. Your father and I are doing the promo for the new broadcast, and you need to be in a few of the shots."

"Mother! The party is for the whole weekend. Everybody's here. I can't just *leave*. I should have never called you."

"I don't care who's there. I need you here tomorrow. I'll arrange for the plane to pick you up at the airport first thing in the morning. My assistant will call you with the time."

"Can't the pictures just be of you and Daddy this time? I don't want to leave."

"Don't argue with me, young lady," Samantha said angrily, now giving the conversation her full attention. "I will see you tomorrow."

There was silence on the line as Samantha waited for a response. She could hear music and laughter in the background.

"Jasmine, is that understood?"

"Yes," came the huffy reply.

"And, Jasmine."

"What?"

"Stay out of the newspapers please."

On the day her father was murdered, Jasmine took an overdose of sleeping pills. Her stomach was pumped, and she was shipped off to a drug rehabilitation facility in Arizona. She spent twenty-eight days listening to the children of the rich spew the pathetic details of their drug-addled lives onto the terra-cotta-tiled floor of the group therapy room. And now she was home. More angry and alone than ever before.

Don't you think you should at least go in and say hello to your mother?" Etta asked as Jasmine walked past her to the staircase.

Without turning around or altering her stride, she replied curtly, "I said I'll talk to her later. Please have someone bring my bags up."

Her bedroom suite was the size of a three-bedroom apartment. It had a private marbled bath with a Jacuzzi tub and gold fixtures, a book-lined study, a walk-in closet dripping from ceiling to floor with clothes and accessories from the trendiest designers, and a king-size bed strewn with stuffed animals and antique dolls and flanked by freshly cut flowers in crystal vases, which were mysteriously replaced every Monday afternoon.

When Jasmine entered the suite, she immediately felt like a trapped little bird in a luxurious gilded cage.

There was a tap on the door, accompanied by, "Jasmine, honey, it's Mommy."

"Come in," came the exasperated reply.

Samantha entered with a smile and outstretched arms. "Welcome home, honey. I missed you," she said while hugging her rigid daughter. "How was it? Are you feeling any better?"

"It was horrible. Why did you send me there?"

Samantha released her from the embrace. "Because you almost died. I had just lost your father, and I didn't want to lose you too."

"Would you have even noticed?" she asked coldly.

"Don't be ridiculous. Of course I would notice. What are you talking about?"

"You know exactly what I'm talking about."

Jasmine busied herself with emptying the contents of a Louis Vuitton overnight bag onto the bed.

"No, I don't. Please explain yourself, young lady."

Jasmine turned sharply to Samantha. "Daddy and I were just props to you. Pieces you trot out when the cameras are rolling or you need to impress some large donor. The perfect Cleaveland family. Well, look at us now. Not so perfect, are we? My daddy is dead, and I wish I was too. But you look great. You must be very happy now. Daddy is out of the way, and now everything belongs to you."

Jasmine's last words were greeted with a stinging slap across her cheek from Samantha.

"Just because your father is no longer with us does not mean you can speak to me like that," Samantha said, causing the stinging on Jasmine's cheek to intensify. "I will not be spoken to in that tone. Do you understand me?"

A look of terror crept across Jasmine's face as her mother loomed, ready to strike again. For the first time she saw evil on her mother's hardened face. She saw a gleam in her eye that was unfamiliar. Menacing, almost dangerous. Her beloved father was no longer there to serve as a buffer between the two of them. She was suddenly afraid to be alone in a room with her mother.

"You hated him, didn't you?" Jasmine finally said, holding her burning cheek. "And you hate me too."

Samantha softened her stance and smiled warmly. "You know that's not true, don't you, honey? I love you. You are all I have in the world." As she spoke, she took a step closer to Jasmine.

Jasmine moved quickly backward. "Stay away from me," she said with a slight tremble in her voice. "Don't come near me. I hate you."

"I know you don't mean that, darling," Samantha said with a smile. "You're just tired. I'll let you rest now. We can talk more later."

Samantha turned toward the door and walked the expanse of lush rose carpet. She then spun around on her heels and said, "Your father is gone now, Jasmine. I won't tolerate any more of your nonsense. It's just you and me now. Understand?"

Tour buses rolled through the grounds of New Testament Cathedral, filled with tourists who gawked at fountains at every turn, crosses hewn from Italian marble, amphitheaters, and at the center, the glass cathedral. It was an ecclesiastical Disneyland. The eyes of the world were focused on the ten-acre plot of heaven in downtown Los Angeles. News vans dotted the compound, chronicling for the world the week of activities before the grand opening of what was now the most famous building in the world.

The week's agenda included dinners at the Cleaveland Estate with the mayor, governor, and other assorted dignitaries and a prayer breakfast with clergy from every faith. Samantha was center stage every second of the week. She had outfits laid out for every event and a cadre of staff to assure that each went off without a hitch.

Samantha sat at the head of the table in a glass conference room with twenty religious leaders from around the world, who had assembled for the highly publicized prayer breakfast. They each had been flown in on private jets, courtesy of New Testament Cathedral, and accommodated in hotel suites around the city. The conference room had been transformed into a formal dining room, complete with imported linens, vases with elaborate floral arrangements, silver, and an army of servers.

Chatter in the room was interrupted by a gentle tapping of a fork on a crystal water goblet. "Thank you all for joining us on this historic occasion," Samantha said, standing to her feet. "I am honored to be surrounded by some of the most powerful spiritual leaders of our great country and the world."

Seated to her right was Rabbi Sherman Gottlieb from Temple Shalom in New York. To her left was the Reverend Joseph Bentley, president of the National Baptist Convention. Next to him was Reverend Henry Phillips, pastor to the last three presidents of the United States. Each of the twenty prominent people around the table was the head of his or her faith, and together they represented millions of dollars of free publicity.

"God has called me to serve as the head of this great ministry," she continued. "It's not a position I sought or ever wanted. I was very happy serving and supporting my husband, the late Reverend Dr. Hezekiah Cleaveland. I thought I would be doing that until the day I died. But God had a different plan for my life."

As she spoke, waiters dressed in black waist-length jackets filled water glasses and poured coffee into waiting Wedgwood cups.

"Many of you knew my husband. He spoke very highly of everyone at this table. He would be pleased that you each have come to share this occasion with us. He was a great man, and I miss him deeply, but as everyone at this table knows, we are all presented with challenges on a daily basis that we have no control over. They are tests designed to prove ourselves as worthy servants to an almighty and all-knowing God.

"It is my mission in life to prove myself worthy of the tasks God has laid before me. With your prayers and God's guidance, I am confident that we will succeed in building New Testament Cathedral into one of the greatest ministries the world has ever known, one that serves as a messenger of God's word and as a place of refuge for those in need of God's love and direction."

Samantha went on, recounting the early days of the church with a nostalgic smile. "Fifteen years ago Hezekiah and I started this ministry in a little storefront on Imperial Highway, only blocks from where we are now sitting. There were twelve members at the first church service we held. We rented the nine-hundred-square-foot space from the owner, who ran a neighborhood grocery store next door.

"We never imagined back then that the ministry would grow to include millions of supporters and viewers worldwide, a twenty-five-thousand-seat glass cathedral, and broadcasts in thirty-four countries, and that it would be ranked as one of the fastest-growing churches in the world. Please, if you will, stand and join me in a toast to my husband, the late great Hezekiah Cleaveland."

Everyone at the table reached for the nearest glass and stood to their feet.

"To Pastor Hezekiah Cleaveland," Samantha said, hoisting her glass. "This is for you, my darling. We did it. May your soul find peace and rest cradled in the loving arms of our Lord."

As she spoke, a glimmering tear could be seen on her perfect cheek. Everyone at the table was moved by her undying devotion to the man she apparently loved so deeply.

"To Hezekiah!" everyone chorused in response to her heartfelt toast. "To Pastor Hezekiah Cleaveland!" Glasses were raised around the room in honor of the man whose life had been cut short by the beautiful widow standing at the head of the table.

***

Danny was asleep in the guest room. His wound had been attended to by Gideon, who had cradled him in his arms until he drifted into sleep. Gideon now paced the floor of his study. With each thought he had of Samantha, his anger increased and his steps grew more rapid.

The idea of losing Danny so soon after he met him caused his stomach to churn. *I'll destroy her,* he thought as he walked the length and width of the room. *I'll expose her for the murderer she is.*

Gideon's mind whirled as he contemplated his next move. Each idea he devised proved to him to be inadequate punishment for the woman who had tried to rob him of the love he had searched his entire life for. Each scheme was too tame, and each punishment too humane for someone who had killed a man and had lied to a world of gullible believers, who only wanted her to be the perfect wife and mother she professed to be.

Gideon sat down at the desk and removed from the top drawer the file containing the e-mails between Hezekiah and Danny. He pulled a random sheet of paper from the file and read the e-mail printed at the top.

My love,

I have to fly out tonight to San Francisco for two days. I wish there was a way for you to join me, but Samantha will be with me. I will miss you more than you will ever know. I will call you as soon as I can get a free moment from her.

Hez

Danny's reply, printed on the same sheet of paper, came seven minutes later.

I will miss you too. I don't know how much longer I can be without you.

Hezekiah wrote back immediately. His reply occupied the bottom of the sheet of paper Gideon held.

It won't be much longer, I promise. As soon as I return, let's talk about how we can be together permanently. You are all I need in this world. Please don't ever leave me. I have to go now. You will be in my thoughts the entire time I am away.

I love you,
Hezekiah

Gideon leafed through the stack of e-mails and pulled out another sheet of paper. He read the first e-mail on it.

I loved being in your arms last night. Do you realize that we've known each other for a year and that was the first time we ever spent the entire night together? I love being in your apartment, but I'm not so sure if your cat, Parker, appreciated me being there. ;-)

Danny's response came one hour and twenty-two minutes later.

Sorry it took so long for me to respond. We had a crisis at the drop-in center. A homeless guy came in covered from head to toe in blood. Turns out he was mugged in the park earlier. Paramedics came, and he's fine now. I loved waking up in your arms this morning. You were sound asleep when I left. You looked like a little boy curled up in the sheets with

Parker nuzzled at your back. I think he likes having you there. Are you coming back tonight?

Hezekiah wrote back immediately.

I can't tonight, my darling. I wish I could, but we have the mayor and his wife coming to dinner tonight.

Danny's response was short and simple.

I understand.

Gideon could feel the disappointment in Danny's short response. At that moment he vowed to never disappoint Danny. It suddenly became very important that Danny never again feel the emptiness he had experienced with a married man. That he never be second in line for the love he deserved. That he never be alone in his bed or in his heart.

Without thinking, Gideon reached for his cell phone at the corner of the desk. He searched for Samantha's private telephone number, which she had given him in preparation for his last interview.

Before he knew it, the telephone was ringing. He had no idea what he was about to say to the woman he now hated so deeply.

"Hello."

Gideon did not respond to the familiar sultry voice.

"Hello? Who is this?" Samantha said, growing impatient.

"Pastor Cleaveland, this is Gideon Truman."

"Gideon. I'm surprised to hear from you. I thought after our last interview I may have offended you."

"You mean after you threw my crew and me out of your home."

"What did you expect? You practically accused me of having something to do with my husband's death."

"Did I?"

"I don't have time to play word games with you, Mr. Truman. Why are you calling me? I hope you're not expecting another interview."

"No, I won't need another interview from you. I have all I need to know about you to compile a very . . . revealing exposé."

"Would you please get to the point."

"All right, Pastor Cleaveland. I will. Danny St. John is alive."

There was silence on the phone.

"That's right. You and your gorilla should have checked his pulse before you left him for dead in Griffith Park."

"A word of advice, Mr. Truman. You're in over your head with me. If I were you, I would forget you ever heard of Danny St. John. My husband was killed for being involved with him, and now it looks like you are at risk of becoming the next one."

"Is that a threat?"

"No, sir. It is not. It is, however, a warning."

"You don't frighten me."

"That's unfortunate, because you really should be."

Gideon stood from his desk, still clutching the second sheet of paper with the e-mails.

"I have evidence of Hezekiah's affair with Danny in my hand, and now I know that you tried to kill Danny to cover up the affair."

"Did he also mention to you that he was trying to blackmail me?"

"Yes, he told me. He admits that was a mistake. But that didn't give you the right to try to kill him."

"I think it did. Anyway, it's his word against mine. You can't prove any of this. The only thing you have is a little frightened boy who let my husband fuck him."

"You seem to forget that you confessed to that 'little boy' that you killed your husband."

"Who's going to believe him?" Samantha laughed into the phone.

"It doesn't matter if anyone believes him. Just the hint of a scandal like this will have the media digging to uncover every secret in your life. Your credibility will be destroyed, and with any luck, you'll spend the rest of your life in prison."

"I can assure you that is not going to happen, Mr. Truman. You underestimate me."

"And I can assure you I am going to do everything in my power to make sure that it does."

Samantha laughed again. "Are you sleeping with him too? He's a bigger whore than I first imagined. Although, I must admit, he is quite lovely. Please tell Danny we have unfinished business. And now, my dear Mr. Truman, so do you and I."

Chapter 6

Hattie Williams had a taste for sweet potato pie. The morning had come and gone, filled with the routines that served well to keep her body active and her mind stimulated. Morning scriptures were read from the weathered leather Bible that had belonged to her mother. A fresh load of crisp white sheets, pillowcases, and towels had been hung to dry in the morning sun. A coat of lemon wax had been applied to the many wood surfaces that held the memories of her life. Now it was time to consider what she would prepare for dinner.

Even though Hattie lived alone, she never deprived herself of a full meal at dinnertime. The same love and skill she had used to prepare meals for her husband and their three children were applied each day to herself.

Her kitchen was awash in midday sunlight. Handmade sheer curtains provided little cover from the warmth that poured through the windows. The creamy yellow–tiled counters and the white- and minty-green-checkered linoleum floor were regularly scrubbed so clean with Pine-Sol that meals could have easily been served on them. "Just because we're poor doesn't mean we have to be dirty," her mother would say. Her house always had a fresh hint of lemon in the air because of the furniture polish and the often used cleaning solution.

A circa 1950s toaster and coffee percolator and a vintage white KitchenAid mixer lined the countertop, as they had for the last fifty-some-odd years, poised and ready for duty. No microwave contraptions had ever crossed the Williamses' threshold. "If it can't be warmed up in the oven, then I don't want it in my house. I ain't in that much of a hurry to eat" was Hattie's motto.

Wrapped in her floral-print apron, Hattie reached in the root cupboard and retrieved three large sweet potatoes. Hands that were more accurate that the most precise scale estimated that she held a total of one and a half pounds. "That should do it," she said out loud. The large pot of boiling water on the O'Keefe & Merritt was already filling the room with steam. Hattie washed each potato under cold water, sliced each one into fourths, and then dropped the pieces into the pot.

She made the pie just as her mother and her mother's mother had made it. No need for a recipe. No need to Google the ingredients. This recipe, like so many other family recipes, was etched on the strands of her DNA. *Four beaten eggs, one tablespoon of vegetable oil, and one tablespoon of vanilla,* she thought as she blended the ingredients. *Half a cup of brown sugar and half a cup of maple syrup.*

"Now, where did I put my cinnamon and nutmeg?" she asked out loud, rummaging through her spice rack. "There they are. A teaspoon of cinnamon and a quarter teaspoon of nutmeg."

Hattie emptied the ingredients into the mixer and added a half teaspoon of salt and a cup of heavy cream. Her internal kitchen timer went off, and just as always, the potatoes in the pot were like butter under the knife she inserted in them. After draining the potatoes, she peeled them. The potato skins yielded under her touch, and she added the soft orange potato flesh to the mixer.

The machine whirled and whisked just as efficiently as it had the day she made her first coconut cake fifty years ago. Hattie hadn't made a homemade crust in years.

Since the day she discovered store-bought crust, she had never looked back. "That little white Pillsbury Doughboy always does just fine," she proclaimed, rightly reasoning.

She removed a pie crust from the refrigerator, pressed it into a pie plate, then carefully poured in the sweet potato filling. With the pie crust filled nearly to the brim with the creamy, sweet goodness, Hattie checked the oven to make sure it was a perfect 375 degrees. When she opened the oven door, her face was met with a gust of heat. *Perfect.*

She slid the pie dish into the oven. As she closed the heated tomb containing the pie, she felt the familiar lightness in her head. She knew immediately what was in store for her in the forty-five minutes it would take to bake the pie. Hattie wiped her moist hands on her apron and slowly made her way to the kitchen table. *Cleanin' up is gonna have to wait till the Lord's done showing me what he wants me to see,* she thought.

Before the full weight of her body had rested in the vinyl chair, the vision began. The image of Hezekiah Cleaveland appeared in the sun-drenched window. He was in his usual black suit, with the tie cinched at his neck.

"Pastor," Hattie said with a gasp. "My dear, sweet pastor."

Hezekiah did not respond to her gentle greeting. Instead, he seemed focused on an energy that came from just out of her range of view. Hezekiah looked lovingly at the source of the energy. He slowly reached out his hand, beckoning for someone to come into Hattie's view. And then she saw him for the first time. A young man slowly appeared. She immediately felt the love and intense affection pouring from them both.

"Is that him, Pastor?" Hattie said softly. "Is that who all this love is for?" Even though he did not speak, Hattie clearly heard the word *yes* echo through the kitchen. Gripped by the scene unfolding before her, she didn't notice the aroma of sweet potato pie filling the kitchen.

A burst of light suddenly leapt from the scene at the point where the tips of their fingers finally touched. At that moment, as she became enveloped by the love exchanged between the two, a tear escaped from Hattie's eye.

"I'm so glad you found love in this world, Pastor," she said. "All anybody wants on this earth is to be loved." Hattie, for the first time, looked away from the window and said, "Thank you, Lord, for blessing him with love before you called him home."

When Hattie's eyes returned to the vision, the figures had shifted. Hezekiah was now shielding the man from a force that was slowly eclipsing the love that was there only moments earlier. A billowing haze obscured the two men from her view. Hezekiah was pleading for the energy to leave them as he protected the cowering figure. Hattie immediately knew the source of the destructive power that now dominated the scene. It was an evil that she had felt on so many Sunday mornings. It was Samantha Cleaveland.

Suddenly Hezekiah vanished. The young man was now left cowering and vulnerable in the mist that surrounded him. Hattie could see the fear in his eyes and feel the terror pouring from his spirit.

"Help him, Pastor Cleaveland!" she shrieked. "Please help him. He needs you." But Hezekiah was nowhere to be seen.

The man began to thrash violently on the ground, as if he were being beaten. She saw blood trickle from his mouth as each invisible blow was leveled.

"She's going to kill him, Pastor," Hattie called out again. "You have to do something! You have to stop her."

But the blows continued with steadily increasing force, until the young man lay on the ground, motionless. Hattie felt helpless and weak sitting in the chair. She was an unwilling witness to such mayhem and evil.

"Lord, why did you show me this?" she cried out, squeezing her eyes tightly closed. "I don't want to see this. He was a beautiful young man, and Hezekiah loved him so much. Why would you let her kill him too?"

When Hattie finally opened her eyes, the image had begun to gradually fade. She sat trembling and wept into a crumpled paper napkin, retrieved unconsciously from a holder at the center of the table.

When the image had completely vanished, she could once again see the tranquility of her vegetable garden and the freshly washed laundry on the clothesline gently dancing in the breeze. Hattie gripped the soaked napkin in her hand and said out loud, "You've got to stop her, Lord. It's just not right."

Suddenly the smell of cinnamon and brown sugar jarred her back into the kitchen. "Oh, Lord," she said mournfully. "Has it been forty-five minutes already?"

Victoria Johnson stopped her silver Mercedes at the iron gate that guarded the Cleaveland estate. She looked scornfully at the security guard as he approached her window.

"Good afternoon, ma'am," the uniformed man said. "May I help you?"

"You can start by opening the gate."

"Is Pastor Cleaveland expecting you?" he responded politely.

"Don't you have a list you can check, instead of wasting my time?"

Victoria was Samantha's oldest friend. She was the wife of the Reverend Sylvester Johnson, Pastor of First Bethany Church of Los Angeles. Victoria was the only pastor's wife with whom Samantha had never competed. The women were equals in every way, including their shared loathing for the men they had married. There were no secrets between them.

Samantha's wealth far exceeded that of Victoria's, but their penchant for spending the alms of their followers was equal in every way. Weekend shopping trips to Paris, personal jewelers, and the latest five-figure designer bags were all theirs on demand. Victoria's claim to fame was not her oratory skills or her ability to manipulate the masses with her cunning. Instead, it was her beauty. Tall, svelte, and elegant, Victoria put all women in her presence to shame, with the exception of Samantha. Her luscious veneer hid the foulmouthed alcoholic who simmered just beneath the surface. Samantha was her friend and confidante; but the bottle was her confessional; and alcohol, the priest to whom she confessed her sins.

"May I have your name, ma'am?" the guard continued, undaunted by her growing irritation.

"Who does your list say Pastor Cleaveland is meeting at one thirty?" she replied snidely, pointing to the iPad the guard was holding like a shield.

"Mrs. Victoria Johnson."

"Good boy. Now, open the gate."

"Yes, ma'am," said the now befuddled guard. "May I please see your identification? It's for Pastor Cleaveland's protection. I'm sure you understand."

The calming effects of the vodka and tonic Victoria had consumed before leaving her home just over the hill were beginning to wear off, causing her nerves to fray.

"If you don't open that fucking gate right now, I'm going to ram this brand-new Mercedes-Benz right through it. I'm sure you'll *understand,*" she sneered through gritted pearly teeth.

"Yes, ma'am," sputtered the guard as he sprinted back to the gatehouse. "Right away, ma'am."

The gate, embroidered with the steel initials HZ, glided open. As Victoria sped past the guard shed, she yelled out the window, "And don't call me 'ma'am'. I'm not your goddamn mother."

The grounds were surrounded by an eight-foot-high white stucco wall. Lower points in the wall allowed passersby brief glimpses of the magnificent estate. Meticulously manicured grounds surrounded the home and seemed to spill down the hill into the skyline. To the left was a freshly painted green tennis court with sharp white lines. A whitewashed gazebo stood to the right and overlooked the Pacific Ocean, and a two-story guesthouse could be seen tucked behind a grove of trees. At the final curve of the driveway the trees unfurled like theater curtains, and the house could finally be seen. It was an off-white Mediterranean villa sitting on a sloped crest with spectacular views of the city and the ocean. Double stone stairways ascended to the grand main entrance under a covered porch, the roof of which was held aloft by four twenty-foot-high, white carved pillars.

Victoria was greeted at the door by Etta. "Good afternoon, Mrs. Johnson. Pastor Cleaveland is waiting for you in the conservatory."

Victoria whisked by Etta without really acknowledging her presence. Her only greeting was, "Bring me a gin and tonic."

The conservatory was three walls of glass and a glass roof attached to the back of the mansion. The sun, the lush green grounds, and the crystal-blue sky served as the wallpaper. Exotic plants and flowers, stone fountains spewing ribbons of water, wicker furniture, and ornately carved statues filled the room.

"You need to fire that fucking rent-a-cop at your gate. Son of a bitch wasn't going to let me in. Thought I was gonna have to suck his dick just to get my lunch."

Samantha laughed as Victoria approached and air kissed her cheeks. "He's just doing his job, girl. He probably thought you were my psycho killer."

"What psycho killer? Do you have another stalker?"

"Oh, you know, girl. There's always plenty of nuts to go around. Security has been on high alert since that ugly Hezekiah incident."

"Oh, that. Do the police think you're still in danger?" Victoria asked, resting in an overstuffed wicker chair. "Where's that woman with my drink?"

As she spoke, Etta silently entered the sun-washed room, carrying the requested beverage on a silver tray.

"It took you long enough. Just put it there."

"I'm sorry, Mrs. Johnson. I had too—"

"Never mind, Etta," Samantha interrupted. "Now, leave us alone and close the door behind you. I'll let you know when we're ready for lunch."

As Etta walked to the door, she heard Samantha say to Victoria, "That woman is so incompetent."

"Then why don't you fire her?" Victoria asked, knowing that Etta could still hear them.

"Because of my dearly departed husband. Five years ago, due to his ridiculous sense of loyalty, he put a clause in his will that said if I fired her within a year of his death, she would get three hundred thousand dollars. I'd rather keep her here and make her life miserable for a year than give her that kind of money."

Etta quietly closed the door.

"The bastard is dead, and he's still fucking you. That reminds me, girl," Victoria said, leaning forward in her seat. "What ever happened with that blackmail business? Did you ever hear from him again?"

Samantha looked over her shoulder at the door to ensure they had their privacy before responding, "I guess it was a hoax. I never heard from him again."

"You must be relieved. But how do you know he won't try it again? I told you I've got people who'll sniff his punk ass out and make him regret he ever heard of you."

"I'm not worried about that."

"Why not? You never know what could get in that crazy fuck's head a year or two from now. Why take any chances?"

Samantha smiled wryly and said, "I'm not worried, dear, because I have people too."

Victoria leaned forward in the chair. "Ooh, good for you, Sammy. You can't be too careful, especially after the way Hezekiah fucked you over. If Sylvester ever did that to me, he'd come up dead too. For the life of me, I don't understand how you just stood by while that son of a bitch was fucking a man."

"I didn't just *stand by,* Victoria. I couldn't. There was too much at stake. If that had come out, I would have lost everything. And you know me better than that."

"You knew? What did you do? I hope whatever it was, you scared the shit out of him."

"Oh, I did more than that," Samantha said casually.

"Go on and tell me, girl. What did you do?"

"Let's just say I arranged it so he would never fuck anybody again."

Victoria paused briefly to ponder the true meaning of Samantha's words. She took a sip of her drink, then another. "Are you saying what I think you're saying? And, believe me, I pray to God you are," she said wickedly.

"I'm saying exactly what you think I'm saying," Samantha said coldly.

"You didn't?"

"I did."

"Sammy, you had him . . ."

Samantha leaned forward and whispered, "What else could I do? He was about to cost me everything. The church, the house, my reputation. He gave me no choice."

"I'm speechless. I don't know what to say. I never knew you had it in you."

"Never underestimate what a desperate woman will do. All those years I never cared who he fucked, until he made the mistake of telling me he was going to leave me and the church for a man. What a fool. I had to stop him, and that was the only way."

"Fuck, yes, that was the only way. Son of a bitch. What was he thinking?"

"That's the point. He *wasn't* thinking. So, unfortunately for him, I had to do the thinking for both of us."

"Well, for what it's worth, Sammy, I think you made the right decision. How did you do it? I might want to do the same thing to Sylvester one day."

"Never mind that. I've already told you too much."

"Now look at you. You're the pastor of one of the largest churches in the fucking country. This Sunday you're going to preach in your new cathedral. You're richer than the goddamn queen, and you got away with it all smelling like a rose. Goddamn, I envy you."

"I'm not completely done yet," Samantha said, standing and walking to the glass wall and looking out over the grounds. "I've still got two small pieces of business to take care of before it's all over."

"Handle your business, girl," Victoria said, raising her glass in a toast. "Handle your business."

"You know I will, Victoria. Now, let's have lunch. I'm starving."

Gideon quietly peered over the redwood gate into Hattie's back garden. Hattie was bending over a row of plants that were bulging with yellow squash, okra, collard green stalks, and tomatoes. The yard was as tidy as the inside of her home. Pristine white sheets billowed on the clothesline. The grass was neatly manicured, and a six-foot pink brick wall guarded the sacred ground and its high priestess.

Gideon could faintly hear the hymn Hattie was singing as she scooped tomatoes from the vines and dropped them into a wicker basket hanging from her arm.

"There is a fountain filled with blood drawn from Emmanuel's veins; and sinners plunged beneath that flood lose all their guilty stains. Lose all their guilty stains, lose all their guilty stains; and sinners plunged beneath that flood lose all their guilty stains."

As Gideon listened, he vividly remembered his grandmother singing that very same song when he was a small boy in Texas. He could almost see her standing on the front pew of the little wood-framed church, wearing her favorite white straw hat with the bursting blue and yellow silk flowers.

"The dying thief rejoiced to see that fountain in his day; and there may I, though vile as he, wash all my sins away. Wash all my sins away, wash all my sins away; and there may I, though vile as he, wash all my sins away."

Gideon was lost in the hypnotic spell of the hymn when he heard, "Don't just stand there, boy. Come in."

Hattie's back was to the gate where Gideon stood. She had not looked up or turned around before she spoke, but she knew who was looking at her over the redwood gate.

Gideon was jolted back into the present by her words and called out, "I'm sorry, Mrs. Williams. I knocked on your front door, but you didn't answer, so I thought I'd check back here to see if you were home. I hope I didn't startle you."

"Not at all. Take a lot more than you standing at my gate to startle an old lady like me. Now, come in. The gate's unlocked."

Hattie stood and turned to Gideon as he approached. The wicker basket swinging on her arm was filled with tomatoes. Her plastic garden clogs had left footprints in the moist soil.

"Now, what brings you back here, Mr. Truman? I wasn't sure if I'd ever see you again."

"I had a few more questions I wanted to ask you, if that's okay. It will only take a few minutes."

Hattie was pleased to see Gideon again. She quickly noted the air of desperation in his spirit as he spoke. "That's fine. I want to help you. I told you the last time I saw you, somebody's praying for you. Your grandmother, in fact. Have you talked to her lately? She misses you something terrible."

"I have not."

"Call her, boy. You need her more than she needs you right now."

"Yes, ma'am. I think you're right. I promise I will call her."

"Now, as you can see, I got lots more tomatoes and squash to pick before it gets dark," Hattie said, pointing to the plants at her feet. "So what can I do for you?"

Gideon was embarrassed. "I'm so sorry, Mrs. Williams. That was very inconsiderate of me. Your garden is lovely. May I help you pick vegetables while we speak? I haven't been in a garden since my grandmother's. It used to be my job to water it every day, after school."

"She was lucky to have you. I'm on my own now that my children are grown. They like to eat the food but never lift a shovel to help back here."

"I remember one summer my grandmother was away for three weeks. The last thing she told me was to not forget to water the garden. Without her there to remind me, I did forget, and when she came home three weeks later, every plant had died. To this day I haven't forgiven myself for that."

"You should, 'cause she never held it against you. There's a basket over by the fence, there by the flowers. Use that one."

Gideon navigated the rows of vegetables like a farmer in Gucci loafers. He reached around a bush with stalks of vibrant pink flowers springing from its core. "These flowers are lovely, Mrs. Williams," he called out to her as he reached for one of the buds. "What are they called?"

"Don't touch those, boy, 'less you want to die where you're standing," Hattie called out abruptly. "Those are foxgloves. One of the most poisonous flowers God put on this earth. Just a nip of the stem would kill you."

"I'm sorry. Why do you have them here if they're so dangerous?"

Hattie smiled. "Never know when they might come in handy."

Gideon's hand froze, suspended only inches away from the beautiful flowers. He looked curiously at the blossoms, then at Hattie, and took a cautious step away from the bush. Now with basket in tow he returned to the row of squash. "Shall I pick these, ma'am?" he asked, pointing down at the bushes of deep green leaves shielding yellow orbs.

"Good place to start," she replied. "Fit as many as you can in the basket."

"Mrs. Williams, I don't know if you remember, but the last time we spoke, you left me with a sort of warning. You told me to be careful because I was heading toward someone who was more dangerous than I could imagine."

"I remember. Have you met that person yet?" Hattie asked as she pulled another tomato from the vine.

"I believe I have," Gideon said cautiously.

"And who is it?" she asked as another tomato made its way into her basket.

"Pastor Samantha Cleaveland."

"I also told you, you was about to meet someone that you've been looking for your whole life. Have you met them yet?"

Gideon's hand froze on a squash when he heard the question. "Yes, ma'am. I think I have met them," he answered slowly.

Hattie heard the caution in his response. "I'm very glad to hear that, son. Very glad." Hattie stood upright and walked over to Gideon, who was crouching before a plant. She placed her gentle hand on his shoulder and said, "Never be ashamed of who you love, son. Just thank God for giving you someone to love."

Gideon looked up at Hattie. He couldn't conceal the moisture that had formed in the corners of his eyes. He simply said, "Thank you, ma'am. That means more to me than you can imagine."

"Good," Hattie snapped with approval and returned to the tomato plants. "So what's this about Samantha Cleaveland?"

Gideon felt somehow emboldened within the confines of the pink brick walls and in the presence of Hattie Williams. He stopped picking the vegetables and stood to his feet. "Mrs. Williams, I don't want to shock you, but . . . I believe Samantha Cleaveland killed her husband."

Gideon paused, waiting for a reaction from the old woman, but there was none. She simply continued to pluck tomatoes gingerly from the vines.

"I also believe, or rather I know," he stammered and cleared his throat, "that Hezekiah was involved in an affair . . . with a man . . . which is why she killed him."

Still no reaction.

"I also believe, ma'am . . . again, that is, I know . . . that Samantha tried to kill the man Hezekiah had an affair with so that he would not go public with his story."

Gideon was shocked, but also frightened, by the lack of response to his seemingly outlandish allegations. He waited patiently for her to lash out and demand indignantly that he leave her garden.

Instead, Hattie kept her back to him and continued to slowly fill her basket. Then, finally, he heard a mournful whisper. "I know, baby. I know."

There was silence in the Eden-like garden. A white butterfly pirouetted around the petals of the foxgloves. The flutters of a thousand ladybug wings whispered on the back of a gentle breeze that swept through the vegetables.

"You know?" Gideon finally said, breaking the spell the silence had cast. "How do you know?"

"God tells us all things, son. Some of us just listen better than others."

"But, Mrs. Williams, if you knew, why didn't you tell someone?"

Hattie finally stood and faced him. They now stood only yards apart across neatly hoed rows of vegetables.

"And say what, son? That I had a vision of Samantha killing her husband in my kitchen window."

Gideon saw clearly the anguish and pain in the old woman's face as she spoke.

"I know why God put me on this earth," Hattie continued. "Not to interfere with His work or to tell people how they should live their lives. He put me here as an intercessor. Do you know what that is?"

Before Gideon could answer, Hattie spoke again. "He put me here to pray for others when they can't pray for themselves. To put my spirit between them and the evil that threatens to destroy their souls. To intercede and plead their case before God when they don't even know they're in danger. Now, what God ultimately does is not for me to say. From the first day I met Hezekiah T. Cleaveland, I was on my knees, praying for him. I saw he was in danger, and I prayed for God to save him, but . . ."

Gideon saw the tears forming in Hattie's eyes. Her voice began to tremble as she spoke.

"I prayed that God would spare him, but he had a different plan." Hattie wiped a tear from her cheek with the apron that was cinched around her waist. "I did my job, son. I did exactly what God put me on this earth to do. No more and no less."

Gideon felt her pain, but he pressed on. "But you voted to make her pastor. Even though you knew what she had done?"

Hattie sat the basket of tomatoes on the ground. The weight had become too much for her to bear. She looked at the flowers and said, "I thought it was the only way for the church to survive. Hezekiah gave his life for that church, and millions of people around the world depend on it for their spiritual nourishment. She was the only person who could keep it alive."

Again silence took control of the garden. The ladybugs rested their wings, and the butterfly settled on the petal of a flower.

"Considering all that has happened since his death, do you still feel you made the right decision?" Gideon asked delicately.

Hattie looked at the butterfly and simply said, "I don't know, baby. I just don't know anymore."

"Gideon, please, I'm begging you to leave her alone. She's too dangerous."

"I can't do that, Danny. She has to be stopped. She's killed once, that we know of. She tried to kill you, and she's threatened me. I can't just walk away."

Danny sat upright on the chaise lounge when he heard the words. The sun was just setting behind the Hollywood Hills. Danny and Gideon were sitting by the pool in Gideon's backyard. Parker purred as he lay curled in a gray ball on the tiled terrace between the two men.

"What do you mean, she threatened you? When did you talk to her?"

"Yesterday. I spoke with her yesterday."

Danny bolted from the chaise. "Gideon, no!" Danny exclaimed.

Gideon stood and grabbed Danny's arm to prevent him from walking away. "I had to," he said, pulling Danny back down on the chaise. "I had to let her know that I'm on to her."

"Did you tell her I was still alive?"

"Yes."

"Are you trying to get me killed?" Danny said, yanking his arm free. "I'm as good as dead now that she knows. Don't you understand? She admitted to me that she killed Hezekiah. She can't risk me talking to the police."

"I won't let her hurt you, Danny. I won't let her get anywhere near you."

"How can you protect me? You can't be with me twenty-four hours a day, and I can't stay locked in this house for the rest of my life."

"You won't have to. As soon as I get enough evidence to tie her to Hezekiah's death, I'm going to expose her on national television. If that doesn't work, I would kill her myself before I let her harm you."

Danny could not conceal his fear. He looked Gideon in the eye and said, "So you believe me? You believe that she killed Hezekiah and that she tried to kill me?"

"Of course I believe you. I always have. By telling her I know everything, she will think twice before trying to do anything to you again. Don't you see, baby? I put myself between you and her."

"Why would you do that, Gideon? This is my problem. I don't want anyone else to get hurt."

"Can't you guess why I did it? I'm in love with you, Danny St. John. I would do anything to protect you. Including risk my own life."

"You can't love me, Gideon. You don't know me," Danny said dismissively.

Gideon grabbed Danny's shoulders and turned him toward his face. "You're wrong, Danny. I know you better than anyone. You are the man I've held every night as you fell asleep in my arms. You are the man who helped me realize there's more to my life than fame and 'the next big story.' I've found myself in your eyes, Danny. You've shown me that I am able to love, because I feel love every time you touch me. You can't look me in the eye and tell me you don't feel the same way, because I know you do."

Silence fell between them. The only sound that could be heard was the gentle gurgling of the spa in the distance and the purr of Parker at their feet.

Danny finally spoke. "You're right, Gideon. I do love you. I'm just afraid."

"Afraid of what? You shouldn't be afraid to love."

"I'm afraid I'll lose you, just like I lost Hezekiah. I loved him, and look what happened. She took him from me, and now she's threatening to take you. I couldn't take that, Gideon."

"She's not going to take me from you. I promise. No one will ever be able to separate me from you. I've searched my entire life for you, and now that I have found you, no one is going to come between us."

Danny wanted to believe him. He needed to believe him. He had never imagined that so soon after Hezekiah's death, he would be within a breath's length of a man so warm and so loving. A man who summoned the same feelings of love from deep in his heart. It had taken a lifetime for him to find Hezekiah and only a second to lose him. And now the same feelings of warmth, security, and love were upon him again. This man had simply appeared in his world, unannounced and with no warning.

The loneliness and despair he had felt in the months after Hezekiah's death had been slowly replaced with comfort and hope. The same reflection he saw in Hezekiah's eyes was there in Gideon's. Danny felt he existed once again when Gideon looked at him. He existed because Gideon could see him. He was alive because Gideon could feel the warmth from his weary body. There was value in his words because Gideon could hear him and said the same words back to him.

Danny trembled as Gideon pulled him closer. "I love you, Danny St. John," he whispered. The words seemed to skim across the glassy surface of the turquoise pool, then echo through the palms and spill down the hill into the canyon below.

"I love you, Gideon Truman," Danny whispered back, finally releasing the words from his heart. "Please don't leave me."

Chapter 7

"I've been trying to reach you all day. Why haven't you returned my calls?"

"I've been busy, David," Samantha replied sharply. "In case you haven't heard, I'm opening one of the largest churches in the world this Sunday."

David sat down behind the desk in his home office. He was relieved to hear Samantha's voice, despite the sharp tone in her response. The office was dark except for the glow from a laptop computer. A picture of Samantha beaming in front of the new glass cathedral filled the screen. The caption below read, "Pastor Cleaveland welcomes you to New Testament Cathedral." The remains from his third brandy sat dripping condensation onto a leather blotter.

"I just wanted to hear your voice. How are you?"

"Never mind that," she snapped. "Are you alone?"

David looked at the closed door. He could hear Scarlett rattling pans in the kitchen. "Yes. Scarlett is in the other room. Why? What's wrong?"

"I got a call from Gideon Truman. He told me that Danny St. John is still alive. That's what's wrong."

"Alive!" David exclaimed. "Are you sure? That's fantastic! That means I didn't kill him."

"No, David, that is not *fantastic,* you fool. If he talks, you and I will stand trial for attempted murder."

"But it was self-defense. He was blackmailing you. You thought he had a gun."

"None of that matters. I can't be involved in anything this sordid. The press will eat me alive. There'll be a drawn-out court case, and even if I'm found innocent in the end, I will most definitely lose everything."

"But . . . maybe he won't talk. He is just as guilty as you," David said pleadingly. The entire conversation had unfolded in his head long before the words were spoken. He knew and feared where it was leading. "Maybe we scared him enough that now he'll just disappear," was his feeble attempt at heading off the inevitable.

"It's too late for that. I told you Gideon Truman is the one who told me. So obviously, he's not too afraid to talk."

David let out an exasperated sigh, and the full weight of his body sank into the desk chair. With a trembling hand, he reached for the drink on the desk and in one gulp downed the remains. The taste of melted ice cubes was followed by the smooth, earthy flavor of brandy.

"You need to give him the money. Give him more than what he asked for," David said pleadingly.

"And what about Gideon?" was her matter-of-fact reply.

"Offer him money too. Every man has a price."

"I won't pay those sons of bitches a fucking nickel, and I'm disappointed that you would suggest it. This is obviously too much for you to handle, so I'll deal with it myself."

"Wait a minute, Samantha," David said, jumping to his feet. "Don't hang up. I'm just trying to come up with possible solutions."

"There's only one solution, and I think you know what it is."

Samantha skillfully let her last statement hang in the air to allow the full weight of its implications to settle in.

"You can't be saying what I think you're saying," David finally uttered.

"It's the only solution."

"But . . . are you talking about . . . murder?" he whispered.

"I'm talking about keeping us out of jail so we can continue to do God's work."

"I can't do it, Samantha."

"So you were lying to me when you said you would kill a thousand men for me and that you would do anything I told you. I guess you were also lying when you said you loved me."

David's hesitation came as no surprise to Samantha. She was used to the weak constitutions of men. She had mastered the art of manipulating fainthearted men to do her bidding after years of moving Hezekiah with the nimble hands of a master puppeteer.

Before they married, Hezekiah's dream had been to be a missionary in Uganda. Samantha had dutifully agreed and had encouraged his dream, until their wedding day in the little church in Compton. From that point on she had employed every tactic she had learned from watching her mother mold and transform her father into the pastor of one of the largest churches in the city at that time. And just as they were for her mother, sexual coercion, guilt, flattery, and threats were the tools she employed to make Hezekiah into the man she needed him to be. In time, she convinced him to open the small church in the storefront on Imperial Highway, and New Testament Cathedral was born.

After years of practice there was nothing Samantha could not convince a man to do on her behalf. There was no mountain too high to climb and no pit too deep to fall into for the love and approval, or even the simple approving glance, of Samantha Cleaveland. Those who were gay, straight, black, white, and every hue in between were susceptible to her mesmerizing smile and smoldering sensuality.

"You know I wasn't lying," David responded with force. "I love you. I worship you. I would do anything for you, but—"

"If you really loved me, David, you would not allow them to do this to me. You're weak and a liar. Just like Hezekiah."

"Don't compare me to him!" David shouted. "Don't ever compare me to him. I'm more of a man than he ever was."

Samantha stepped up the pressure. "No, you're not. He wasn't much of a man, and neither are you." Her timing was perfect, as usual.

"I didn't say I wouldn't do it. I'm just—"

"Never mind, David. I should have never expected more from you. You're wasting my time now. Go back to your wife and daughter and have a blessed life."

"Don't hang up, Samantha!" he shouted. "I'll do it, damn it. I'll do whatever it takes to prove how much I love you."

At that moment the office door flung open and Scarlett seethed in the threshold. "Who are you talking to, David? Is that her?" she shouted.

David turned abruptly and placed his hand over the mouthpiece. "What are you screaming about?" he asked angrily. "I'm on the phone."

"I heard everything you said. Are you talking to Samantha Cleaveland?"

David returned to the call. "I have to go. I will call you later."

"Is that Scarlett?" Samantha asked cautiously.

"I have to go now," he repeated.

"Don't say anything about this to her, David."

"Don't worry. I won't. I'll talk to you later."

"I heard you," Scarlett said, approaching David. What will you do to prove how much you love her? What did she ask you to do?"

"That's none of your business, Scarlett. You're being ridiculous. I can't talk to you when you're this hysterical."

"You're in love with her. She's out of your league, David. She'll chew you up and spit you out, just like she does everyone in her life."

"You don't know what you're talking about. I suggest you get out and leave me alone."

"I won't leave you alone!" she shouted even louder. "You're my husband, not hers! I'm warning you, David. She's evil. She'll destroy you if you get too close to her."

"Shut up!" he shouted, raising his hand, as if to strike her. "Shut your fucking mouth! You lied to me all these years about Natalie. God only knows what else you've been lying about, so how can you judge anyone?"

"I've told you a thousand times I lied only to protect Natalie. It was a mistake. I should have told you the truth."

"It's too late for that now."

Scarlett walked closer to David. She raised her hand and placed it gently on his cheek. "It's not too late, David," she said pleadingly. "It's not too late to save our family."

David violently pushed her hand away. "Family," he replied mockingly. "We are not a *family*. Natalie is not my daughter, and she never was."

"I never told you she was."

"You also conveniently didn't tell me she was the bastard child of Hezekiah Cleaveland. Always protecting your own ass, regardless of who gets hurt. And believe me, Scarlett, you hurt me deeply. But to be honest, I don't think that really matters to you. What really matters to you is that you maintain that ridiculous victim routine you've crafted your whole fucking life. 'Poor, poor me. Look at how poorly the world has treated me. Look at how Hezekiah abandoned me. Look at how cruelly Samantha treated me. Now look at how my no-good husband is treating me, even after I told him the truth. The world is so cruel.' Well, I've got a news flash for you, Scarlett. I don't care anymore," he said sarcastically. "Boo the fucking hoo. My advice to you is that you should do whatever it takes for you to sleep at night, and you can fucking bet I'm going to do the same."

With his final words spoken, David pushed her aside and exited the room.

"She's going to destroy you, David!" Scarlett shouted to his retreating body. "She's going to destroy you, just like she did Hezekiah. I'm not going to let her destroy my life again, David!"

"Ladies and gentlemen, my guest tonight is Pastor Samantha Cleaveland," the host said with a British accent. "For the one or two of you out there who don't know who she is, I'll tell you. Pastor Cleaveland has the distinction of being one of the most popular pastors in the world and is the head of one of the largest congregations in the United States."

Samantha sat across the acrylic desk from Jonathan Moran. His boyish looks were broadcast live to the home of millions each evening on CNN. Studio lights and the electric blue set made his cheeks look unnaturally rosy.

"Welcome, Pastor Cleaveland. Thank you so much for joining us this evening. I have to tell you I have been looking so forward to meeting you in person."

Samantha wore a Versace floral two-piece lace suit with four crystal buttons, a notched collar, and long sleeves with scalloped cuffs. "Thank you, Jonathan. It's a pleasure for me to be here." Her black hair caught every ray of artificial light that pointed in her direction.

"I don't mean to gush," the host continued, "and I hope you don't mind me saying, but you are an exquisite woman. I, like most other people in this country, have seen you on television, and I thought you were stunning, but my heavens, you are even more beautiful in person. I hope that doesn't offend you."

"Not at all," Samantha said, flashing only a portion of her signature smile. "On the contrary, I'm flattered."

"Good. Now that that's out of the way, and you've reduced me to a jabbering schoolboy," he said with a shy smile, "let's talk about what's going on in your life. I know you most likely would prefer not to talk about it, but I feel like we must. You lost your husband, Pastor Hezekiah T. Cleaveland, in one of the most horrific and astonishing ways anyone could possibly imagine. I guess there's no delicate way to put it, but he was killed right in front of you, in the pulpit of your church, New Testament Cathedral, in Los Angeles. I can't even begin to fathom what that must have been like for you."

Samantha indulged the tiresome host and responded, "I don't mind talking about it, Jonathan. It seems the more I talk about it, the quicker I've been able to heal. Sometimes I can't believe it actually happened. One moment he was standing in front of me, full of life, and the next, he was lying in my arms, breathing his last breath. I still have a hard time accepting the fact that he's actually gone. It all happened so quickly."

"Do you have any idea who did this?"

"The police have very few leads. They've warned me that the more time that passes, the more unlikely it is that they will be able to identify his killer."

"That must make you furious. I mean, that this—I hesitate to even call him a person—that this animal is still out there and could possibly never be apprehended."

"It did at first, and that's the natural response when a loved one is taken from you unnecessarily. I'll admit I initially wanted him to be arrested and to suffer the same fate he inflicted upon my husband. But the more I prayed about it and the more I was able to let go of my anger and turn it over to God, the better I began to feel. The Bible tells us that God will never put more on us than we can bear, and after this test I truly believe that."

"Now, you, in a very short time after his death, were installed as the pastor of your church. Some of my colleagues in the media have been very harsh and have criticized you for not waiting an *appropriate* amount of time after his death. Some have called you, and I'm quoting here, 'power hungry.' How do you respond to those who have said that you're just not ready and this was simply a desperate move on your part to hang on to the religious empire you and your husband built?"

"I would say that everyone is entitled to their opinion," Samantha said, unfazed. "But at the end of the day that is all it is, an opinion. If they knew the facts, I don't think they would say those things."

"Then, please tell us the facts. What possessed you to step into the position of pastor only two short months after your husband's death?"

"The simple answer is that I was asked by the board of trustees to take over the position. Whether it's true or not, they felt I was the best person to continue the work of our ministry in the absence of Hezekiah. Believe me, I wanted nothing more than to go to my room and lie under the covers for the rest of my life after it happened, but God had a different plan for me. So when they approached me with their decision, I was shocked and, I must admit, a bit terrified."

"Why terrified? Weren't you always deeply involved in the day-to-day operations of the church, and you're an ordained minister, correct?"

"That is correct. I am an ordained minister, and I hold a doctorate in theology from Brighton Theological Institute. I also have an MBA."

"I don't think anyone has ever questioned your qualifications. I've heard you speak on several occasions, and each time I was so moved, you left me on the verge of tears. It's more the timing of the appointment."

"What most people don't realize is that Hezekiah and I built New Testament Cathedral together."

"Really? I, for one, didn't know that."

"Yes. Hezekiah was a charismatic and bigger-than-life man. He had an uncanny mastery of the scriptures, and I truly believe he had a special connection to God. But the day-to-day operations of the church, the television ministry, and all the national and international components of the work were primarily my responsibility. Even many people who are intimately involved with us had no idea of the depth and breadth of my involvement in the church, and to be honest, I preferred it that way."

Jonathan looked at his guest with a doubting eye as she spoke, but the cameras chose not to share his skepticism with the nation.

"I enjoyed being the 'wind beneath his wings,' as the song says. He was my husband, and he was called by God to be the head of our household and the church. I was very content living in his shadow."

Jonathan couldn't stand being part of the obvious deception and decided to quickly change the direction of the conversation. Samantha's glow had slowly begun to dim for him.

"Now, this is a very exciting week for you. You recently completed the construction of your new cathedral, and this Sunday you'll hold the first worship service there."

"That's correct," Samantha said, sensing the almost imperceptible decline in his juvenile infatuation. She proceeded with her usual charm, but now it was tempered by caution and humility.

"This was Hezekiah's dream." As she spoke, images of the cathedral, the beautiful couple waving from the pulpit, and Samantha veiled in black at his funeral flashed on a giant screen between them. "His vision was to build a church that could accommodate the entire New Testament Cathedral family. Now we can all be together at one time, like a family should, and feast together on the word of God. This could have never been built without the love and dedication of my husband and the love and generosity of millions of our supporters around the world."

"Could you tell us how your daughter is doing? This must have been devastating for her."

"That was the most painful part of this entire ordeal. My daughter means the world to me, and the sun rose and set in her father's eyes. She was definitely Daddy's little girl. She is doing much better. She's back in school, and we're surrounding her with love, support, and prayers."

"Tell us a little bit about you, Pastor Cleaveland. I think many of our viewers know what you are, but they don't know *who* you are, if that makes any sense to you. What is it in you that has kept you going all these years in a field that I'm sure has many difficult moments?"

"There's not much to tell, Jonathan. I'm your average PK who was raised in the church. The church has been a part of my entire life. My father was a pastor, and his father was a pastor. From the moment I laid eyes on Hezekiah, I could see the spirit of God around him, and I knew immediately that he was going to be my husband. From then on, we dedicated our entire lives to the ministry, and now, without him, I promised God and myself that I would continue and not give up the fight."

"That's all well and good, but what is it that motivates you? I mean, what makes you get up in the morning and think, *I'm going to dedicate my life to others, put myself second and other people's needs first?*'"

"I love people, Jonathan, and I made a promise to myself to make sure that everyone I encounter feels the love of God through me. Our hands are God's hands. Our voice is God's voice. I deeply believe that everyone is put on this earth for a reason, and I want to see everyone live life to the fullest and absolutely reach their potential. That's the fundamental message of God, and that is the foundation of this ministry."

"What do you say to the critics who accuse you of spending millions of dollars to build a shrine to yourself?" he asked bluntly.

"If they only knew the sacrifices I've made in my life, they would never make such accusations," she scoffed. "I have never benefited financially from this ministry. The donations that come in go directly into spreading the love of God to a world so desperately in need of it. I have dedicated my life to helping others and have even sacrificed loved ones to keep this ministry alive and to grow it into what it is today."

Samantha could see the glow of admiration slowly resurfacing in the host's countenance. It was undeniable that Jonathan was back in the Samantha fan club after her last passionate sermonette. *Probably has a hard-on under the desk,* she thought as he reached across the acrylic divide and caressed her hand.

"Well, Pastor Cleaveland, you are an amazing woman, and I feel like a better person just being in your presence. Thank you so much for taking the time to speak with us during what I am sure is a busy week for you."

"It's been my pleasure," Samantha responded, covering his clammy hand with hers. "Thank you so much for having me."

***

White boxes of vegetarian chow mein, hot and sour soup, fried prawns, and barbecued pork sat in the center of the dining room table, along with wooden chopsticks, little packets of soy sauce, and two tightly wrapped cellophane bundles of fortune cookies, hot mustard, and cheap paper napkins. Cynthia and Percy sat silently eating, only occasionally asking the other, "Could you please pass the chow mein?" or "Is there any more shrimp?"

Cynthia hadn't cooked a meal in their kitchen in over two months. All her energy had been consumed by plotting to remove Samantha from her lofty throne. Plan after plan had been intricately devised, including blackmail, anonymous death threats, lobbying each member of the board of trustees to change their vote, and a smear campaign designed to tarnish the Cleavelands' reputation to the point that not even Samantha could recover.

Each plan had required countless days to work out the fine details and only moments for Cynthia to discard for being either too risky, too easy for Samantha to recover from, or too likely to backfire in her own face. Now, sitting at the table across from Percy, Cynthia had no viable scheme for removing Samantha from the helm of New Testament Cathedral.

She shifted strands of noodles from one side of her plate to the other with her splintered disposable chopsticks, sipped Pellegrino, dabbed her lips with a paper napkin, and occasionally took a bite of the tasteless Americanized Chinese takeout.

"How was your day?" Percy finally asked to break the deafening divide.

There was no response.

"Cynthia, honey, how was your day?" he repeated.

"It was fine," came her simple, yet polite, reply.

"What did you do?"

Cynthia laid her chopsticks on the table and resigned herself to the fact that she had to have polite dinner conversation with her unambitious husband.

"I had a hair appointment this morning. After that I went shopping and bought a few things. Then lunch with my sister. Came home, ordered Chinese, and now I'm here with you. Is that enough detail for you?"

"I don't want to argue, Cynthia. I was only trying to be polite."

"I know, darling," she replied apologetically. "I'm sorry. I just have a lot on my mind. How was your day?"

Percy reached across the table and gently touched her arm. "No need to apologize. Things are crazy this week at church. I've already given five VIP tours of the grounds. I've lost track of how many interviews I've done. Today Samantha and I had lunch with the mayor, and tomorrow the governor is flying down for a personal tour. I think you may be wrong about Samantha, honey. So far I think she's doing a very good job. Did you see her on Jonathan Moran's show? She had him eating out of the palm of her hand."

Percy babbled on, oblivious to the steam that was rising just across the table from him. Cynthia tried her best to control her anger.

"Samantha has her flaws. Don't we all? But one thing you have to admit is that she knows how to raise money. Because of all the coverage she's been getting, donations this week alone have broken every record. We got a check for half a million dollars today from a venture capitalist in Silicon Valley, and another from Texas for a quarter of a million. Both of them said they saw her on Moran's show and felt compelled by God to send her money. That woman could get water from a rock if she was thirsty enough."

This last spewing of praise was enough to make Cynthia jump to her feet. "Shut up!" she shouted. "You fool, please shut up!" As she yelled the words, Cynthia swept her arm across the table, sending boxes of tepid food, utensils, plates, and glasses slamming against the dining room window. "Would you please stop ranting about how great that woman is? You're making a complete fool of yourself. She's making fools of everyone around her, and I will not allow her to make a fool of you as well. Stop kissing her ass. Can't you for once stand up for yourself and be a man?"

"And just what do you suggest that I do?" Percy asked calmly. "She's our pastor, and we have to support her."

"She's *your* pastor. That woman is not *my* pastor. You should be pastor, and I'm going to do everything in my power to make sure that happens."

"Damn it, Cynthia," he said, pounding his fist on the table. "You've been saying that for months now, and I'm sick of it. How do you propose to make that happen? It's over. She's the pastor, and that's final."

"It's not final. I wouldn't be surprised if she had Hezekiah killed just so she could become pastor. Did you ever think of that?" she asked smugly. "She probably paid someone to kill him. I wouldn't put anything past her."

"Now you're just being ridiculous."

"Am I? Think about it, Percy. Who is the only person in the world who stood to gain anything from his death? Her! And who would have lost the most if that story about him being gay had ever come out? Her! And do you think it was a coincidence that he just happened to get killed the day before the story was scheduled to run? I don't! If you hadn't accidentally killed that reporter, I can almost guarantee you that she would have."

As Cynthia spoke, the words came to her like an epiphany. Words born from anger, frustration, and hate somehow had a surprising air of truth to her. Percy did not allow his face to show it, but the words held a grain of possibility for him as well.

"That's just crazy," he said, trying to convince her and also himself. "Samantha would never do anything like that. She loved Hezekiah."

"You know as well as I do, Percy, that Samantha loves only three things. Herself, money, and the spotlight."

Again, the words smacked of the truth. Percy found it more and more difficult to deny their veracity.

Chow mein noodles slid down the window, leaving slimy trails, as they spoke. The fried shrimp and barbecued pork lay on the carpet like spent shells on a scorched battlefield. The city lights in the distance slowly began to blink on one by one as the evening sun set on the horizon.

Cynthia continued. "You at least have to admit that even if she did love him, which I seriously doubt, she has always craved the spotlight. You know she resented being in his shadow. That's why she's treated everyone around her like dirt. Over the years you've had to have noticed how she found it harder and harder to contain her contempt. It was inevitable that one day her anger would reach a boiling point and someone would be hurt. And I think that someone was Hezekiah."

Percy found it impossible to counter the argument in the face of Cynthia's surprising clarity. It couldn't be proved, but there was almost an undeniable logic to her reasoning. Samantha was the only person who gained from his death. Samantha would have suffered the most if he were exposed as a homosexual, and Hezekiah had confided to him that he was thinking about leaving the church. *I wonder if he told Samantha?* he thought as Cynthia continued with her stream of logic.

While she spoke, Percy recalled the conversation he had had with Hezekiah shortly before he died.

"What's going on with you, Hezekiah?" Percy had asked as the two men stood naked under the steaming shower after a workout at the gym.

"What do you mean? I've never been in better shape."

"We've worked together for years now," Percy had said, pressing. "Not only are you my pastor, but you're also my friend, and I'd like to think you feel the same. I know when something is troubling you. Why did you tell the board of trustees to start thinking about your replacement? What's going on?"

"I can't talk about it right now, but I'm not sure if I'll be able to continue as pastor for much longer."

Percy stood naked and shocked before the pastor. "Are you sick?"

Hezekiah turned his back to Percy and continued to soap his body. He was not prepared to have the conversation. "No, it's nothing like that. I'm fine. I'll be honest with you, Percy. I'm struggling with a moral dilemma that I don't think I'll ever be able to resolve."

"Hezekiah, nothing could be that bad. Maybe you should talk about it with someone. Have you considered seeing a therapist? I know several ministers who are seeing a guy in Anaheim who's supposed to be excellent."

Hezekiah had never confided in a therapist, although he had made the recommendation to many members whose problems required more time than he was willing or able to give. "I don't think he could help me with this," Hezekiah said with a resolute expression on his face. "Everything is more complicated than you could ever imagine."

"No problem you could have is too complicated for God. Let me get you the therapist's number. Give him a call. Whatever is going on might not be as bad as you think."

"Okay, Percy. I'll call him. But if I do leave, I want you to take over as pastor. You're a good man, and you're the only person I would trust with New Testament."

"Don't even think in those terms yet, Hezekiah. You know I'm honored, but I pray it doesn't come to that."

The two men had then showered in silence to the sound of water echoing through the tiled room.

"Percy, are you listening to me?" Cynthia said, interrupting his recollection of that day in the shower with Hezekiah. "You have to admit what I'm saying is true."

Percy stood from the table and began to pick up the dinner from the floor. He methodically plopped sticky noodles and shrimp covered in lint onto a plate he retrieved from near the window.

"You're not responding, because you know what I'm saying is true," she asserted. "Why haven't the police been able to find any leads? It's because they're looking in the wrong place. She's fooled them, like she's fooled everyone else."

Another strand of logic assaulted his ears.

"She didn't pull the trigger, but I know she had something to do with it. And what about Reverend Willie Mitchell? Have you even thought his suicide may have some connection to all of this? It can't be a coincidence that he killed himself right after Hezekiah was assassinated. You know he would have done anything for Samantha. Even kill someone."

"Reverend Mitchell was in the sanctuary when Hezekiah was killed." Percy was relieved to find a hole in her logic. "There's no way he could have done it."

"I'm not saying he did it. But he certainly knew enough of the type of people who would have done it."

It was true. Willie Mitchell loved Samantha and would do her bidding, if only for the honor of being in her presence and inhaling the air that had once been in her lungs.

His hate for Hezekiah was matched only by his love for Samantha.

"The police haven't even thought to link Reverend Mitchell's death with Hezekiah's," Cynthia said. She was relentless. "And you more than anyone has to know that if Lance Savage had lived and that story had run, the board of trustees would have sent Samantha packing. You unwittingly did her a favor by killing him."

Stooped over a pile of noodles on the floor, Percy froze when he heard those words. "Don't be cruel, Cynthia," he said, standing and facing her. "I told you it was an accident. I didn't mean to kill him, and I certainly didn't do it for Samantha."

"I know it was," she said gently. "And I know you didn't do it for her. I'm just saying that there are way too many coincidences, and Samantha seems to be the sole beneficiary of them all. Every road leads to her doorstep, and I think it's about time someone put up a few roadblocks to stop her before she hurts anyone else."

Percy placed the plate of soiled food on the table and slowly walked to the window. Night had fallen during the course of their exchange, and the city was now a bed of sparkling lights laid out before him.

From his silence, Cynthia knew she had broken through his barrier of denial. She knew he could not deny the soundness of her deductions. She allowed him the necessary moments to join in her conclusions before she spoke.

Percy stared off into the distance. Could she be right? he thought. Did Samantha kill Hezekiah? Why did Reverend Mitchell kill himself? Did Samantha drive him to suicide?

The questions seemed unending. But he grudgingly conceded that Cynthia was correct. All roads did seem to lead directly to Samantha.

"You know I'm right, don't you, Percy?" she finally said calmly.

"I don't know any such thing," Percy said with his back to her, to hide the doubt on his face. "Even if you are, there's absolutely no way to prove it. There's nothing that can be done."

"We could talk to the police," Cynthia said patiently.

Percy turned sharply. "We can't talk to the police. Remember I killed a man, Cynthia. I can't risk getting myself wrapped up in this. One slip of the tongue and I could spend the rest of my life in jail."

"That's true," she conceded. "Then what can we do? We can't just let her get away with it. There has to be justice."

"Don't bother pretending to take the high road, Cynthia," he said curtly. "This has nothing to do with justice for you. It's all about making me pastor and you first lady."

"Okay, I won't deny it, and I'm not ashamed of it, either. I still believe you will make a much better pastor than her. If justice is served in the process, all the better."

Percy began to pace in front of the window. He nervously rubbed his forehead as the full weight of Cynthia's accusations settled on his chest.

Cynthia watched him intently as he avoided her gaze. "Regardless of the motivation, the question remains the same," she asserted. "What are we going to do about it?"

"There's nothing that can be done. Our hands are tied," he said, facing her. "If what you said is true, and I'm not saying I think it is, but if it's true, then she will most likely get away with murder."

"Your hands may be tied, but mine aren't."

"What do you mean by that?" he asked nervously.

"I mean that I have nothing to hide. I didn't kill anyone. I've done nothing wrong. I can do whatever I feel is necessary to deal with her."

"You're in no position to take the moral high ground," he said snidely. "Lance Savage told me how you had sex with him in a car just to get him to run the story."

The words had the same effect as a punch in her face. She staggered slightly from their impact. So much had already been exposed that she dismissed the need to deny the allegations. "Yes, I slept with him, and I'd sleep with him again," she said defiantly. "Don't you see, baby? I did it for you."

"You did it for yourself," he scoffed. "You were willing to sell your body to be first lady."

His words didn't sting anymore. "I was willing to sell my body to make you pastor," she said.

"Well, whatever the reason, it certainly backfired. Didn't it?"

"Only a slight setback."

"You think three dead men is 'only a slight setback'?"

"Yes. Collateral damage. I'm not happy about it, but it was obviously God's will."

"I find it hard to believe God had anything to do with this."

"Now you are being ridiculous. 'All things work together for good to them that love God, to them who are the called according to his purpose.' Don't you see it, baby? You've been called by God to be the pastor of New Testament Cathedral."

Percy was weak from her steady barrage of logic, pleading, and now scripture. He couldn't find the strength to resist her anymore. "What are you planning on doing about it?"

She removed the space between them and held the weary man in her arms. "Don't worry about that, Percy. The less you know about what I'm going to do, the better it will be for you."

Percy melted in her arms. He clutched her for his life amid the Chinese debris, the strewn plates, and the toppled water glasses.

"Leave her to me, Percy. I've decided to put an end to this whole horrible situation. Trust me, baby. I won't allow her to destroy anyone else's life."

Chapter 8

Gideon and Danny walked hand in hand along the shore at Playa del Rey. Gentle waves washed up to their feet, forming rippling lines in the sand as the water receded. It was just after seven in the morning. The beach was deserted except for the occasional jogger with a dog in tow and a random squawking seagull searching for sand crabs the waters had deposited on the shore. Whenever the occasional jogger approached, their hands would gently part and the two men would transform themselves into colleagues, or possibly brothers, simply enjoying the morning air together. When the joggers were far enough in the distance, their hands would join again, converting them back into the lovers they had become.

"I'm going to interview the members of the board of trustees again," Gideon said as the two walked barefoot in the sand. "I feel like I only scratched the surface with them. Scarlett Shackelford in particular. I think she knows a lot more than she's saying."

"What do you mean?" Danny asked innocently.

"She used to be Hezekiah's personal secretary. I'd like to know why she left. There's something there. I can feel it. Did Hezekiah ever mention her to you?"

"Only once," Danny replied. "He was telling me something about his daughter, Jasmine. I can't remember what it was. And then he said something about Scarlett's daughter. Something about how cute she was and that he envied her father for having such a lovely little girl. It was a bit strange at the time, but I didn't give it much thought until you mentioned it just now. Do you think it means anything?"

"I'm not sure, but I'll see if I can get some answers out of Scarlett. What was his relationship like with Jasmine? Did he ever discuss it with you?"

"He loved Jasmine. He always worried about her. He thought she hung with the wrong type of friends. Apparently, she liked to party, but he was always so busy, he couldn't keep track of her. He complained that Samantha showed very little interest in her. He once told me she treated Jasmine like an object that she put on display whenever a scene called for it. He always regretted that she had been raised, for the most part, by nannies and house staff."

"Did you ever go to his house?"

Danny hesitated before he responded. He, in fact, had been to the Cleaveland estate on one occasion. Hezekiah and Danny had been seeing each other for six months. Samantha was in Washington with Jasmine, accepting an award for her work on women's issues around the world.

"I want you to see my house, Danny," Hezekiah had said out of the blue while the two lay twisted and tangled in each other's arms one afternoon after they had made love in Danny's bed.

"I'd like to see it sometime, but it's not necessary. How would you explain me to your staff?"

"I don't have to explain anything to my staff. I'm the lord of the manor," Hezekiah had said jokingly. "There's always someone coming and going. They won't give you a second thought."

"Wouldn't it make you uncomfortable having your lover in your wife's house?"

"Maybe a little. But it would be worth it for you to see where I live. I can't explain it, but it's important to me that you see that part of my life. My home is a part of who I am, and I want you to know every part of me. I also want you to come to my church one day. I sometimes search the faces in the audience, hoping I will see you there."

"I understand, Hezekiah. That means a lot to me."

"Good! It's settled," Hezekiah said, sitting upright in the bed. "Let's go to the house now."

"Now?"

"Yes, now. Samantha and Jasmine are in D.C. Etta is probably out running errands. The groundskeepers are most likely done for the day. Now is a perfect time."

After much persuading, Danny agreed to follow Hezekiah in his car to the estate.

As Danny walked on the beach with Gideon, he remembered how he felt when he first entered the house.

Danny had driven his blue 1998 Toyota Corolla behind Hezekiah's silver Mercedes from the West Adams District to the heights of Bel Air. The wrought-iron gates slid open at the sight of Hezekiah's car. Hezekiah gave the guard in the gatehouse a thumbs-up and pointed to Danny's car behind him. The guard nodded cautiously as Danny passed through the gates.

The house was like none Danny had ever seen. The double doors swung open as soon as they had parked their cars, and Etta Washington was standing in the threshold, in her usual black dress and white apron. Danny could see a hint of surprise on Hezekiah's face when he saw her. Hezekiah braced himself and opened Danny's car door. Side by side, the two men ascended the stairs to the main entrance.

"Hello, Etta," Hezekiah called out as they approached the entrance to the house. "This is my associate and friend Michael Thomas. Michael, this is our housekeeper, Etta."

"Welcome home, Pastor Cleaveland," Etta said warmly. "Hello, Mr. Thomas. Welcome to the Cleaveland estate. Will you be staying for dinner?"

"No," Danny blurted. "I mean, I—"

"Thank you, Etta," Hezekiah interrupted. "Yes, Mr. Thomas will be joining us for dinner."

Etta looked on approvingly as the two men entered the house. *There's something . . . almost lighter about Pastor Cleaveland in the presence of that young man,* she silently noted.

The opulent exterior of the house was mirrored in its interior. Sunlight poured through a skylight in the two-story foyer and coated the massive oval-shaped room in a yellow glow. Double living room and dining room doors were to the right and to the left. A round marble table that held a massive floral arrangement sat in the center of the room, and on each side symmetrical stairways caressed the curved walls and climbed to a second-floor landing that overlooked the room. Black wrought-iron banisters provided a stark contrast in the bright room.

Directly ahead hung the first of two Picassos in the Cleaveland home. The painting was in the center of the foyer's rear wall. The dreaming woman's hands rested suggestively in her lap. Her head was slightly tilted to the right, and her closed eyes hinted of erotic sweet dreams. Parts of her deconstructed face provided a glimpse of the thoughts that seemed to give her such serene pleasure.

Antique furniture and European art were masterfully displayed throughout. A well- thought-out furniture arrangement composed of wingback chairs, marble- and glass-topped tea tables, and satin-swathed couches created the optimum setting to impress and entertain the rich, the pious, and the famous. Crystal chandeliers and Lalique vases sparkled throughout, and plush pastel carpets softened the hard edges of each room. A cold, sleek black baby grand piano rested in front of a wall of glass that overlooked the grounds and a shimmering cobalt-blue swimming pool.

Hezekiah escorted Danny through what seemed like an endless chain of rooms, each more beautiful than the one before, pointing out trinkets, paintings, and books that marked significant events in his life.

"You see that Bible on the coffee table," Hezekiah said in the living room. "It's a first edition sixteen eleven King James Pulpit Bible. There are less than two hundred of them in the world. It was a gift to us from Pope John Paul II."

"I'm not sure if I even want to know the story behind that," Danny said, pointing to a painting, Picasso's *Les Demoiselles d'Avignon,* which hung over a fireplace that was almost the size of his bedroom in the West Adams District. The five women's faces resembled primitive tribal masks, and the jagged edges of their pink flesh formed sharp angles that pointed in every direction.

Hezekiah was almost embarrassed when he responded, "I bought that for Samantha on our eleventh anniversary. She insisted on it."

An oil painting of Hezekiah and Samantha was on the opposite wall. Their faces countered the seductive and horrifying image of Picasso's five women across the room. Hezekiah's and Samantha's smiles in the painting absorbed the light that streamed through the room's many windows.

Danny remembered the uneasiness he had felt amid such opulence and wealth. The house didn't reflect the Hezekiah he had come to love. He hadn't seen him reflected anywhere in the home's sixty thousand square feet. After that day, they never discussed the house again and Danny never went back.

"I have been there once," Danny finally said to Gideon as they walked hand in hand along the beach. The warmth of the morning sun had slowly replaced the cool ocean mist.

"What did you think?" Gideon asked cautiously.

"I've never seen anything like it. It was magnificent, but . . ."

"But what?"

"It wasn't Hezekiah. It was all Samantha. You could feel her in every room. I felt sorry for him when I saw him in that house. It was almost like he was a piece of furniture or a painting."

"You mean he seemed out of place?"

"I think he hated it," Danny said, looking at the horizon. "Behind the expensive suits and that television smile, Hezekiah was a very humble man. In a lot of ways he was like a little boy. He was playful and passionate, and he really cared deeply about people. He sometimes told me about problems people in his congregation were facing, and I could see in his face how much it affected him."

"I never knew that about him."

"I don't think anyone knew it. I don't think he fully realized how deeply he cared about others until we met. He told me once that I helped him see who he really was. I understand it now, because he did the same thing for me."

Gideon placed his arm around Danny's shoulder. He could see the conversation was making Danny uncomfortable. "I'm sorry. I'm being insensitive. I know how much you loved him. I just hope one day you'll be able to love me as much. He sounds like a wonderful person who also loved you very deeply, and I'm grateful to him for that."

"There's no need to apologize," Danny said, nestling under Gideon's shoulder. "It actually helps me to talk about it."

"He was very lucky to have found you. People go their entire lives and never have what you two shared. This might sound selfish, but I can't help but think that if it was not for him, I would have never met you, and that frightens me."

"Why?"

"Because the thought of not having you in my life scares me."

"But a few weeks ago you didn't even know I existed, and you were doing just fine."

"That's the thing. I thought I was doing fine, and then you came along and showed me how empty my life was. The thought of living that way for the rest of my life absolutely frightens me. Knowing that I spent so many years chasing my career and never really connecting with another person is very sad."

"You've never been in love?"

"Infatuated, yes. In lust, maybe. But I can't say that I've ever been in love. Certainly not in the way I feel about you."

The two men walked in silence. The range of their feelings ebbed and flowed with the tide. More locals began to trickle onto the sands, causing them to replace their intimate touches with a more respectable distance.

"Danny?" Gideon finally said. "Do you think you could ever love me the way you loved Hezekiah?"

There was no response. A dog barking in the distance punctuated the quiet. The gentle rushing waves pounded like thunder in Gideon's ears, and the calls of the distant seagulls sent a screeching chill up his spine.

"I'm sorry. I shouldn't have asked you that," Gideon said bashfully. "I'm a reporter. I can't help my—"

Danny gently placed a finger against Gideon's lips before the last word could escape and said, "I think I already do."

Samantha held the gun with the skill and intention of a trained assassin. The room was dark and smoky, and shards of light pierced through the crevices in the boarded-up windows. A ceiling fan whirled in slow motion, causing smoke to plume from the floor to the ceiling and then back down to the cold cement.

Samantha's arms were fully extended, with the gun aimed at a target that was just out of view.

"Don't do it!" Hattie sputtered in the grip of a fitful sleep. "Please, Samantha, don't do it."

A patchwork quilt made from the remnants of her life lay in a heap at her feet. She clutched a pillow to her chest, as if shielding herself from the bullet in Samantha's gun. It was 3:12 a.m. Hattie hadn't fallen asleep until 2:00 a.m. A cup of chamomile tea, the crackling voice of a radio evangelist calling for fire to rain down from heaven on evildoers, and the second chapter of Acts had finally coaxed her into a blissful sleep. But the peace and safety of slumber had not lasted.

Samantha took a deliberate step forward. Multiple layers of the sheer black fabric of her dress fluttered and waved from a wind that engulfed the room. Her intentions were clear to Hattie even under the veil of sleep. Samantha took another step forward.

Hattie thrashed her head from side to side on the bed, freeing her gray-streaked hair from tightly clamped bobby pins and plastic rollers. Her feet kicked and flailed, as if she were fighting to keep Samantha at bay.

"No!" was her muddled cry. "I won't let you do it again!"

Samantha was oblivious to her entreaties. The louder Hattie cried, the closer Samantha came to her target. The harder she thrashed and kicked, the more deliberately Samantha moved.

Hattie craned her neck in the bed to see who Samantha had in her sights. She could feel the presence of a man. Was it Gideon? Or maybe the man Hezekiah had pleaded with her to protect. Her body twisted from side to side, but the figure was just beyond her view.

"Stop, Samantha! You can't keep doing this. God, please don't let her do it again."

Samantha continued slow and steady toward her prey. As she moved, the wind blew harder, causing her dress to whip and snap in the gusts.

And then Hattie saw him. A young man standing vulnerable under Samantha's icy gaze, with the gun aimed directly at his head. His face was as clear as if he were standing in the room with Hattie. "Danny!" Hattie shrieked. Even in sleep she knew his name. She knew it as sure as she knew her own. She also knew, and did not question, that this was the man whom her pastor loved so deeply.

Hattie lay flat on her back. Her neck arched toward the headboard. She frantically began pounding the mattress with her clutched fists. "No!" she yelled into her dark room. "No!" She slammed her fists into the bed. "No, no, no, no, no!"

A loud blast from the gun pierced through her dream. She could see sparks coming from the barrel. Behind the flash she saw the dark eyes of Samantha Cleaveland staring defiantly at her. The sight caused Hattie to burst violently from the dream. She bolted upright in the bed. Her forehead was covered in perspiration. Gray hairs pointed in every direction, and plastic curlers lay strewn across the mattress. Hattie cried fitfully as she struggled to free herself from the nightmare. She fixed her eyes on the oval vanity mirror on the opposite wall and saw her shaking, disheveled reflection. The nightgown drooped over one shoulder, and her fingers shook as she clutched her gaping mouth.

"Don't let this happen again, Lord. Why are you testing me? I can't let it happen again."

***

"I gave you her head on a platter, and you treated her like she was made of porcelain."

"I couldn't accuse her of a cover-up on national television. She had just lost her husband. The public would have demanded my head, not hers."

"Bullshit. The public loves that kind of scandal, and you know it. Admit it, Gideon. You're afraid of her."

"Don't be ridiculous," Gideon said incredulously. "Timing is everything with a story like this. As for her husband's death, Samantha Cleaveland is one of the most popular public figures in the country. No reporter wants to be perceived as attacking a grieving widow, especially not one like Samantha."

Gideon and Cynthia sat facing each other in the lobby of the oceanfront hotel. They could see throngs of summer revelers taking full advantage of the afternoon heat from their vantage point in the bay window overlooking the Santa Monica boardwalk. Scantily clad joggers, souvenir-toting tourists, and sticky-fingered children juggling cotton candy and snow cones formed a mob of fun seekers and sunseekers.

Gideon would never admit to Cynthia that he agreed with everything she accused him of. He had kicked himself many times after the interview he conducted with Samantha in her home only weeks earlier.

He had had her in his sights on that day in her living room. Vulnerable, with his lights and cameras pointed at her and exposing every pore.

Gideon recalled the fateful interview that had caused him to question his ability as an investigative reporter.

"Tonight we are honored to have a woman who, until recently, was one half of a couple that for years has captivated the hearts of people around the world," he had said, looking directly into the camera. "Her recent tragedy rocked the religious world to its core. Please welcome Pastor Samantha Cleaveland. Good evening, Pastor Cleaveland, and thank you for inviting us into your lovely home."

He recalled how Samantha had magically transformed into a bigger-than-life character when the camera was rolling. Her skin captured the light around her and sent it back into the room brighter than it had come.

"Thank you, Gideon. It's my pleasure, and welcome to my home," she had said graciously.

"I'm sure I speak for millions of people when I say how sorry I am for the tragic loss of your husband."

"Thank you," she said with a slight nod of her head.

"Let me start by asking you, are the police any closer to finding out who assassinated Pastor Cleaveland?"

"The Los Angeles Police Department has been amazing throughout this entire ordeal, but unfortunately, they are no closer today to finding his killer than they were the day it happened. A part of me feels we may never know who killed Hezekiah. The important thing, however, is that this person will have to answer to God either in this life or the next."

"You are a woman with strong religious beliefs. Are you in any way able to forgive the man, or woman, who did this to you, your family, and all the people who love you?"

"I'm so glad you asked me that." Gideon remembered how Samantha had looked him directly in the eye when she answered. "I have already forgiven him. This has caused my daughter and me immense pain and anguish. There were days when I didn't think I could go on without him. But you know, Gideon, God promised us all that He would never give us more burdens than we could bear. And with that knowledge I was able to get up one morning a few weeks after it happened, put on my makeup, and face another day. Don't get me wrong, though. I still cry every day, and I miss him more than you can imagine, but life must go on, and every day I get a little stronger."

"You mentioned your daughter, Jasmine. How is she handling the loss of her father?"

"Jasmine took her father's death very hard. They were very close. She was Daddy's little girl," Samantha said with a smile. "They were inseparable from the day she was born until the day he died. She couldn't bear to be in the house after he was killed, so she's staying temporally with very dear friends of our family in Malibu. I see her every day, and we pray together on the telephone every evening, before she goes to bed. God and time heal all wounds, and every day she gets a little stronger. As painful as this has all been, I know that someday she will come to understand that this is all a part of God's master plan."

"Can you think of any reason anyone would want to kill your husband?"

Gideon noted that Samantha's suddenly dilated pupils were the only visible reaction to the unexpected question.

"I have thought a lot about this and have had multiple conversations with detectives, who wanted to know the same thing. Everyone loved Hezekiah. He was the kind of person that would give you his last dollar if you needed it. I've never known him to have an enemy. I can't think of anyone who would have wanted him dead."

"New Testament Cathedral is the sixth largest church in the country. Your television ministry generates millions each year. Do you think jealousy may have played a part into this?"

"I would hate to think jealousy was a factor, but anything is possible," Samantha said coolly. "There are many troubled people in the world. We may never know what motivated this person to do what he did."

"Do you think you may have factored into his death in any way?"

"I'm not sure what you mean." Her eyes became a centimeter tighter.

Gideon saw the almost imperceptible shift in her demeanor. He pressed on, unfazed by the icy glare from his guest or the rustling of his producer behind his shoulder. "What I mean is, could you have done something to contribute to the murder of your husband, inadvertently, of course?"

Megan, his then segment producer, clutched her mouth to prevent a gasp from escaping. The four cameramen looked nervously at each other and then zoomed in on Samantha's stone face.

"Anything is possible, of course. I'm sure I've made decisions in the ministry that may have possibly upset some people, but I honestly don't think I've done anything to anyone that would illicit such an extreme response as that. What your viewers need to understand is that, for the most part, the world is filled with people who have no desire to hurt anyone.

"I have traveled all over the world and have met so many people from different cultures, and I'm always amazed to find people just like you and me, all believing in the same God, but maybe calling Him by a different name, who simply want to live their lives without doing harm. There is, however, a small minority of people out there who don't have God in their lives, and unfortunately, they sometimes make misguided decisions that hurt other people."

Gideon found some solace in remembering that he had pushed a little harder. "I find it difficult to fathom that a man as powerful as Hezekiah Cleaveland didn't have any enemies. So do you think this was a random shooting?"

"My husband was human like everyone else. He made mistakes like us all. He's done things that, if he were alive, I'm sure he wouldn't be proud of. But I'll say it again. I don't think he ever did anything that would warrant him being killed. If that were the case, we all would have to walk down the street, looking over our shoulders."

It was at this point in the interview that Gideon abandoned the thought of exposing Hezekiah's affair with Danny. He knew from experience that after her last response the audience would be sitting snugly in the palm of her hand. She was officially immune to scandal. He grudgingly conceded that at that point the interview had turned into pure fluff.

"Let's talk about New Testament Cathedral," Gideon said, flipping the index cards. "Shortly after Hezekiah's death you were installed as pastor. How has the transition from first lady to pastor been for you?"

"I believe it was a blessing for me. The appointment was totally unexpected. I didn't even know I was being considered for the position until I received a call from the president of our board of trustees," Samantha said, batting her mink eyelashes.

"I, of course, was honored," she continued, "and a little concerned whether it was too soon after losing my husband. However, the trustees had faith in me and insisted that it was the best thing for New Testament Cathedral. Initially, I said no, because I felt I needed more time to mourn my loss. But my daughter said something that changed my mind."

"What did she say?" Gideon asked, abandoning all hope for a hard-hitting interview.

"Something very simple. She looked me in the eye and said, 'Mommy, Daddy would have wanted you to be pastor.' So I prayed through my tears and through my grief, and God . . ." Samantha paused and gingerly dabbed the corner of her eye with the tip of her finger. "God spoke to my heart late one night and said, 'Samantha, this is my will. With me, you can do all things.' After I heard that, I knew I had to either live what I've been preaching all these years or just walk away. I decided I would stand on God's word."

Gideon remembered looking down at his index cards so the camera could not catch the smirk on his face. He regretted that he had resisted the urge to ask, 'Were you aware that your husband was involved in a homosexual affair for two years with a man named Danny St. John?' Or 'How do you think the millions of people who send you their hard-earned money every year would feel if they knew you knew about it?' Or 'If the public found out that one of the most loved ministers in the country was gay, it would have cost you millions. What did you do to Hezekiah when you learned of the affair?'

"Pastor Cleaveland," Gideon said, looking up again, "I think your board of trustees made an excellent choice."

An audible sigh of relief could be heard from Megan in the background, signaling her relief that Gideon had become less aggressive.

For the remainder of the one-hour interview Gideon censored any question that would in any way appear accusatory. His questions could have been asked by any novice journalist. Samantha skillfully spun each response to fit her image as the brave grieving widow who set aside her own needs for the good of the church.

"Pastor Cleaveland, it has been a pleasure speaking with you today. I now see why America has fallen in love with you." Recalling this comment hurt Gideon the most. "I wish you, Jasmine, and New Testament Cathedral the best."

"It's been my pleasure."

Now sitting with Cynthia in the hotel lobby, Gideon felt attacked and needed to defend how he had handled Samantha during that interview.

"She made a fool of you," Cynthia said, pressing on with her assault. "And on your own television show. She made you look like just another one of her lackeys. You let me down, Gideon. Not only that, you also let down everyone at New Testament Cathedral. The world deserves to know the truth, and you were the only person in a position to tell it."

"Don't you think you're being a bit melodramatic, Cynthia?" Gideon asked, finding it increasingly harder to protect himself from the barrage of accusations. "The only thing you handed me was a stack of e-mails. That's not enough to build any kind of credible case on."

"So you don't believe they're authentic?" she asked.

"I didn't say that. I'm saying you'll need more than a bunch of e-mails if you want to be the first lady of New Testament Cathedral."

"I never said that was my primary motivation," Cynthia snapped, leaning forward in the wicker chair. "What on earth are you talking about?"

"I'm not an idiot, Cynthia," Gideon responded as his patience grew thinner. "Any fool can see through that ridiculous pious 'good of the church' routine of yours. It's obvious this is all about destroying Samantha so your husband can become pastor and, thereby, you first lady."

Cynthia pressed forward, unashamed of the exposure. "Whether that is true or not is irrelevant. What's important is Samantha should have never been installed as pastor and someone has to do something about it."

"And you've elected yourself as that person?"

"As a matter of fact, I have. There doesn't seem to be anyone else around with the balls to do the job," she said, looking to Gideon with disdain.

"Look, I didn't ask to meet you today to talk about any of your grand schemes," Gideon said dismissively.

"Then why did you ask me to come here?"

"I wanted to ask you what you know about Hezekiah's death."

"What do you mean?" she asked suspiciously.

"I'll be blunt with you, Cynthia. There are some people who think Samantha may have had something to do with his murder."

Gideon felt his relationship with Cynthia had sunk beyond the reaches of discretion. He was desperate for any piece of information that would potentially remove Danny from Samantha's deadly path.

"Do you know anything that might potentially link her to his death?" he asked point-blank.

Just as he spoke the words, a waiter bowed over his right shoulder. "May I get you two another glass of chardonnay?"

"Yes, thank you," Cynthia quickly responded, with Gideon's words still hanging in the air. The waiter departed with a confirming nod of his head.

"My husband and I just had a very similar conversation," she said, finding it difficult to contain her glee. "I've always had my suspicions."

"What type of suspicions?"

"Well, for starters, not many people knew their marriage was a sham. He had so many affairs, I stopped counting. Not to mention the last one was with a man, and he was thinking about leaving the church for him. I called Samantha 'his camera wife.' They were the perfect couple in front of the camera, but when it was turned off, they went their separate ways."

"No one ever told me that."

"No one wants to speak ill of the dead."

"No one but you?"

"I thought we were beyond the bullshit, Gideon. As you said, you're 'not a fool,' and neither am I."

"You're right. We are beyond that. Anything else? You said you had your suspicions."

"Well, there's also the fact that Samantha hated living in Hezekiah's shadow. You could see it in her face sometimes when she was standing behind him. It was only a hint of disdain, but I could see it, and I'm sure others could too."

"But why would she be jealous of him? He made sure she had everything. She's got two Picassos, for Christ's sake, and that god-awful house in Bel Air."

"You have to understand something about women like Samantha. They make men into the successes they are only because they believe the world isn't ready for them to be in positions of absolute power, especially in the church. The faith community is still very chauvinistic. I suspect once she felt the world was ready for her, she figured she no longer needed Hezekiah."

"Is that how you feel about your husband?" Gideon asked unapologetically.

"Perhaps, but you forget the difference between Samantha and me."

"What's that?"

"Samantha is an ordained minister with a doctorate in theology."

Gideon tried to hide his disgust with her frankness. "She obviously didn't do it herself. If you think it's possible that she is responsible, who do you think she could have convinced to do it?"

"That's easy," Cynthia said, beaming. "Have you heard of Willie Mitchell?"

"Yes. The minister that committed suicide."

"That's right. Coincidentally, on the same day Hezekiah was killed," she said with a slight wink. "He was a fool who Samantha had wrapped around her finger. Uneducated and very crass, but also very rich," she said. "Made a fortune in a string of shady real estate deals. He was connected to all sorts of underground gangster types and street thugs. Guys with the balls to do whatever is necessary in order to get the job done," she revealed, looking disappointingly toward Gideon's crotch. "All he wanted in life was to fuck her, and I wouldn't be surprised if she actually let him in exchange for arranging Hezekiah's murder."

"Can you prove any of this?" Gideon asked with a glimmer of hope in his eyes.

"I can't prove a damned thing," Cynthia said with an exasperated sigh. "All I've got are the e-mails, which you say are useless."

The two sat in silence, looking out the bay window at the ocean in the distance. Surfers danced on the cresting waves. The shoreline was dotted with kaleidoscope umbrellas, dripping coolers, and folding beach chairs with heads sticking over the tops.

Cynthia broke the silence. "Sometimes I feel the only way to get rid of her is if the same thing that happened to Hezekiah happens to her."

Gideon looked to her with suspicion but said nothing. The instincts of a seasoned reporter kicked in. This was the time to listen and not to ask questions.

The silence allowed Cynthia's mind to wander. "God forgive me, but sometimes I wish someone would . . ."

"Would what?" he asked, prodding cautiously.

"Someone would put a bullet in her pretty little head," she said while casually scanning the shoreline.

Gideon did not respond. He couldn't without admitting that he had entertained the exact same thought.

The wall safe was tucked discreetly behind a nondescript oil painting that would not catch the eye of a burglar trained in the art of identifying valuable masterpieces. Samantha nimbly turned the dial. With each spin, an almost inaudible click reverberated through her quiet home office.

This room, her office, provided a startling contrast to the decor of the other rooms in the house. A sleek Swedish couch and two modern leather chairs, too perfect and erect to provide comfort, floated on a bloodred island rug in the center of the room. Sparkling modern light fixtures served more as art than as illuminators. Stark teak planks covering the floor directed every step taken in the room to the front of Samantha's desk. The glass desk glowed at the rear of the room from light shining through a floor-to-ceiling window that overlooked the lush grounds of the estate.

With the last turn of the dial, a louder series of clicks indicated that the safe was unlatched. Samantha slowly opened the heavy metal door, revealing a small portion of the hidden treasures she had stashed in secure locations around the world.

A 478.68 carat blue sapphire and diamond necklace, once worn by the queen of Romania at the coronation of her husband, was nestled in a burgundy velvet box. A flawless 10.04 carat black diamond from South Africa in a much smaller velvet box sat atop a stack of stocks, bonds, and deeds to a winery in Napa Valley, a villa in the South of France, and a penthouse in Bangkok.

In the rear of the wall safe were stacks of one-thousand-dollar bills. The stacks were comprised of bundles containing fifty one-thousand-dollar bills held together by a single white paper strip.

The gun that was used to, almost, kill Danny St. John was sitting on one of the stacks of money. Samantha reached past the fortunes and removed it from the steel cave. It was a small matte black Smith & Wesson Centennial 442 snub-nosed revolver. She trembled slightly when she felt the sensuous weight and cold steel in her hand.

Samantha had fond memories of the gun. It held a special place in her heart. It was also the same gun Virgil

Jackson had used to kill her husband. It was the gun that David had used in his bungled attempt to kill Danny. She viewed it as her friend. A friend who would do anything she told it to. A friend who asked no questions and a friend who obediently removed anyone who stood between her and her heart's desires.

Samantha walked slowly across the room to the window overlooking the estate grounds. The sun was just starting its slow decent to the horizon. Her world was quiet and peaceful as she fondly reminisced about the day her loyal friend removed Hezekiah from her life.

It had been a beautiful Sunday morning at New Testament Cathedral. The parking lot was filled with freshly washed cars. Children played on the lawn in front of the church, carefully trying to keep their flowered white dresses and little tan suits clean for as long as possible. Women rushed their husbands up the stairs to the church to get a good seat. The lobby was filled with members waiting to be seated by the ushers. White-gloved ushers handed neatly folded powder-blue bulletins to each person who entered the sanctuary.

The day before, Samantha had arranged for the balcony to be closed to give her hired assassin the privacy he needed. When the sanctuary had reached full capacity, the overflow of worshippers was directed to Fellowship Hall, where folding chairs had been assembled auditorium style. No one liked viewing the service over the television monitors, but they could not refuse the only remaining option.

By 10:50 the choir had lined up behind the now closed double doors to the sanctuary. Except for choir members waiting to enter the sanctuary, the lobby was empty. They waited patiently for the first chords from the organ. Singers nervously fastened buttons on their robes and adjusted the sashes embroidered with the name of the church. The doors flew open and the procession began when the chord was finally struck. Parishioners stood to welcome the jubilant march.

Reverend Willie Mitchell had dropped off the crack-addicted assassin, Virgil Jackson, three blocks away from the church. He had then double-parked his car in the parking lot of the church and had run up the stairs. His seat was waiting for him in the pulpit. As he passed Samantha on the front row, she remembered how he bent over to kiss her check and whispered, “Everything is set.”

Samantha had decided against pearls for her wrist and had instead chosen a diamond bracelet Hezekiah had bought her for Christmas.

The worship service proceeded as it had for the past ten years. The choir sang, the people rejoiced, the cameras rolled, and Hezekiah entered the sanctuary on cue. The cameras followed his precisely sculpted black suit as it floated up the steps to the pulpit. He nodded good morning to the choir as they continued their song.

When the song ended, all cameras focused once again on Hezekiah. Samantha remembered how pious and arrogant he looked on the forty-foot JumboTron screen. The applause subsided, and Hezekiah spoke his first words of the morning.

She remembered them as if they were etched in her brain. “I know a lot of you are not going to want to hear what I have to say this morning, but praise God, I’m going to say it any way.

“Brothers and Sisters, it’s time for us to stop lying to ourselves. It’s time we stop lying to each other, and most importantly, it’s time we stop lying to God. He already knows our hearts, so who do we think we’re fooling? Now, please understand I’m preaching to myself just as much as I’m preaching to you.”

A mixture of laughter and the words '"Go ahead, Preacher" came from the far reaches of the sanctuary.

"Now, one lie is only the tip of the iceberg. Once you tell one lie, you've got to tell ten more to cover it up. Pretty soon we don't even know what the truth is ourselves. We lie about our hair color. We lie about our jobs. We stretch the truth about our income." Hezekiah extended his arms to illustrate the point. "And some of us even lie about who we love."

Samantha shuddered slightly at her office window when she recalled how nervous she was at that point in his sermon. She had looked over her shoulder to the balcony several times, hoping Virgil would act before Hezekiah said something she would regret. She wanted to be remembered as the wife Pastor Cleaveland loved. Not as the woman he had planned to divorce for a man.

Virgil Jackson had entered the now empty lobby unnoticed and had quietly climbed the side stairs of the balcony. The double doors of the sanctuary were closed, and all eyes and ears were focused on Hezekiah and his cryptic sermon.

Hezekiah continued, "I will be the first one to say before God and all of you that I've told my share of lies. I'm just a man. A man who must humble himself daily before God to confess his sins and to plead His forgiveness." Hezekiah picked up the handheld microphone and walked away from the podium. "I, like you, have done some things in my life that I am not proud of."

Countless amens were uttered. Samantha remembered noticing Hattie Williams rocking with her Bible open and reading. A quiet confusion began to work its way through the pews. This was a sermon like none they had ever heard from the pastor. He had lowered himself to the level of mortals. The faces became troubled by his descent, because they needed him to be better than they were.

Hezekiah had put one foot on the steps, preparing to walk down, when two loud shots reverberated through the sanctuary. The first shriek came from someone in the center of the church, as Hezekiah fell backward into the pulpit. Everyone was paralyzed for what seemed like minutes. Women began ducking behind pews, while men shielded them. Screams were soon heard from every part of the auditorium. Hezekiah lay bleeding from bullet wounds to the head and chest. The members in Fellowship Hall gasped as they watched the mayhem unfold on the massive flat-screen.

Virgil stood erect and ran stumbling up the center aisle of the balcony. Samantha saw the shadow of a man running out of the dark balcony.

Samantha smiled slightly when she recalled how she dramatically broke free from a security guard who was trying to protect her. She ran up the steps to her husband. Some members of the choir dashed from the stand, while others crouched, weeping, behind seats. The organist sat frozen in fear on the bench as several people ran screaming out the double doors.

Samantha dropped and cradled Hezekiah's head on the arm of her suit. Her bracelet sparkled from the light in the church's stained glass. She screamed hysterically. "Hezekiah, baby! Hezekiah, don't die! I need you." She resisted the urge to lay her head on his chest, for fear of getting blood on the collar she had so carefully selected. "Hezekiah! Please, God, don't take him from me!"

After a respectable moment had passed, Reverend Willie Mitchell and Reverend Percy Pryce gently separated Samantha from Hezekiah's body and briskly escorted her, crying and thrashing, out the side door. Hezekiah's lifeless body lay at the top of the steps, clutching the microphone, while the security guard tried unsuccessfully to resuscitate him.

By two o'clock the church grounds were filled with police cars and news vans. Satellite dishes pointed to the heavens, and high heels stumbled over electrical cords crisscrossing the parking lot. The police had emptied the sanctuary of parishioners, and the double doors had been cordoned off with yellow tape. Members were now milling in the halls and outside the church, giving and receiving comfort. The final word had already spread that the pastor was dead.

From her window in the church Samantha could see reporters, with microphones and cameras in tow, cornering members for their reaction to the tragedy for the local and national news networks. Television programming around the country had been interrupted to report on the assassination of Pastor Hezekiah T. Cleaveland. The hats, the fresh haircuts, and the pain at New Testament Cathedral were beamed live that day to televisions throughout the world.

Samantha fondly remembered seeing the covered body of her husband being removed from the church. Cameramen scrambled to get a shot of the gurney as it was being lifted into the rear of the van. Crying women, children clinging to their thighs, provided a dramatic backdrop for the parting shots of the vehicle.

Samantha sobbed into a crumpled tissue on the sofa inside Hezekiah's office. The suit jacket Hezekiah had worn that morning was draped over her lap, and blood from his head had dried on her sleeve. Reverend Pryce and his wife, Cynthia, sat on either side of her.

Jasmine had not attended church again that morning. Samantha had instructed Etta to let her sleep in. She hadn't wanted Jasmine to witness her father's assassination. Samantha called home shortly after being taken to the church office. "Jasmine, honey," she said. "This is Mommy. Something terrible has happened. Daddy has been shot. He's dead."

Suddenly Samantha's office door swung open, and Jasmine appeared in the threshold. The whoosh of the door startled Samantha from the fond memory of that wonderful day two months earlier. She turned abruptly from the window, revealing the gun, her friend.

"Jasmine, you startled me," she said with uncharacteristic surprise. "Why didn't you knock?" As she spoke, she slowly put the gun into a desk drawer.

"I didn't know you were in here. I came in to get one of your cigarettes," Jasmine said, watching the gun as it disappeared into the desk.

"I've told you I don't like you smoking. It's a filthy habit."

"Then why do you do it?"

"Because, honey, your mother is under a lot of pressure and—"

"How much longer are you going to pretend I didn't see that gun you just put in your desk?" Jasmine asked suspiciously.

"I'm not pretending. I know you saw it."

"Then would you mind telling me why you have a gun? I thought you and Daddy hated guns. Are you planning on using that on someone?" she asked sarcastically.

"Don't be ridiculous. I have it for protection."

"Protection from what?" Jasmine scoffed. "This place is crawling with armed guards. Sometimes I feel like I live in a prison. I don't believe you. What is the gun for?" she asked insistently.

The two women locked eyes. There was silence in the room. Throughout Jasmine's life she had never felt she knew fully what damage her mother was capable of doing to those she considered a threat or an enemy. She had seen Samantha send employees running from rooms in tears. She had had a front row seat in the theater that was their life. For years she had seen how Samantha manipulated her father. She had sometimes sat in disbelief after witnessing how abusive her mother could be to the house staff and security.

Now seeing her mother standing there with a gun, she realized there was yet another level of cruelty she was capable of. The picture did not surprise or shock her. The image of her mother standing at the window, the blue sky enveloping her in an ethereal glow, actually filled in a missing piece in her view of her mother, the woman with the French-tipped fingernails holding a gun.

"Have you ever used it?" Jasmine asked without any hint of doubt.

"Of course I haven't."

"I don't believe you."

"What are you talking about?" Samantha replied.

"I think you know," Jasmine said coolly.

For the first time Jasmine saw a third dimension to her mother, and it frightened her. She knew all too well the cardboard cutout of the pastor's wife and the loving mother that had always repulsed her. She knew the cruel woman who seemed oblivious to the feelings of others. But now she saw the dangerous woman who, without question, had it in her to kill. In that light, at that window, and with that gun, her mother could not hide her true self.

"I don't want to talk about this anymore," Samantha said, closing the desk drawer. "You should leave."

"You killed him, didn't you?"

Samantha froze for a millisecond. "Killed who, darling?" she said, as if indulging the furtive imagination of a precocious child.

"Daddy," Jasmine said, looking her directly in the eye. The original intent of the question was simply to irritate her mother, but as the words floated between them, they took on a distinct air of possibility and even truth.

"Why would you say a horrible thing like that?" Samantha replied incredulously. "Are you on drugs again?"

"No, I'm not on drugs. I haven't used drugs since I came back from Arizona. Now answer my question," Jasmine said firmly. "Did you kill Daddy?"

"Honey, you know perfectly well I was sitting in the audience when your father was killed."

"Is that the gun he was killed with? Did you pay someone to do it?"

"I want you to stop this nonsense right now." Her tone shifted from that of an indulgent caregiver to that of an accused killer. "I don't want to ever hear those words come out of your mouth again. Do you understand me?"

"For the first time I feel I really do understand you. You had him killed. Why?" Jasmine said, taking a step closer to Samantha. "Did you want to be pastor that bad? Did you finally realize you didn't need him anymore? That you could do it all on your own."

Samantha took a step toward her, narrowing the space between them to only a few feet. Her shoulders stiff and her hands at her sides, as if squaring off with an equally worthy opponent, she said, "I loved your father. I could never do anything to hurt him."

Jasmine laughed slightly. "You hated him. He hated you, and I hate you too."

As the last word escaped her lips, Jasmine felt the sharp sting of Samantha's open palm on her cheek.

"You will not speak to me in that way," Samantha said as Jasmine recoiled from the blow. "I'm your mother, and don't you ever forget it."

"Or what?" Jasmine said, holding her burning cheek. "You'll kill me too?"

Samantha immediately raised her hand and, in a flash, leveled another blow with even greater force. "If you insist on speaking to me like a grown woman, then I will treat you like one. You don't seem to realize how much I indulged you and your behavior only because your father protected you from me. Now that he's gone, there's nothing standing between us. You don't know what I'm fully capable of, and trust me, you don't want to know."

"I think I know now," Jasmine said defiantly. "I know you're capable of murdering the only person in the world I ever loved."

"I'll attribute your ranting to your drug-addled brain. But trust me, if you ever say that to me again, or to anyone else, you will see for the first time exactly who you're dealing with."

"Is that a threat?"

"Yes, it is."

Chapter 9

Percy Pryce made every effort to perform his duties as assistant pastor to the best of his now limited abilities. Conducting marriage ceremonies for young, starry-eyed couples. Officiating over funerals and comforting the families of the dearly departed. Today's tasks included counseling a parishioner who was contemplating suicide after losing his home to foreclosure and, shortly after that, his wife.

The man, whose name Percy could hardly remember, sat across from him in his office at New Testament Cathedral and poured the troubled contents of his heart onto the desk between them.

"The day after I received the foreclosure notice, she just got up, packed a bag, and left. Her mother was waiting in the car out front. The bitch didn't even say good-bye. I'm sorry, Reverend, but this has got me so upset."

"That's all right . . . umm, Brother. I understand," Percy said on auto pilot. "Go on."

Percy could not stop his mind from wandering as the man spoke. The troubled parishioner's words soon turned into a bothersome buzz in his ears. Even though Percy looked at him with sympathetic eyes, he could see only the faint blur of a brown suit and a head with glasses.

Percy's mind drifted to the first day he had heard the name Danny St. John and to the events that followed.

"Hello, Catherine. Sorry I'm late," he had said on that afternoon, when he entered the office of Catherine Birdsong, the church's then chief operating officer.

Percy remembered Catherine's troubled face when he saw her that day.

"You look terrible. Is there something wrong? Have you been crying?" he had asked, approaching her with an outstretched hand. "What has Samantha done to you now?"

The comment was initially said in jest, but as he walked closer, he detected the faint remnant of a tear in the corner of her eye.

Catherine extended her hand and allowed it to be enveloped by Percy's hearty grip. "I'm fine, Reverend Pryce," she said, pointing to the chair in front of her desk, inviting him to sit. "What did you want to see me about?"

"Catherine, you can't fool me. I know something is wrong. We've known each other a long time. I think of you as a friend, and I hope you feel the same about me. Has Samantha done something to upset you?"

Catherine looked away, avoiding his sympathetic gaze. There was silence for a moment, and then she spoke. "Percy, something terrible has happened, and I don't know what to do about it."

"Then tell me about it. Maybe we can figure it out together."

"It's about Hezekiah, but he told me to not discuss it with anyone."

Percy threw his head back and laughed aloud. "How many times have we both heard that over the years? But we each know that sometimes it's necessary to discuss our concerns with others we trust to make sure our perspectives are clear and unclouded by fear. Now tell me. What's going on? Maybe it's not as bad as you think."

Catherine proceeded to recount the antagonistic meeting with Lance Savage. She told him how the reporter had confronted Hezekiah with the information he had on his affair with Danny St. John.

Percy listened attentively, shifting several times in his seat and occasionally interrupting to ask questions, such as "What did Hezekiah say?" and "When is the story supposed to run?"

Catherine concluded her tale with, "I've never been this worried about anything in my life."

Percy's last question was, "Who else knows about this?"

"I made the mistake of telling Kenneth. He's threatened to call Lance and sue the *Chronicle*."

"Don't worry. I'll talk to Kenneth." Percy then flashed a comforting smile and said, "Catherine, it doesn't sound all that bad. You know these crazies come out of the woodwork every few years. This St. John person is probably some nut who's obsessed with Hezekiah. I'll bet if I put a little scare into him, he'll stop spreading these lies."

"That's just it, Percy. I'm not convinced it's a lie. Hezekiah never denied it and swore me to secrecy. Why would he do that if it wasn't true?"

"What kind of mood was Hezekiah in this afternoon?"

"I have no idea," she said fretfully. "He canceled all his appointments. I haven't seen or heard from him all day."

"That's not like him. I'll see if I can reach him on his cell later this evening."

"Please don't tell him you spoke to me," Catherine pleaded. "Tell him you ran into Lance in the hall and he told you."

"Don't worry about that. I won't even mention your name. In the meantime we should meet first thing in the morning with Kenneth and see if we can come up with a plan for damage control, just in case the story does eventually run. Will you set that up?"

"Are you sure he can be trusted?" she asked. "How do we know he didn't leak the story in the first place?"

"Why would he do something as stupid as that? If Hezekiah goes down over this, we'll all be out of a job."

"I know, but I just don't trust anyone," Catherine said. "How's eight thirty tomorrow morning for you, in the conference room?"

"I'll be here."

The two walked toward the door and embraced.

"Oh my God," Catherine said. "You wanted to talk to me about something. I'm sorry, Percy. This has got me so distracted."

"Don't worry about that. We can talk about it later. This is much more important."

The next day Catherine, Kenneth, and Percy met in the conference room. Percy took the seat of power at the head of the conference room table.

Catherine broke the silence at the table and asked, "Where is Hezekiah? Shouldn't he be here to talk about this?"

"I thought the whole discussion might make him uncomfortable," Percy replied. "He doesn't know we're meeting."

"I think that was a mistake," Kenneth said nervously. "If he finds out we discussed this behind his back, he'll be furious." As he spoke, he picked up his cell phone from the table and said, "I don't want any part of this."

Reverend Pryce leaned forward. "Wait a minute, Kenneth. There's no reason for him to find out. I just wanted us to put our heads together and come up with a plan. This meeting never took place as far as anyone outside this room is concerned."

Kenneth looked at Catherine for signs of agreement. She signified yes by nodding.

"All right. I'll stay. But if he finds out about this meeting, I'll deny I was ever here."

"Good then," Percy said with slight relief. "I spoke with Hezekiah, and it's not alleged. He confirmed the whole story. There is in fact a Danny St. John, and they are involved in a sexual relationship."

"How long has it been going on?" Kenneth asked.

"He said for about a year. If that story is printed, all hell is going to break loose."

"We're all aware of that, Percy. But there just might be some way to convince Lance Savage to kill the story." Kenneth looked at Catherine. "You know Lance better than we do. What do you think? Can he be bribed, frightened off?"

Catherine shook her head. "I don't think there's any way he's going to let this slide. I've seen him in action. He's relentless once he gets his hands on anything sensational. He stands to build a national reputation on this."

"Come on, there's got to be some way," Percy interjected. "Every man has a price. We just have to find out what his is."

"The construction budget has one million dollars in discretionary funds," Kenneth said to no one in particular. "I think we should offer to buy his silence. That's the only way."

Catherine sat silently while the two debated the plan's merits. The conversation progressed more rapidly than she had wished. She finally spoke. "I think we're getting ahead of ourselves here. What I'd like to know is, who leaked the story in the first place? That's what's most important."

Percy looked at her impatiently and said, "That's irrelevant. It's out, and now we have to deal with the consequences."

"I disagree," Catherine protested. "Let's say we are able to silence Lance. Whoever the source is could easily find another reporter to pick it up. Eventually, we'll have to buy off every reporter in the city."

Kenneth leaned back in his chair and said, "She's right. Whoever this person is, they are obviously very close to Hezekiah and have something to gain by him not being the pastor. Any ideas?"

"It could be anyone," Catherine said. "Even one of us."

Catherine's last words unleashed a flurry of retorts. Kenneth bolted to his feet. "If you're suggesting I'm responsible, you're crazy. I'll be out of a job if this ever gets out."

Percy raised his voice. "I take personal offense at your accusations, Catherine. I've devoted the past five years of my life to this church, and I deserve better than that."

Kenneth held up his hands in an appeal for calm. "Hold on, everybody. Let's not accuse each other. Who else could have gotten that close to Hezekiah to know about this?"

"How about Dino, his driver?" Catherine asked. "He must know about it, but I think he would rather take a bullet in the head than see any harm come to Hezekiah."

Everyone nodded in consensus. Puzzled expressions formed on their faces as they pondered who the Judas might be.

Catherine, with great caution, broke the silence. "I know this might sound crazy, but I'm going to say it, anyway. What about Samantha?"

The puzzled looks quickly changed to shock and horror.

"Catherine, how could you even think something that horrible?" Kenneth said. "Samantha worships the ground Hezekiah walks on. She would rather die than see him publicly humiliated."

Catherine recoiled in her chair. "I know. You're right. I just wanted to put it out there."

"Well, please don't ever say anything like that again," Percy said in a fatherly tone. "She's going to be hurt enough when she learns about the affair. I'd hate to see her hurt even more if a rumor like that started circulating."

Having been chastised, Catherine said, “I’m sorry. I’m not suggesting she did it, but we have to look at all possibilities.”

“Look, this idle speculation isn’t getting us anywhere,” Kenneth said with his hands clasped in front of his face. “We could be here all day trying to figure out who did this. I say we go back to our original plan and offer Lance money. If the story resurfaces again later, then maybe we’ll have more time to flush out the source. But not now. We don’t have the time.”

“Kenneth is right,” said Percy. “If we’re going to act, we have to do it quickly.”

“Are we all in agreement, then?” Kenneth asked.

Percy said yes, but Catherine simply stared out the window.

“Catherine, what about you? Do you agree or not?” Percy asked.

“I don’t think it’s going to work, but if that’s our only option, then yes, I agree.”

Kenneth clapped his hands and said, “All right, then. I’ll meet with Lance this afternoon and make the offer and hopefully—”

“Wait a minute, Kenneth,” Percy said, “I want to come with you. I’d like to have a few words with him myself.”

“You don’t want to upset Lance,” Catherine said. “He’s in control. If you threaten him, he’ll turn you down flat.”

“I won’t threaten him. I just think we should hedge our bet with a little intimidation. Let him know that if he reneges on the agreement, there will be serious consequences.”

“It’s risky, but it might help in the long run,” said Kenneth. “Okay, Percy. As soon as I set up a time for the meeting, I’ll call you.” Kenneth stood and said, “Wish us luck, Catherine. We’re going to need it.”

Percy now wished he had never heard the name Danny St. John. He regretted getting involved and taking the lead in trying to get the reporter to drop the story about Hezekiah.

I should have stayed out of it, he thought as the man across from him wrapped up his tale of financial and marital woe. I should have let the Cleavelands just deal with their own mess themselves.

Now his life would never be the same. A man had died at his hands. His own wife was the source of the e-mails that had launched the newspaper article. And in spite of the fact that she knew he had killed a man, she was more determined than ever for him to become pastor.

"Reverend Pryce . . . ," said the parishioner sitting across from him at the desk in his office.

Percy did not hear him.

"Reverend Pryce . . ." the man said again. "So what do you think? Should I beg my wife to come back to me?"

The second call pulled Percy back to the counseling session. "Yes, I'm sorry, Brother. I . . . I . . . Yes, you should call her. She's just afraid and confused right now. Call her and tell her you forgive her, and let her know how much you love her. Tell her you two can work this out together."

"Thank you, Reverend Pryce," the man said, standing with Percy. "That's exactly what I needed to hear. Thank you."

As the man exited the room, Percy sat down behind his desk. He knew the parting words of advice he had just given were more for himself than for the man whose problems he hadn't heard.

I do love her so much, he thought warmly. *She's just afraid and confused.*

The waters off the California coast between Catalina Island and Long Beach were calm and tranquil, the occasional wave causing the yacht to rock gently from bow to stern. The rear deck held a series of wooden chairs and chaise lounges with blue-striped cushions. A brown lacquered table with chrome pedestal legs held a vase filled with orchids, a bucket filled with champagne and ice, and two flutes.

Cherrywood covered much of the walls of the main cabin below deck. A big-screen television was positioned on a wall next to a state-of-the-art sound system. Overstuffed tan chairs and couches had been placed seemingly in no particular order around the large space. A wet bar complete with stools and taps was in one corner of the cabin.

It was 199 feet of floating elegance, complete with six staterooms, a formal dining room, a six-person sauna, a Jacuzzi on deck, and a wine cellar, and had a range of 5,380 nautical miles.

Samantha and David sat looking out a bank of tinted windows at the endless Pacific Ocean, while the three-man crew labored above deck, unseen and unheard. They each held a glass of champagne.

"You can't screw it up this time, David," Samantha said calmly without looking in his direction. "There's too much at stake."

David did not speak. He took a gulp of champagne and stared blankly at the horizon. The gentle rocking of the boat intensified the churning in his stomach.

"Danny St. John has been living with Gideon Truman for the past four weeks. You'll find them at his home in Hollywood Hills."

"How do you know that?" David asked, looking in her direction.

"I know everything about Danny and Gideon. I have a man in Switzerland that will tell you the number of hairs on anyone's head in the world for the right price."

"What else do you know about them?" David regretted asking the question as soon as the words left his mouth.

"I know that Danny has a hundred twenty-seven dollars in his bank account. I know that he's estranged from his mother. That he has a cat named Parker, and that he's a social worker at a nonprofit agency that works with the homeless. What else would you like to know?" she asked confidently.

"How about Gideon?"

"He has a net worth of twenty million dollars. His only living relative is his grandmother in Texas. He's never been in a long-term relationship. Before he met Danny, he occasionally hired male prostitutes, who would visit him in hotels downtown. I also know the alarm system on his home has been temporarily disabled."

"Disabled?" David said in disbelief.

"That's correct."

"I don't believe you."

"You would be surprised how responsive the manager of his security company was to an anonymous offer of ten thousand dollars to accidentally allow his service to lapse for one week," she said with a disdainful smile. "It's a shame what some people will do for money these days."

David looked away in disgust.

"It has to be done this week, David. I want it done before the cathedral opening this Sunday. I don't want this hanging over my head that morning. I need to be able to focus on my sermon and nothing else."

David was silent.

"Do you understand me, David?" she asked. "You have to do it this week."

David had resigned himself to the promise he had made during the throes of passion they had shared. Her intoxicating scent in the cabin caused his senses to reel. He was weak in her presence. He was weak in her absence. Just the thought of her made his legs wobble. But the thought of killing a man caused his nerves to fray. Now the thought of killing two men had left him in a state of unbridled panic.

"Isn't there any other way you can shut them up? Did you try offering Gideon money?"

"Weren't you listening when I said he's worth twenty million dollars? Plus, now that he's fucking Danny St. John, he won't be able to listen to reason. Look what Danny did to Hezekiah, for God's sake. He was willing to walk away from a multimillion-dollar ministry and, even more amazing, away from me," she said without a hint of modesty. "I'm sure Gideon is no match for him."

"He can't be that great."

"You didn't look in his eyes. For a moment I thought I was looking in a mirror," she said admiringly. "He's stunning. I understood as soon as I looked at him why Hezekiah fell in love with him."

As she spoke, David felt his head sway with the rhythmic motion of the boat. With each wave the cabin seemed to spin to the left and to the right, then to and fro. He sensed the beginnings of a debilitating panic attack. David fumbled in his coat pocket for the vile of pills that had grounded him so many times before. But they were not there.

"What are you looking for?" Samantha asked as she saw him grope his pants and jacket pockets.

"My pills," he said guardedly. "I need my pills."

"What kind of pills?" David had her full attention now.

"Diazepam."

"Why do you need Valium?"

"Panic attacks, all right!" he snapped. "I've had them my entire life."

David had had his first anxiety attack when he was eight years old. He had innocently placed his hand his chest and for the first time had felt the gentle beating of his heart. He instinctively knew that it was the source of his life and that if the beating stopped, he would die. For the next hour his mind had been awash with frightening thoughts of what he could do to make sure his heart continued to beat. But at eight years old, he could not find the answer. The more he thought, the faster his heart would beat. And the faster his heart beat, the less he was able to control the frightening images that flooded his mind.

Then, finally, the sight of his young body lying lifeless there on the living room floor sent him running for the comfort of his mother's arms. She calmed his fears and wiped away his tears as only a mother could. Since then, whenever David found himself in situations that presented him with pressure he was unable to handle, his head would begin to spin, his heart would race, and sweat would pour from his brow. Diazepam, Prozac, Zoloft, Paxil, and Cymbalta were now called on to replace the comforting arms of his mother.

"Here. Drink this," Samantha said, waving a half-full brandy snifter in his face.

David's trembling hand took the glass, and he quickly downed the quivering brown liquid.

"You can't fall apart on me now, David," Samantha said, closely studying him. "I need you to get ahold of yourself."

"I'll be fine," David said, panting. "Just give me a minute and I'll be fine."

David stood before the bank of windows and took three deep breaths through his nose, the way his psychiatrist had instructed him. "I'm better now," he said self-consciously. "They usually pass pretty quickly."

Samantha stared at the man standing at her window, surrounded by the deep blue sea. She expertly recalculated the level of care, flattery, and physical attention she would need to apply to ensure that he would do her bidding.

"David, darling, are you okay now?" she asked gently.

"I told you, I'm fine."

"Good. I need you to keep a level head. At least until Sunday. Are you going to be able to do this for me?" she asked, turning her back to him. "If not, then I'll have to . . ."

David could feel her slipping away. "I told you I would do anything for you," he said, placing his hand on her shoulder. "I don't want to, but if this is what it will take for us to be together, then I'll do it."

Samantha turned to him. They were now only a breath's length away from each other. "I'm afraid, David. You won't let me down, will you?" she asked, gently brushing his cheek. "I need you to be strong for me."

David slowly wilted under her touch. The cabin began to whirl, and his heart raced again. Not from panic this time, but from lust. The warmth of her breath caused him to shudder. He could feel her touch pierce his body down to the soles of his feet. No need for Xanax or his mother's arms when Samantha was near him. The overwhelming complexities of life and the reality of murder became insignificant trivia, easily swept from his mind when she was within his reach.

"Thank you for agreeing to speak with me, Mrs. Shackelford," Gideon said politely. "I know this has been a difficult time for everyone at New Testament Cathedral, especially for the members of the board of trustees."

"I'm sorry I don't have much time," Scarlett said, directing Gideon into her living room. "I have to pick up my daughter in an hour."

"Oh, you have a daughter? Is that her there?" Gideon pointed to a photograph of a little girl, with pink barrettes dangling from pigtails, sitting on the fireplace mantelpiece. "She's adorable. What's her name?"

"Natalie," Scarlett replied guardedly. "Please sit down. So what is this about? Why do you need to speak with me?"

Gideon took a second look at the picture on the mantel. There was something familiar about the cute little girl in the photograph.

"As I mentioned on the phone, I'm doing a story on the life of Hezekiah Cleaveland. I've had the opportunity to speak with Samantha, Hattie Williams, and a few other members, but I don't think my story would be complete if I didn't interview all the members of the board of trustees."

Scarlett did not respond.

Gideon sat in the comfortable chair she had directed him to. From his vantage point he could see the little girl in the photo staring down at him just to Scarlett's left. "Would you mind if I recorded our conversation?" he asked, pulling a small recorder from his breast pocket. "My handwriting is so bad, I sometimes can't read my own notes."

Scarlett looked suspiciously at the little device. She made a mental note to watch her tone and to show no emotion. "Not at all."

"How long have you been a member of New Testament Cathedral?"

"I joined a few years after it was founded. It's been about eight years now."

"At that time it was still a small church. Why did you choose it as your church home?"

"I was actually an employee at first. I was Pastor Cleaveland's assistant for a year before I joined the church."

"Really? I didn't know that. What was it like working for the Cleavelands?"

"I didn't work for the Cleavelands," Scarlett replied, bristling. "I said I was Pastor Cleaveland's assistant."

"I see. Well, what was it like working for Hezekiah?"

"He was a good boss. Very compassionate. Very professional. I didn't have any complaints."

Gideon knew instinctively there was more to the story, and proceeded with caution. "What were your duties at that time?"

"I was primarily his scheduling secretary. I managed his calendar and made all his travel arrangements for speaking engagements outside of the city, and I handled some personal things, like doctor's appointments, car maintenance, small things like that."

"Why did you quit?"

Scarlett hesitated. She had not anticipated this line of questions. "I'm not clear what this has to do with Hezekiah."

Her slightly defensive tone did not go unnoticed by Gideon. "Understanding your role at the church and with Pastor Cleaveland helps me establish a context. I hope I haven't offended you in any way." Gideon watched closely for her verbal and nonverbal responses.

"I'm not offended at all," she said as she crossed her legs on the couch. "I left when I married and became pregnant with my daughter."

"I see. So that was five or six years ago. Is that when you married David?"

"No, David is my second husband. He's not Natalie's father," she responded and looked nervously at her watch. "Her father and I divorced when she was two years old."

"I'm sorry. How did you become a member of the board of trustees?"

"Hezekiah asked me personally."

"And why do you think that is?"

"I'm not sure. I suppose he trusted me."

As she spoke, Gideon looked at the photo of the little girl again, and now it was clear. She looked remarkably like Hezekiah. "She really is a lovely little girl. Was your first husband related to Hezekiah?"

"No," Scarlett replied with a puzzled look. "Why do you ask?"

"I'm sorry, but I couldn't help but notice the resemblance between your daughter and Hezekiah." Her nervousness served as the answer to his questions. "She has his eyes and nose."

Scarlett turned and looked at the picture over her shoulder to avoid eye contact. She did not respond.

"Do you have any other children?"

"No, she's an only child." Scarlett looked at her watch again.

"What was your relationship like with Samantha Cleaveland?"

"I didn't have much contact with her. She had her own assistant."

"If I can be frank with you, Scarlett . . . May I call you Scarlett?"

She responded with an affirmative nod of her head.

"Thank you. As I was saying, I've spoken to several people, and some have told me in confidence how difficult Samantha can be. That the woman the public sees is actually nothing like the Samantha Cleaveland they know behind the scenes."

Scarlett did not respond but simply looked down at the recorder that sat on the coffee table between them.

"This can be off the record if you would prefer," Gideon said, pressing the STOP button on the recorder. "I would really appreciate anything you can tell me to help me get a true picture of Hezekiah and Samantha. I can assure you that I will attribute nothing to you that you do not approve in advance."

Scarlett stood and walked to the sliding-glass door behind the couch. She crossed her arms and looked out into the yard.

"Samantha Cleaveland is a horrible woman," she finally said.

Gideon remained silent.

"The only things that are important to her are money and power. I don't know what's going to happen to the ministry now that she is pastor. I'm sure it will keep growing, but at what cost?"

"You're a beautiful woman, Scarlett. Did Samantha have a problem with you working so closely with Hezekiah? Is she the real reason you quit as his assistant?"

"Yes," was her anguished reply. "She made my life miserable. Hezekiah tried to shield me from her, but the more he tried, the more hostile she became toward me." As she spoke, a tear fell from her eye. She tried to wipe it away discreetly, but Gideon recognized the gesture even with her back turned.

In a split second Gideon calculated his next move. He weighed the risk of asking her the question he already knew the answer to, and reasoned there was nothing to lose.

"Scarlett, is Natalie Hezekiah's daughter?"

Scarlett was too weak to form a believable denial. The lies, the death, and the betrayal had taken their toll. If only her life could have been as neat and tidy as the perfect living room. She slowly lowered her head and was silent.

Scarlett had arrived in Los Angeles as a young girl from the South. Her mother had wanted a better life for her, so she had sent her to live with relatives in California. She had been smart and beautiful her entire life but had never really known it. Her shyness was often mistaken for conceitedness. Boys found the shy Southern girl captivating. Her naïveté and her soft voice garnered proposals of marriage long before she turned eighteen.

Scarlett thought back to when she was nineteen, to the day she found out she was pregnant with Hezekiah's baby.

Gideon could see that she was crying at the window. He stood and walked behind her and gently placed his hand on her quivering shoulder and asked again, "Is she his daughter, Scarlett?"

Scarlett could no longer contain her tears. She covered her mouth and sobbed, "Yes," into her cupped hand. "She is Hezekiah's daughter."

"It's okay, Scarlett," Gideon said in his most comforting voice. "Your secret is safe with me. Does your husband know?"

The question caused her sobs to intensify. Gideon's heart told him to stop, but his reporter's mind urged him to push harder. Through his touch on her quivering shoulder, he could feel her pain. She was so gentle and fragile, he felt any additional pressure would cause her to shatter into a million pieces on the peach carpet.

Against the gentle pleading of his heart, he pressed on. His instincts told him David knowing about Natalie accounted for a large portion of her pain. "How did David react when you told him?" he asked gently.

"He was furious," she said through tears. "I can't blame him. I made a mistake by not telling him sooner. He feels embarrassed that Hezekiah and Samantha knew and he didn't. It was stupid of me. I just didn't know how to tell him." The entire time she spoke, she kept her back to him. "I've made a mess of everything, but I didn't mean anyone any harm. I just wanted to protect my daughter."

Gideon had interviewed enough battered women to recognize some of the signs. Overwhelming guilt, shuddering under the touch of a man, blaming herself rather than the perpetrator. The signs were there.

"What did he do when you told him?"

There was no answer.

"Did he hurt you, Scarlett?" he asked with the voice of a seasoned therapist.

"No," she said in a dismissive tone. "David would never hurt me. He's much too gentle to hurt anyone."

"Then what happened?"

Gideon allowed the words to linger in the air. He knew there was no turning back for Scarlett. Once the floodgates of confession had been opened, few could resist the rushing tide.

"He's threatening to leave me for . . ." She hesitated and seemed to brace herself for the next words.

"Leave you?" Gideon said, tenderly goading her.

Scarlett took a deep breath and said, "Yes. For Samantha Cleaveland."

Gideon froze. It was unbelievable on so many different levels. The glamorous grieving widow already connecting with another man. The pastor stealing another woman's husband. The board of trustee member giving birth to the pastor's illegitimate child. It was almost too much for him to grasp. Blackmail, love triangles, and murder. The seasoned reporter who thought he had heard everything was now presented with a story so fantastic that even Hollywood would be challenged to do it justice.

"Are you sure?" Gideon asked with the deepest sincerity. "Why would Samantha do that to you?"

"You don't know her," she replied with a mixture of scoffs and tears. "She doesn't care who gets hurt as long as she gets what she wants. She almost destroyed my life once, and now she's trying to do it again. I c-c-ould . . ." she stammered. "If I had the chance, I would kill her."

It was well after midnight. Hattie sat in her favorite floral wingback chair in her living room. The steam from a cup of chamomile tea that sat on the tea table released a wisp of mint into the quiet, dark room. Hattie had raised three children in this house. Her husband had died years earlier, and she now lived alone. The newest piece of furniture in the entire home was a small ottoman that her husband had purchased twenty years earlier so she could elevate her leg and take the pressure off her arthritic knee.

There was a chill in the air. The only light came from the dial of a transistor radio sitting on a hutch across the room. A minister she had never heard before chirped his message of damnation to insomniacs, who were either enthralled by his words, too tired to turn the dial, or otherwise preoccupied.

No need to turn on the heater, she thought while pulling her terry-cloth robe tight around her chest to ward off the cold. *Lord willing, I'll be asleep soon.*

It was in the midnight hours like this that Hattie had been guided through decisions that shaped her life. Alone and in the dead of night. The world was asleep, and the air was clear of the blizzard of thoughts that often distort the mind.

Her philosophy was that since the beginning of time there had only ever been one man and one woman. Adam and Eve. There was only one mind, and we all drew our wisdom, inspiration, and creativity from the same source. If one person had an idea, then every person on the planet had access to that very same idea. If one person suffered, then we all suffered. If one person succeeded, we all succeeded.

Hattie had inherited the gift of empathy, and the particular wisdom that accompanied it, from her grandmother. It placed Hattie in the unique position of knowing the hearts of people and being able to anticipate their actions. Only a few people knew she had this gift. Her grandmother knew the moment she laid eyes on the gurgling little baby girl. Pastor Cleaveland realized it when she told him he was going to be one of the most famous men on earth.

Now, on this quiet night, Hattie could feel the universe had something to tell her. She sat patiently in the chair, tolerating the ranting preacher on the radio. If my arthritis wasn't acting up on me, I'd get up and turn him off, she thought. But it was, so she sat captive to his misguided perspective on the Gospel. Her defense was to reduce his voice to nothing more than white noise as she sipped the herbal tea and quietly hummed one of her favorite hymns.

"Walk in the light, beautiful light, come where the dewdrops of mercy shine bright. Oh, shine all around us by day and by night, Jesus is, Jesus is the light of the world."

Hattie knew her Bible, and she knew the truth. She had never relied on anyone to tell her God's will. "If one man knows the truth, then we all know the truth. God ain't telling one man a secret that he ain't willing to tell everybody," she often noted. Hattie discounted any preacher who said, "God told me to tell you . . . ," because she knew it wasn't true and would invariably be followed by him or her reaching into her pocketbook. "God don't have favorites," she often said. "If he has a message for anyone on this earth, believe me, child, he will tell them personally. God doesn't need a middleman."

"If the gospel be hid, it's hid from the lost, my Jesus is waiting to look past your faults. Arise and shine, your light has come. Jesus is, I know that He is the only light of this world."

As the hymn fell almost silently from her lips, she felt a familiar stirring in her stomach. This always meant that either a vision was coming or she would soon need a sip of Metamucil. Considering she had had only cottage cheese and a few slices of canned peaches for dinner, she assumed a vision would soon play out before her.

She gently placed the cup of tea on the table and looked straight ahead into the darkness. Hints of furniture and the shadows on her drawn shades from the trees standing guard outside her window were all she could see.

Slowly, a form began to appear in the middle of the room. At first she couldn't see what it was, but as the moments passed, it became clear it was taking the shape of a human. She freely opened her heart and mind to what was to come.

Before the image was fully formed, she knew exactly who it was. The room took on a ghostly glow, which emanated directly from the form. She felt a rush of cold sweep through her body. Hattie gripped the armrest to brace herself for the visitor. She felt waves of hate rush over her as the image became clearer.

Then, in an instant, Samantha Cleaveland was standing in the room. Hattie had never seen an image so clearly. Samantha was looking directly at her with a foreboding glare. There was something threatening in her stance. Her feet were firmly planted on the oval braided rug in the center of the room. Her shoulders were square, and her fists were clenched at her sides.

Hattie looked calmly at the figure and waited for it to reveal the purpose of its visit. She could feel the hate. She'd felt it before on so many Sunday mornings. Then Samantha slowly raised her hand and pointed directly at Hattie. The gesture sent a shiver down Hattie's spine. Samantha took a step toward Hattie.

"Don't come any closer," Hattie said out loud.

Samantha stopped as Hattie's voice sliced through the cold in the room. Her expression said she wanted to come closer, but she could not.

"What do you want?" Hattie asked firmly.

There was no response. Instead, Samantha took another bold step forward. Hattie sat upright in the wingback chair. She reached to her left and took a leather-bound Bible from the table and rested it in her lap.

"I know what you did to Pastor Cleaveland," Hattie said in a clear attempt to provoke the spirit. "God knows what you did."

Samantha took another step forward. It happened so quickly that Hattie noticed only that the distance between them had become shorter. She opened the Bible in her lap. This was no ordinary vision. Up until now she had witnessed only visions that seemed as though they were playing on a television screen. This time was different. She could actually feel Samantha in the room. It was almost as if she could reach out and touch her. Hattie was, for the first time, a part of the vision.

She knew the spirit was trying to intimidate her, but she was not afraid. "Don't hurt anyone else," Hattie said boldly. "This has got to stop. Stay away from that boy, Danny. Hezekiah loved him. He won't let you hurt him."

Samantha began to laugh. There was no sound, only the mocking expression on her face. Her presence was so strong in the room that Hattie had to brace herself so as not to become overwhelmed by it. She was determined, however, to stand her ground.

"God is going to stop you," she said. "I'm praying with every ounce of me for God to stop you."

Samantha took another defiant step closer. She was now standing only four feet away.

Hattie stood from the chair. Her arthritic knee functioned as well as it had when she was twenty years old. She looked Samantha directly in the eye and said, "This has got to stop now." Hattie raised the Bible between them and began to pray. "In the name of Jesus, I rebuke you. I bind you by the power of God."

She said the words over and over. The intensity of her speech increased with each repetition. As she spoke, Samantha took a step backward. One after another, Hattie unleashed a barrage of scriptures and declarations. The more she spoke, the farther Samantha moved away. But Hattie was relentless. With every step back that Samantha took, Hattie took one step forward.

The hate pouring from Samantha did not diminish. The room remained cold, and her finger stayed fixed on Hattie. Then, as slowly as the figure had appeared, it began to fade away. The two women's eyes remained locked the entire time. After a few moments, the figure disappeared completely. The last thing Hattie saw was Samantha's eyes peering at her through the darkness.

Hattie made her way back to the wingback chair and collapsed onto the seat. Suddenly the pain in her knee shot through her entire body. She realized she was panting for breath and her hands were shaking. She felt a bead of perspiration roll down her cheek.

In all the years she had been having visions, never once had she been presented with an image that frightened her as much as this one had. The sight of Samantha standing in her living room, pointing at her, had made Hattie's heart pound against the walls of her chest.

She clutched the Bible to her breast and said, "Lord, you have to stop her."

Chapter 10

New Testament Cathedral felt like the center of the universe this week. The campus was filled with tourists who had traveled from far and wide to witness the opening of the new sanctuary. Mobile homes, tour buses, cars, and limousines were lined up at the entrance, waiting for their turn to drive along the campus's cobblestone streets and to come that much closer to Samantha Cleaveland. Each vehicle was greeted with a hearty "Welcome to New Testament Cathedral," from the armed security guards. "Would you mind stepping from the vehicle while we search it? We can't be too safe these days."

No one protested. Everyone understood that there was still a killer on the loose and that every measure had to be taken to protect Samantha Cleaveland. The first few steps into each new building took guests through metal detectors. Visible gun bulges could be seen under the arms of discreet men and women in black suits and dark sunglasses as they talked into their wristwatches while walking the grounds and looking inconspicuous.

It was now only three days until the first Sunday morning in the new sanctuary. All the hotels within a ten-mile radius of the church were fully booked. The opening was being covered in the media like a long-awaited movie premiere. It was a phenomenon due to the dramatic fashion in which Hezekiah had died and the theatrical way in which Samantha lived.

Samantha stood at the window of her glass office, surveying the grounds. From there she could see people pointing up at her office on the fifth floor, above the main entrance of the sanctuary. She could see them all clearly, but fortunately, they could not see her through the heavily tinted windows. If they could, they would have been offended by the disdain in her eye and the dismissive slant of her mouth as they craned their necks to see her.

Samantha's world was governed by deception. As a child, she had to be perfect at all times. She was the daughter of a pastor, and her mother would accept nothing but the best from her and for her. She was a beautiful little girl. Long, naturally wavy hair, perfectly chiseled features, and eyes as black as onyx, which seemed to look straight through you. She played with the other children at church in the hallways, in Fellowship Hall, and on the lawn at the back of her father's church, but her mother on many occasions had reminded her, "Samantha, you're not like the other children. Always remember you're better than they are. You're the daughter of Pastor Herman Jedediah Armstrong. Don't ever forget that."

It was a working-class congregation. The members came from the poor neighborhoods and the housing tenements that surrounded the church. The faithful would come every Sunday, and on the first Sunday of each month they would give 10 percent of their monthly earnings to Pastor Armstrong. Ten percent from one person's salary in that neighborhood didn't amount to much, but 10 percent from over three thousand households allowed Pastor Herman Armstrong and First Lady Adeline Armstrong to drive his and hers Mercedes-Benzs, live in the city's upper-middle-class neighborhood, and send Samantha to the finest private schools.

Samantha's clothes were always a little nicer than those of all the other children at church. Her education was better, and the food on her table much finer. She soon learned the value of the masses. They were there to meet her needs. The parishioners who filled the sanctuary each Sunday were there for her. They were there to buy Samantha her first car at sixteen. They were there to purchase her mother a new fur coat each winter. They were there to wrap her father's wrist in Rolex watches and adorn his pinkie finger with diamonds.

Church was the family business. Pastor Armstrong christened the babies, married the young couples, and prepared the dead, in the family-owned and family-operated mortuary, for their final resting place. The church even had its own credit union. It was the first in the community, which meant the Armstrongs held the deeds and pink slips to many of the members' homes and cars. The church was a one-stop shop, and all the proceeds kept the Armstrong family cradled comfortably in the arms of luxury.

Samantha had always known she could never inherit the family business, because she was a girl. She did, however, inherit something much more valuable. Her mother's ability to manipulate and control the men in her life. Pastor Armstrong was a strapping and elegant man. His pearly smile and fiery sermons would seduce the women and inspire the men each Sunday morning. But behind closed doors it was apparent who ran the business. Adeline Armstrong managed all the church and family finances, which were one and the same. She dressed her husband in the finest Brooks Brothers suits and draped him in gold-embroidered robes. Sunday morning was theater, and Adeline was the director and producer.

Samantha Cleaveland was already a master at the game by the time Hezekiah Cleaveland entered the picture. He didn't have a chance against her. On the first day she saw him, as a young visiting preacher in her father's church, he wore an ill-fitting suit. But there was something about him. The women in the audience hung on his every word. The men looked on with envy, admiration, and a healthy tinge of jealousy. In an instant, she decided he would be her husband. He would be the man who would serve as pastor of her church. He would be the man who would father her children. This was the man who would keep her in the finest clothes, cars, and homes. He was raw and unrefined, but he was charismatic and beautiful. Just the right man to play the role in the production that was to be her life.

She wasted no time in re-creating him. He was immediately integrated into the Armstrong dynasty and taken under her father's wing. Adeline coached her on the fine art of training him to be the man who would keep her in the only life that she knew.

But Samantha's skills surpassed those of her mother. The difference between the two women was that Samantha was willing to do whatever it took to get what she wanted. Adeline had limits. Oral sex was not a part of the equation. "Ladies don't do things like that," she had once told her daughter. But Samantha mastered the toe-curling and eye-rolling skill and used it as yet another tool to control. "Don't ever steal, honey. God hates a thief," was another of her mother's instructions. Samantha, however, felt that if she wanted something, she had a right to have it, no matter who it belonged to. *It's not really stealing if it was always supposed to be mine,* she had often thought.

"Marriage is a sacred bond, darling," Adeline told Samantha on the night before her wedding. "Always be faithful to your husband, no matter how much you are tempted." Samantha was never tempted by sex or passion. She could take it or leave it. She did, however, know that sex was one of the easiest ways to persuade men to do her bidding, whether it was Hezekiah, Reverend Willie Mitchell, David Shackelford, or any other man she needed at the time. If money wasn't enough to convince them, then she always had her body as the ultimate bargaining tool.

Adeline didn't believe in divorce, and she instilled the same belief in Samantha. "Now, honey, you know we don't believe in divorce in our family," she told Samantha on the eve of her wedding, dispensing more motherly advice. "When you say 'until death do us part' tomorrow in front of God and all those witnesses, make sure you mean it. My great-grandmother, my grandmother, and my mother all buried their husbands. I plan to bury your father someday, and now you have to plan on doing the same with your husband. There's no turning back now."

"I will, Mama," Samantha replied, gently touching her mother's hand. "I love Hezekiah. I will never divorce him."

At the young age of sixty-five, Reverend Herman Jedediah Armstrong died of a heart attack in his church office, on top of his forty-six-year-old secretary, with his pants around his ankles. The funeral was lovely, and Samantha noted that her mother had never looked more radiant.

"Excuse me, Pastor Cleaveland." The voice on the intercom startled Samantha as she looked from her office window.

"Yes? What is it?" she asked curtly.

"I'm very sorry to disturb you, Pastor Cleaveland," the assistant said timidly. "Trustee Scarlett Shackelford is here to see you. She said it's very important. I told her you were not available, but she insists."

Samantha looked curiously at the phone but did not respond. In all the years she had known Scarlett Shackelford, she had never been in a room alone with her. There was no need. She was the mother of Hezekiah's bastard child, and because of that, Samantha was resigned to the fact that Scarlett would always have a piece of Hezekiah that she could never buy, steal, or control. For this reason alone she had always hated Scarlett.

"Shall I make an appointment for her at another time?" said the intercom.

"No. Send her in."

A slight gasp of surprise could be heard from the intercom. Samantha rarely saw anyone without an appointment. "Yes, Pastor Cleaveland."

Samantha continued to look out the window as she waited for the door to open. Pretty, delicate, meek, and mild Scarlett was, ironically, the only woman on the planet who caused Samantha to doubt her beauty. Of all the affairs Hezekiah had had, Scarlett was the one that had affected him the most. On the day Samantha found out about the affair and the baby, she told Hezekiah to end it immediately. For the first time, he protested about ending a relationship. Not because he thought there could ever be a future for him with Scarlett, but rather because he knew that she would be devastated, and he never wanted to hurt Scarlett.

On so many Sundays mornings after the child was born, Samantha could see Hezekiah scanning the church audience from the pulpit for the mother and child.

Scarlett entered the room and closed the door behind her. Samantha took a seat at her desk facing the window.

"So you finally told David about Natalie. I had assumed you and I were going to take our little secret to the grave."

"He had a right to know," Scarlett said, standing in the middle of the spacious office.

"Why? What good did it do you, Scarlett? It only hurt him and destroyed your marriage. You know he's very angry with you now. You should have kept your mouth shut."

"The truth didn't destroy my marriage. You did."

"You overestimate me. The moment you told David was the moment your marriage ended. I had nothing to do with that," Samantha said and turned to face Scarlett. "You made that decision on your own, and now you have to live with the consequences."

"Consequences?" Scarlett scoffed. "What do you know about consequences? You've never had to pay for any of the damage you've done to anyone."

"Oh . . . and how do you know that much about my life?"

"Because you splash your entire life in front of the world every opportunity you get," Scarlett said, looking directly at her.

"Don't believe everything you see on television, my dear."

"Don't 'my dear' me. You forget, I know who you are."

"Did you come here to insult me or to discuss this like adults?"

"You're sleeping with my husband, and you expect me to discuss it calmly, like an adult?"

"Your husband would have never come to me if you hadn't opened your mouth. You never once considered how your affair with my husband affected me, did you? It was all about you and your delicate feelings. Well, fuck you and your feelings. He was my husband, and you had no right to touch him, and now you and your daughter are paying the price for it."

"Is that what this is all about?" Scarlett asked, taking a step forward. "Revenge?"

"I suppose in a way it is. You tried and failed to take my husband, and I tried and succeed in taking yours. Don't worry, though. When I'm done with him, I'll send him back to you, at least what's left of him."

"I came here to speak with you woman to woman, Samantha. I apologize for what I did to you. I know it was wrong."

"Apologize?" Samantha said indignantly. "You have my husband's child and then blame me for how your life turned out, and all you can do is *apologize* five years later. You're not the victim, Scarlett. Hezekiah and David bought that whole poor Scarlett routine, but I don't. You're nothing more than a manipulator. I offered you money, and you turned it down. I offered to relocate you to another city, and you turned that down too, because you wanted Hezekiah. Hezekiah is dead, so now you can't dangle that little girl in front of him anymore. Now you just have me to contend with. Take your best shot at me, and you'll see just how little the world will care about your bastard child."

"I'm not here to threaten you, Samantha."

"Then why are you here?"

"To try to appeal to you one woman to another. You've made your point with my husband, and I guess on some level I deserved it. I'm asking you to not take advantage of him or our situation. David loves me, and you know that. You have everything and can have any man you want. Don't do this, Samantha. I'm not asking for myself. I'm asking for Hezekiah's daughter. Don't make her suffer for our mistakes, and whether you like it or not, she's here and she deserves a chance at happiness."

"I don't owe you or your love child anything," Samantha sneered. "You should have thought about all this before you slept with my husband. Now I want you out of my office. As a matter of fact, I want you off the board of trustees and out of this church. Consider yourself excommunicated."

"You can't remove me from the board without a unanimous vote of the members, and you know that."

"And just how difficult do you think that will be for me to get?' Samantha replied coldly. "They'll vote exactly how I tell them to vote."

"You know you can't control Hattie Williams."

"When she finds out about your little secret, she may be more easily persuaded."

"I can't believe you would use this against me. Haven't we all suffered enough?"

"As a matter of fact, no, I don't think you've suffered enough. I went easy on you when this all happened, because at the time I had other things that needed my attention. But since you've decided to reopen this whole sordid mess, I have no choice but to deal with it and with you."

"Deal with me?" Scarlett said with a hiss. "You arrogant . . . I tried to do the right thing and speak to you like a reasonable human being, but I see that was a mistake. So now I'm giving you fair warning. If you don't keep your hands off my husband, you will regret it."

"Is that a threat?" Samantha asked with one eyebrow raised. "If it is, you better be ready to back it up, because I don't take threats lightly."

"Yes, it is a threat, Samantha, and yes, I am fully prepared to back it up."

As time passed, Cynthia Pryce's obsession with Samantha only increased. There was not a day when she was not consumed with thoughts of removing her as pastor. One scheme after another was dissected, dismissed, and resurrected when no other viable plan could be devised.

Percy and Cynthia had come to New Testament Cathedral from a neighboring church. They were a young and optimistic couple who wanted nothing more than to serve God and Hezekiah Cleaveland. In the early days the relationship was ideal. Percy fit in nicely as Hezekiah's right-hand man. He performed weddings, funerals, and christenings when Hezekiah was not available. The church in those days was smaller and had a more intimate feel. Everyone knew everyone's name or, at the very least, recognized their face.

Cynthia initially loved the role of wife of the second in command. The position came with more power and prestige than she had ever experienced in her life. When she was a college student from the wrong side of the tracks in South-Central L.A., the extent of her exposure to wealth and fame was watching soap operas and people like Hezekiah and Samantha on her parent's television in the city's projects.

But she was beautiful and cunning. There wasn't a loss she couldn't transform into a win for herself, and there was no man she couldn't have if she chose him. She met Percy in her sophomore year at the Bible Institute of Los Angeles. He was the young graduate student in the theological seminary. She was the popular undergrad whose primary purpose for being on the campus was to find a husband. When she first laid eyes on Percy as he walked across a bustling cafeteria, he catapulted to the top of her list of eligible candidates. Tall, chocolate, holding an armful of books, and the eyes of every girl in the room watching him as he walked by.

No formal introductions had been necessary. One day she boldly sat next to him on the quad and simply asked him, "Do you believe in love at first sight?"

Percy's stammering response was, "Yes, I s-suppose do."

From nearly that moment on they were inseparable. He worshiped her from day one and continued to do so in spite of all they had been through together. She was woven into his DNA. Percy couldn't face a day without first looking into her eyes and feeling the warmth of her body.

He couldn't sleep at night if she was not near. She was his touchstone. The reason he woke and the reason he lived. God was good, but for Percy, Cynthia was essential.

As the church grew, Cynthia began to resent the subservient role her husband's position had transformed into. He was the backup plan. The second best. The one to call "only if Pastor Cleaveland isn't available."

"Why do you let them treat you like that?" soon became the precursor to many of their conversations. "They don't appreciate you," was another, and as was, "You're nothing more than his lackey."

Cynthia also took note of the increasing wealth accumulating just beyond her reach. One day the chauffeur-driven Escalades showed up in the church parking lot and the Cleavelands stepped out, as if they had had uniformed drivers their entire lives. Then increasingly expensive pieces of art began appearing on walls and tables in Hezekiah's and Samantha's offices. Then came the chartered jets for overnight trips for Samantha. But the final straw was the Cleaveland estate.

Hezekiah and Samantha had hosted an open house for the members of the board of trustees and seven-figure supporters of the ministry. The display of wealth was shameless. The mammoth size of the house was bad enough, but on top of that Cynthia was stunned by the army of servants and the priceless works of art scattered around the house. Peacocks, fountains, tennis courts, and swimming pools—they were all too much for her to take.

It was on that day that it became Cynthia's life mission to replace Samantha as the first lady of New Testament Cathedral.

"Are you okay, Cynthia?" Percy had asked her in the car on their way home from the open house that evening. "You haven't said a word since we left the party."

Cynthia had sat silently, looking out the passenger window, as the car took them away from the rarefied heights of Bel Air.

"I'm disgusted, just sick, and I don't understand why you aren't too," was her icy reply when she finally spoke.

"I know it was a little over the top, but that's just how Samantha is."

"A little over the top! Two Picassos. Did you see that security system? It alone must have cost at least a million dollars."

"Don't let it upset you," Percy said, missing the point of her anger.

"You can't think that all of that was okay. Especially with them giving you a lousy five hundred and fifty thousand a year. I can't believe you're not as angry as I am."

"Honey, we've always said we aren't doing this work for the money. It's about spreading the gospel. It's about ministering to the sick and—"

"You don't have to remind me what the work is about," she snapped. "I went to the same racist, Bible-thumping, dogma-preaching college that you went to, remember. I know the speech, so don't lecture me. You know as well as I do there's no justification for spending that kind of money, especially when it's coming to you in ten-dollar increments from old ladies and widows living off their husband's pensions. It's reprehensible."

Cynthia neglected to mention the near orgasm she had had when she entered Samantha's walk-in closet. The closet was larger than her living room and dining room combined. The walls were lined with designers she had seen only in magazines. Shoe racks filled with shoes in every color seemed to cascade like rainbows from the ceiling. There were two sets of matching Louis Vuitton luggage, hats, purses, scarves, and gloves. Cashmere, leather, chiffon, and silk spilled from the walls like sweet honey from the rock.

Cynthia wanted it, and she wanted it all, but she never fully admitted it to herself. The calling of God was the perfect camouflage for the true desires of mortals. The wealth flaunted in her face and just beyond her reach made her fingertips ache.

"They ought to be ashamed of themselves. And did you see the way everyone was fawning over them?" she ranted on during the car ride home. "I thought that one woman was going to cream her panties in the foyer when she saw that Picasso."

"Cynthia, please! Is that really necessary?"

"I'm sorry, but the entire evening left a horrible taste in my mouth."

Now, years later, the rancid taste of jealousy was still in her mouth.

From her dining room table, Cynthia dialed Scarlett Shackelford.

"Scarlett, it's Cynthia. How are you, dear?"

Scarlett was still reeling from her confessions to Gideon and her confrontation with Samantha. David had not been home in two nights, and Natalie was beginning to ask questions.

"Not good, Cynthia. This is not a very good time for me. Can you call me back later?"

"This will only take a minute."

Scarlett plopped down on the sofa and said, "Okay, but could you please make this quick? I have a terrible headache."

"This is about Samantha."

"I assumed so," Scarlett replied scornfully. "You put me in a very awkward position, Cynthia. I thought you had the votes locked up. I held up my end, and you couldn't even get your own husband to vote against her. I looked like a fool at the meeting. I thought you could count on Hattie's vote."

Scarlett shivered when she recalled the night the board of trustees installed Samantha as permanent pastor.

The board of trustees had sat nervously around the table in the recently christened Pastor Hezekiah T. Cleaveland Memorial Conference Room. The special closed meeting had been convened at the request of Reverend Kenneth Davis. The only item on the agenda was the selection of the permanent pastor of New Testament Cathedral.

Kenneth sat at the head of the table as the convener of the meeting. Hattie Williams's wooden cane rested on the conference table. Her purse, filled with Kleenex, peppermints, and a pocket Bible, rested on her lap. Reverend Percy Pryce sat to her left, three chairs down. Despite his best attempts at appearing calm and detached, he could not hide the glimmer on his upper lip, which betrayed the churning in his stomach.

Kenneth nervously checked his watch. Scarlett Shackelford sat stiffly three chairs to his right. The pills she'd taken before leaving home that evening had effectively erased the remains of her shattered emotions.

"I don't think she's coming," Kenneth said, checking his watch again. "It's already twenty past eight. We were supposed to start at eight."

"Maybe we should start without her," Percy said softly.

"She'll be here."

All heads turned to Hattie.

"How do you know that?" Scarlett asked coldly.

"Because she's already in the building," Hattie said. "I can feel her."

Scarlett rolled her eyes and said impatiently, "I say we call the meeting to order right now and get this over with."

As she spoke, the security guard swung one half of the double doors open and Samantha appeared in the threshold. Kenneth and Percy leapt to their feet, while Hattie and Scarlett remained seated. Before entering, Samantha made eye contact with everyone at the table.

"Good evening, Brothers and Sisters," she said confidently. "I apologize for my lateness, but I was attending to church business. Please sit down, Brothers."

Reverend Davis walked to the console and poured a glass of water. "Would anyone else like a glass before we get started?"

A chorus of "No" and "No thank you, Reverend," followed, and he made his way back to the head of the table.

Samantha sat four chairs to the right of Scarlett, which placed her the farthest from the head of the table. She crossed her legs and leaned back in the high-backed leather chair.

Kenneth placed the glass of water beside a single sheet of paper, five pens, a stack of index cards, and a small tape recorder. After pressing the RECORD button on the tape recorder, he said, "I now call this special meeting of the Board of Trustees of New Testament Cathedral to order at eight twenty-five on this day of our Lord and Savior Jesus Christ. Thank you all for coming on such short notice. As you know, we are convened to decide an issue of the utmost importance. The sole agenda item is who will serve as the permanent pastor of New Testament Cathedral."

Samantha raised her hand and was immediately acknowledged by Kenneth.

"I would like to know what prompted this sudden need to appoint a permanent pastor," Samantha said calmly. "It was my understanding that I would be given ample time to demonstrate to this body and the congregation at large that I am fully capable of serving in that position on a permanent basis. Is one month the trustees' idea of 'ample time'?"

No one spoke as Samantha waited patiently to see who would lead the charge. Finally, Percy leaned forward and clasped his hands together on the table. "Pastor Cleaveland," he said, clearing his throat. "This is in no way a reflection on how we feel about your leadership during this trying time. I think I speak for us all when I say under the circumstances we feel you have done an amazing job in holding the congregation together and keeping the vision of Pastor Cleaveland alive and on track."

"Then what is this all about?" Samantha asked, her question punctuated by a flick of her French-tipped nail on the table.

Kenneth stepped in. "It's just that some of us feel we may not have fully factored in your feelings when we placed you in this position. We . . . I mean I, feel we may have acted too hastily, and selfishly, I might add. You just lost your husband. The center of your life. Reverend Pryce is willing to step in and give you the time you and Jasmine need to—"

"Reverend Davis, I am very aware that I just lost my husband," Samantha interrupted, "but contrary to popular belief, he was not the center of my life. God is the center of my life, as I hope He is yours. I loved my husband, but I also love New Testament Cathedral. I helped found this church when it was in a storefront on Imperial Highway before any of you ever heard of the Cleavelands or the Cleavelands had ever heard of any of you." Samantha leaned into the table. Her tone became firmer, and the words came more rapidly as she spoke. "Hezekiah and I built this ministry from the ground up, and now you think just because he's gone, you can snatch it from under my feet."

"Now, hold on, Reverend Cleaveland," Percy said, jumping in and gesturing with both hands. "No one is trying to snatch New Testament away from you. We all recognize the significant contributions you have made to this church, and we all appreciate everything you've done to make New Testament what it is today. We're only thinking about what's best for you. That's all. This is not an indictment against you."

"You 'appreciate' my contributions," Samantha said snidely. "I don't need your appreciation, Percy. It means nothing to me. Let me ask you something. How many millions of dollars have you brought into the ministry this year? How many new members have you brought into the church?"

Percy stiffened his back and said, "This isn't about money. It's about doing what's right by you. Hezekiah would have wanted us to look out for you, and by placing you in this position prematurely, we failed him. You can wait a few years, can't you? Give it time, Samantha. You need time to heal."

"Let's be honest, Percy. This isn't about me at all. It's about you, isn't it? Did your wife put you up to this?" Samantha said, looking him directly in the eye. "Because let's face it. You don't have the balls to come up with a ridiculous plan like this on your own. Hezekiah always said you were a small-minded, weak little man, and I see now that he was right."

"That's uncalled for, Samantha," Kenneth interjected. "Please, I know this is a difficult conversation for us to have, but let's at least try to be civil with each other."

"*Civil?* You expect me to be civil when you jackals have plotted behind my back to steal my church? Well, let me say to you all, if you think you are going pat me on the head and brush me aside, you are sadly mistaken."

Kenneth cleared his throat and said gently, "I'm afraid we do have the authority, Samantha. According to church bylaws, section IIA, it is the responsibility of this body to select the pastor."

Kenneth reached for the single piece of paper in front of him and read aloud, “A pastor shall be chosen and called whenever a vacancy occurs. A Pastor’s Selection Committee shall be appointed by the church—that’s us—to seek out a suitable pastor. The pastor’s election shall take place at a meeting called for that purpose. That’s this meeting. The pastor—for the time being, that’s you, Samantha—the pastor shall be an ex officio member of all church standing committees, except the Pastor’s Selection Committee.”

Kenneth returned the paper to the table and said, “Because you are the interim pastor of New Testament Cathedral at the time this agenda item will be called to a vote, you will, unfortunately, not be allowed to vote on this matter.”

“May I speak?” Scarlett said loudly.

Kenneth leaned back, relieved that someone else had entered the fray. “Please, Sister Shackelford, go ahead. You have the floor.”

Scarlett spun her chair to face Samantha and said, “I’m not basing my vote on you or your feelings. I actually don’t think you need time to heal. Do you know why? Because I think you’re relieved that he’s gone.”

“Sister Shackelford!” Kenneth shouted.

“Let me finish,” Scarlett said deliberately. “My decision is based on the fact that I don’t think you are fit to be pastor. You are an evil woman who has demonstrated over the years that you are more than willing to destroy anyone and anything that stands between you and whatever it is you want at the time. New Testament Cathedral deserves better than that, God deserves better, and I know I deserve better. I’m ready to call this to a vote.”

With her final words spoken, Scarlett spun her chair back to its original position. Samantha sat stunned and speechless.

Kenneth held his breath, waiting for Samantha to respond, but she remained silent. Kenneth then leaned forward again and said, "We haven't heard from everyone. Mother Williams, do you have anything to add before we call for a vote?"

Hattie remembered the vision she saw in her garden, of Samantha standing in the pulpit, with thousands of lost souls standing at her feet, crying and raising their hands to the heavens. She clutched the handle of her cane and simply said, "I have nothing to add. I'm ready for the vote."

"Very well, then," Kenneth said, reaching for the index cards and pens. "Please write your choice for pastor of New Testament Cathedral on these cards. Fold it in half and pass it back to me when you're ready."

"May I ask a question before we vote?" Samantha said calmly.

"The discussion is over," Scarlett said. "Let's vote please."

"Hold on, Scarlett. Let her speak. Go ahead, Samantha. You have the floor," Kenneth said, leaning back in his chair.

Samantha looked at Percy and said, "Reverend Pryce."

"Yes?" he said suspiciously.

"Do you know someone named Lance Savage?"

Kenneth jerked forward in his chair and lunged toward the tape recorder. He quickly pressed the STOP button and, in doing so, knocked over his glass of water. Water splattered down the center of the table, soaking the single sheet of white paper and forming a puddle around the tape recorder

"Oh, God, I'm sorry," Kenneth blurted out. He jumped from his seat and ran to the console for the cloth napkins. When he returned, the water had begun to drip onto his chair. Kenneth dabbed and blotted the table, his chair, and around the base of the tape recorder until much of the spill had been absorbed.

Samantha watched him curiously and noted his unexpected reaction to the name Lance Savage.

I'm so sorry, everyone," Kenneth said with a shaky voice. "I'm so sorry. I didn't mean to do it. It was an accident. I'm . . . I'm sorry."

Percy retrieved more napkins from the console and wiped the remaining drops of water, all while coolly saying, "It's all right, Reverend Davis. Calm down. It was a just a little accident. Calm down."

Kenneth sank back into the damp leather chair and said through labored breaths, "Samantha, I don't see what that has to do with the matter on the table."

Samantha returned her gaze to Percy. "Answer my question, Reverend Pryce. Do you know Lance Savage?"

Percy looked helplessly at Kenneth and then back at Samantha and said, "No . . . I don't believe I know anyone by that name."

"Judging by Kenneth's reaction, I think you do," Samantha insisted.

"You're stalling, Samantha. What does this have to do with anything?" Scarlett said impatiently.

"To be perfectly honest, Scarlett, I'm not sure. But I'm curious. You see, my assistant gives me a monthly report on the church telephone records. I like to know if anyone is making any unauthorized calls. We had a problem with that a few years ago. You remember that, don't you, Mother Williams?" Samantha continued methodically. "Anyway, in doing so, she noticed two calls were made to Lance Savage." Samantha looked around the room and added, "Did I forget to mention Mr. Savage was the *Los Angeles Chronicle* reporter who was found murdered in his home on the canals in Venice?"

She then looked back at Percy and said, "The calls were made from your extension to his cell phone and home. And, ironically, they were made on the very same day he was murdered. Quite a coincidence, don't you think? I've been meaning to ask you why you called him, but I've been so busy burying my husband and running the church."

There was silence in the room. All eyes were now on Percy. Kenneth sat stiff in his seat. The remnants of the spilled water had soaked the seat of his pants. Beads of sweat formed on his brow, and his heart pounded in his chest.

Samantha broke the silence. "Looks like you might not remember right now. That's okay, though, because, you see, if I'm not going to be pastor any longer, I'll have plenty of time on my hands to solve little mysteries like this." She leaned back in her chair and said with a smile, "All righty, then, Reverend Davis. I think I have my answer. Now let's get on with that vote."

Kenneth's hand shook as he passed the cards and pens to Hattie, Scarlett, and Percy. He kept one for himself. He used a dry napkin to wipe the sweat from his brow, only to have it replaced by even more.

Scarlett was the first to hand back her folded card. Hattie was next. Percy's hand rested on the table, with the tip of the pen suspended only centimeters above the card. Scarlett, Hattie, and Samantha watched him as the pen finally began to glide along the surface of the card. He stopped and started several times before he finished. He then opened his fingers slightly, and the pen dropped to the table with a thud that echoed off the walls of the conference room.

Percy stared at the card without moving. All he could think of was his wife's final words as he left their condo for the meeting. "Call me as soon as it's over," she said, brushing imaginary lint from his lapel at the door. "And, Percy," she continued, "don't screw this up."

Samantha leaned toward the table and said, "Fold your card, Reverend Pryce, and hand it back to Reverend Davis."

Kenneth's card was soggy from the droplets of water that had remained on the table in front of him. He was the last to fold his card and add it to the stack of four.

"Thank you, everyone," Kenneth said nervously. "Here we go."

"Wait a minute, Reverend Davis," Samantha said calmly.

"Yes, Pastor Cleaveland?" Kenneth said humbly.

"I think it might be a good idea if you turned the recorder back on. For the record."

"Of course . . . yes, of course. I'm sorry. I forgot."

"No need to apologize again," Samantha said.

Kenneth reached forward and pressed the RECORD button. "Okay, where was I?" He opened the first card and read out the name written on it. "Samantha Cleaveland." He opened the second card and said, "Samantha Cleaveland."

Scarlett looked bewildered and betrayed. The numbing effects of the medication she'd taken began to wear off rapidly with the reading of each card.

Kenneth unfolded the third card and let out a gush of air. "Percy Pryce," he said with a hint of disappointment.

The last card seemed to levitate above the table in front of him. He reached for it, hesitated halfway, and then picked it up. He looked around the room at each person. Scarlett looked at him with a longing glare. Hattie's eyes were closed. She still clutched the head of her cane. Percy's eyes were closed as well.

Samantha looked at him with the cold, narrowed eyes of a woman who was about to lose everything.

Kenneth opened the final card and read it. He then closed his eyes and released a puff of air. "Samantha Cleaveland," he said, dropping the card to the table. "Let the record show that Samantha Cleaveland is as of this day the permanent pastor of New Testament Cathedral. Congratulations, Pastor Cleaveland." He then slapped the table with his open palm and added, "This meeting is adjourned."

Samantha stood immediately and walked over to Kenneth. She reached over his shoulder and pressed the EJECT button on the tape recorder, and the little cassette popped up.

"I'll take this," she said.

Without making eye contact with anyone there, Cynthia spun on her heels and left the room.

The others sat in stunned silence, and then, one by one, they slowly exited the conference room. The last one to leave turned off the lights.

In less than one hour Samantha had been installed as permanent pastor. Scarlett now sat on the couch in the living room with the phone to her ear as Cynthia pleaded her case.

"I *never* said I had Hattie's vote," Cynthia said emphatically.

"I assumed you already had a majority when you told me about this scheme."

"I thought I did, but Samantha outsmarted us."

"You mean, she outsmarted *you*. I held up my end of the deal. I voted against her. You're the one who was supposed to have the other votes lined up."

"I know, and I apologize for that."

"I don't need your apology. It's too late now," Scarlett answered.

"That's why I'm calling. I don't think it's too late."

"It is. She outsmarted you. Percy will never be pastor of New Testament Cathedral."

"It's not too late!" Cynthia blurted. "Don't say that."

"Why? There's nothing you can do to stop her. She has the trustees following her now in lockstep. She even got Hattie's vote. I never dreamed *that* would ever happen."

"I agree. That old lady surprised me," Cynthia said with a hint of introspection. "I'll never forgive her for that."

"The congregation loves Samantha. The world loves her," Scarlett continued bitterly. "When the people see her this Sunday, standing in the pulpit of that glass cathedral, she will be set for life. Everyone will be eating out of her hands."

"I just don't want to believe it's over. The world has got to know just what kind of woman she is. If people only knew the secret she kept before Hezekiah died, they would see her in a different light."

Scarlett sat upright on the edge of the couch. "What secret?" she asked cautiously. "What are you talking about?"

There was no need for pretense or deception at this point. Lance Savage was dead. Hezekiah was dead. Reverend Mitchell had killed himself. Percy had all but given up on the idea of being pastor. There was nothing to lose.

"It was about Hezekiah. Samantha knew about him."

"What about Hezekiah?" Scarlett said, urging her on.

"Hezekiah was having an affair with a man," Cynthia blurted, with no regard for the impact her words would have. She sent them blindly into the phone, almost forgetting there was another person on the line. "Danny St. John is his name. Hezekiah was going to step down as pastor on the Sunday morning he was killed. Samantha knew it, and I think she stopped him before it was too late."

Scarlett stood to her feet as the words swirled in her head. She could not form the words to respond.

"Hello, Scarlett. Are you still there?"

"You're a liar!" Scarlett shouted into the phone. "How could you say a horrible thing like that?"

"Because it's true."

"It's not true. It's impossible. Hezekiah loved women, and he loved . . ." Scarlett stopped.

"No one doubts that he loved women. But that didn't stop him from also loving men. At least Danny St. John."

"How do you know this?"

"I printed hundreds of e-mails from his office computer," Cynthia replied confidently. "I'll show them to you if you don't believe me."

Within an hour Cynthia was standing in Scarlett's living room. Scarlett hadn't sat down since she hung up the telephone. She had managed to stop the room from spinning when the doorbell rang.

"Here they are, Scarlett," Cynthia said, handing her an unmarked envelope. "It's all there. Read it for yourself."

Scarlett snatched the envelope from Cynthia and frantically removed the small stack of papers.

"That's only a sample of the e-mails between them," Cynthia said.

Cynthia studied Scarlett as she read each page. She could see her hand trembling and then the tears flowing. Scarlett tried to contain her sobs as she leafed through the irrefutable evidence.

She read the inflammatory text of e-mail number seven.

> I love you, Danny. I love you more than I have ever loved anyone in my life. I want to hold you when you are not here. I want to hear your voice call my name when we make love. You are everything to me.

Scarlett dropped the page to the floor, where it landed on top of the first six pages. Then she read e-mail number thirteen.

I've never seen that look in her eye before. She looked like she could kill me.

Seventeen minutes later the entire contents of the envelope lay at Scarlett's feet. She was numb after reading the last e-mail. Her eyes were glazed as she stared blankly into the fireplace.

"Disgusting, isn't it? Are you okay, honey?" Cynthia asked. "You don't look so good."

Scarlett did not respond. The words from the scattered sheets of paper swirled in her head, forming a vortex of pain and betrayal. "This can't be true," she said to no one. "This just can't be true."

"I'm sorry, but it is," Cynthia said coldly. "He was gay, and Samantha knew all about it. The evidence is right there at your feet."

At that moment Cynthia saw Scarlett for the first time since she had entered the house. She saw a trembling woman whose reaction to the news far exceeded that of a disappointed parishioner. It looked more like . . .

"Oh my God," Cynthia said, staring at the trembling woman. "You were in love with him."

Scarlett let out an anguished cry when she heard the words. Her fists repeatedly pounded the cushions on the couch. "No, no, no!" she yelled over and over again.

Cynthia's eyes were wide open as she looked on in astonishment. She watched as the beautiful woman shuddered and wilted into a trembling puddle on the couch. Cynthia rushed to her side and placed her arms around her. "Honey, I'm sorry. I had no idea how you felt. It's okay. I'm so sorry."

Cynthia looked up at the picture of the little girl that was sitting on the fireplace mantelpiece as she held the crying woman in her arms. She immediately saw Hezekiah's crystal-clear eyes looking back at her. Cynthia slapped her hand over her gaping mouth, her arms still wrapped around Scarlett. It was all clear now. She understood the source of the grief and pain in her arms.

"He was her father," she whispered through her clenched fingers into Scarlett's ear. "Hezekiah was your lover." Cynthia continued without waiting for a response. "The bastard. How could he have done this to you?"

"I loved him," Scarlett sobbed into the arms that held her. They were anonymous arms. She couldn't even recall whom they belonged to. She knew only that they were the anchors that held her to the ground. Without them she feared she would float away into oblivion.

Cynthia's mind returned to her original mission after the initial shock subsided. "Does Samantha know?" Cynthia asked shrewdly.

"Yes," Scarlett answered. "She knew everything at the time. She wanted me to have an abortion. But I couldn't. I just couldn't do it. That's my little girl. I love her. I know Hezekiah loved her too. I just know he did."

"I'm sure he did, honey," Cynthia replied. "In his own way."

Scarlett jerked out of her arms. "Not 'in his own way,'" she sneered. "He did love her."

"I didn't mean it that way," Cynthia said apologetically. "I know he must have loved her very much. How could he not? She's beautiful."

Scarlett stood and walked over to the fireplace. She took down the framed photograph and gently touched the glass. "She looks like him. She even sounds like him."

"You can't let Samantha get away with this," Cynthia said, walking over to her and placing a hand on her shoulder.

"There's nothing I can do. It's over. He's gone."

"Of course there's something you can do. You can make sure she suffers. She made you suffer. Now it's time for her to pay for it."

"I don't care anymore," Scarlett said, pulling away. "God forgive me, but I think we would all be better off if she were dead."

"Do you really mean that?" Cynthia asked softly.

"Mean what?"

"That we'd be better off if she were dead."

"I don't know what I mean anymore," Scarlett said, wiping the tears from her eyes. "I'm just so tired. I don't have the energy to fight anymore."

"I know you're tired, honey, but you're not alone anymore. I'm here. We can stop her together."

"Why do you care so much? This has nothing to do with you."

"But it does. My husband served under them for years, and he lied to us. I feel betrayed. She is not fit to serve as pastor."

"Oh, right. How could I have forgotten? You want Percy to be pastor. This is about you."

"No, it's about doing what's right. It's about correcting the mistake that was made when she was installed as pastor. It's about exposing the lies they told us and the world all these years. She is evil, and we have to stop her."

"But how?"

Cynthia slowly walked to the sliding glass door and looked out onto the yard. The lawn sprinklers were showering the perfectly green grass with water. A hummingbird hovered over a rosebush, then quickly darted between the buds before whizzing off over the redwood fence into the next yard.

"I've thought of so many different ways to deal with her, but I'm afraid there's only one that will really work."

Scarlett took a hopeful step toward her and asked, “What is that?”

“It has to be irreversible. It has to be quick, and it has to be permanent.”

“What are you saying?”

“I think you know exactly what I’m saying. It has to be something that she can’t recover from. It has to be lethal.”

Scarlett looked at her with a puzzled expression. “Are you saying what I think you’re saying?”

“I’ve tried everything else, and nothing has worked,” Cynthia explained. “I tried exposing the homosexual affair, and that failed. I tried securing the votes on the board of trustees, and that didn’t work. This is the only option left.”

“I can’t believe you’re saying this,” Scarlett said. “She’s evil, but no one deserves to be . . .”

“I think she does, and deep down inside, I believe you do too.”

“You’re not God, Cynthia. Only God can decide who lives and who dies.”

“I agree. But don’t you believe God uses man to execute His divine plan? How do you know this isn’t God’s plan and that we’re not a part of it?”

“Because God would never ask us to do anything that horrible.”

“That’s not true. God does call on believers to make painful sacrifices on His behalf. Look at Abraham and Isaac.”

“This is crazy, and I don’t want to discuss it anymore,” Scarlett said, turning away. “And you should put the thought out of your head as well. It’s wrong, and you know it.”

“I’m sorry, but I don’t think it’s wrong. What they did to you is wrong. What Hezekiah did with that man is wrong. What they did to my husband is wrong. This is justice. Pure and simple.”

"Who made you the arbitrator of justice? You are not God," Scarlett said, putting emphasis on each word.

The two women stood on opposite sides of the room with their eyes locked. After a few moments of tense silence, Cynthia took a deep breath and said, "You're right. I don't know what I was thinking. Please forget I ever brought this up. I'm sorry. Just the thought of her makes me a little crazy."

Scarlett walked over to Cynthia and placed her arms around her. "I understand," Scarlett said, holding her close. "She has the same effect on me."

The pounding bass of Kanye West's latest release made the floor vibrate as dancers humped, gyrated, and twirled in the frantic glow of pulsing spotlights. The hottest new nightclub on the Sunset Strip was filled to overflowing with what appeared to be all of Los Angeles's young, rich, somewhat notorious, and shameless wannabes. Bottles of Cristal and Dom Pérignon flowed from the bar up to the mezzanine, to the private booths occupied by the richest and most infamous of the crowd and their hangers-on.

Jasmine Cleaveland sat at the center of one of the booths, which was crammed with a gaggle of partying girls as beautiful as she was and with men who were as pretty as the women. The fourth bottle of Cristal on Jasmine's tab was delivered to the table. Powdered cocaine, Ecstasy, and an assortment of synthetic designer drugs were passed between the members of her party and consumed freely.

It was just after 2:00 a.m., and the club was in full swing. Jasmine slurred her words and dribbled her sixth glass of champagne as she laughed and hung her body from one of the male occupants of the booth.

"I'm bored with this place," she said, slurring. "I'm tired of looking at all these wannabes. Let's go somewhere quiet."

"No problem, baby," said the young man, whose name she did not know. "Let's go to my place. It's quiet there, and I've got some chronic dat's da bomb."

As the two stumbled from the booth, Jasmine threw an exaggerated kiss to her entourage and said over the pounding music, "Later, bitches."

Jasmine braced herself against the young man as they descended the club stairs and maneuvered through the frenetic crowd. They bumped and scooted their way to the exit and finally made it out into the early morning air. She could barely stand on her own and required the shoulder and arms of the man who was desperate to direct her to his waiting vehicle.

Gideon sat in his car across the street from the club entrance and saw Jasmine as she exited the club. He had followed her from the Cleaveland estate earlier that afternoon. He had spent the afternoon and evening watching her from a distance. First on Rodeo Drive, where she loaded Gucci bags and other shopping bags into her convertible BMW. Then at dinner with a young girlfriend at a trendy restaurant in Santa Monica. Next was a small bungalow in West Hollywood, where, judging from the steady stream of traffic at the door, he assumed she bought drugs. That was followed by a string of bars in Beverly Hills and Hollywood and finally the club on Sunset Boulevard.

Gideon had wanted to talk to her for weeks, but he hadn't figured out how to get past the gauntlet of secretaries, assistants, and body guards that typically surrounded her. He was determined this evening to approach her but was waiting for just the right moment.

As Jasmine exited the club in the arms of an exceptionally large man, who appeared to be in his mid-thirties, Gideon could see she was intoxicated and was having trouble walking on her own. The two stumbled together down a side street and into a residential neighborhood, where he lost sight of them. Gideon quickly exited his car and dashed across Sunset, darting through a parade of cars filled with young people still cruising the boulevard.

When he reached the corner, he saw the red security lights of an SUV flashing halfway down the block. He then saw the man lean Jasmine against the vehicle as he fumbled to open the door.

"Jasmine!" Gideon called out, without even thinking what his next words would be. "Jasmine, wait!" he called again, sprinting toward the couple.

The man looked over his shoulder as Gideon approached.

"Are you all right, Jasmine?" Gideon asked when he reached them, motivated by paternal instincts that he had had no idea he had. "I think you should let me take you home."

"Hold up, man," her companion said, placing a firm hand on Gideon's shoulder. "Who the fuck are you? The young lady is with me."

Gideon ignored the man and spoke directly to Jasmine. "Jasmine, let me take you home. You're in no condition to be out alone."

"She's not alone, OG. She's with me," the man said in a more aggressive tone. "You need to take your old ass home to bed before you get hurt."

Almost lifeless, Jasmine was now slumped against the car, oblivious to the scene developing next to her. The street was dark and deserted except for occasional clubbers making their way to their cars.

Again, Gideon ignored the increasingly agitated man. "Come with me, Jasmine. I'm taking you home." Gideon reached for her arm and was stopped short by the firm grip of the man, who was now standing between them.

"Take your fucking hands off her," the man said, pushing Gideon backward. "You better step the fuck off."

Gideon stepped aggressively toward the man and placed his hand in his jacket pocket, hoping the gesture would cause the man to pause. But it did not. The man quickly pulled Gideon's hand from his pocket and raised his clenched fist toward Gideon's face. At that instant a car drove past and flashed headlights directly into Gideon's face. For the first time the man could see who he was talking to, and froze mid-swing.

"Oh, fuck," the man said. "You dat nigga from the news. Gideon . . . Gideon Truman."

"That's right, and I'm also her uncle," Gideon said without thinking. "And I'm taking her home to her mother. If you know what's good for you, you'll step aside." With that last line, Gideon placed his hand back in his pocket.

The man took two steps back and raised his open palms in the air. "No problem, brotha. I was just going to take your niece to her house. She was partying pretty hard, and as you can see, she's in no condition to drive. I was just looking out for her."

"Good lookin' out . . . brotha," Gideon said snidely, "but I can take over from here."

"That's cool, man," the man said, taking another step back. "Just wanted to make sure she got home safe. That's all. No harm, no foul." He looked at Jasmine and said, "You got my digits, shorty. Call me." Within seconds he climbed in his car and disappeared into the night.

Gideon put his arm around Jasmine and slowly walked her back to his car. Every step was labored as her head bobbed from side to side and was accompanied by garbled words that Gideon could not understand.

When he finally had her resting securely in his passenger seat, he said, "Okay, little girl, let's get you to your mother. She can send someone to pick up your car tomorrow."

"I don't want to go home," Jasmine told him, slurring. "I can't let her see me like this."

"I'm sure it won't be the first time. You'll be fine."

"No!" she blurted. "No . . . I can't go home."

"Okay," Gideon said reluctantly. "Do you have a friend I can take you to?"

"No," she replied. "Take me back to the club. I can stay there until . . ." As Jasmine laid her head on the headrest, her words trailed off and she slowly drifted into sleep.

"Jasmine," Gideon said, jostling her arm. "Jasmine, wake up."

She did not respond. Gideon scanned the street, which was now empty of revelers. It would be hours before the morning light would begin to push the night aside. Gideon wondered what he had gotten himself into as he looked at the sleeping girl in his passenger seat.

I can't just sit here, he thought as his own signs of fatigue began to surface. Gideon started the car, and quickly made a U-turn onto Sunset Boulevard and was heading toward his home in Hollywood Hills with his notorious and intoxicated passenger.

Gideon stopped the car in front of his home. Danny was inside, surely asleep. Jasmine was in the car. *Oh God,* he thought. *Danny is going to be angry with me for bringing her here. I hope he understands I had no choice.*

Gideon guided the listless jumble of flesh up the stairs and to his front door. The door swung open before he could place the key into the lock, and Danny was standing in the threshold.

"Gideon," Danny said, "where have you been? I've been calling your cell all night. I've been worried sick. I thought something had happened to you. Are you all right?"

"I'm fine. Help me get her to the sofa."

"Who is this?" Danny asked, reaching under Jasmine's dangling arm. "She's drunk."

"Just help me get her in. I'll tell you everything in a minute."

Gideon and Danny gently deposited the bundle on the couch and stood simultaneously as they caught their breath,

"Who is this? Where have you been? Are you all right?" Danny quizzed.

"I'm fine," Gideon said, retrieving a throw blanket from the hall closet and placing it over Jasmine. "Danny, you're not going to be pleased, but this is Jasmine Cleaveland. Hezekiah's daughter."

"What!" Danny blurted.

"I'm sorry. I didn't know where else to take her."

"You should have taken her to her mother. She created this mess. Let her deal with it."

"She didn't want to go home. She didn't want Samantha to see her like this."

"That's not your problem. It's their problem."

"I know. I just felt sorry for her."

"Is this what you do? Bring stray cats home?"

"What are you talking about?"

"You brought me here. Now her. She's a mess," Danny said, looking down at a sleeping Jasmine. "It's no wonder, with a mother like that."

"I know it's very sad."

"What are you going to do with her?"

"I don't know," Gideon said, taking Danny's hand. "I guess we'll let her sleep it off. I would like to try to talk to her about her father when she wakes up. Would that be uncomfortable for you?"

"Yes, it would be very uncomfortable."

"You don't have to meet her when she wakes up, but it might be good for you."

"And what purpose would that serve?" Danny asked skeptically.

"You both loved Hezekiah," Gideon said, squeezing his hand tighter. "It might help you to talk to someone who misses him as much, if not more than you do. It could be good for you to speak with someone who understood him like no one else in the world."

"Are you crazy?" Danny said. "I was her father's lover. She would freak out if she knew her father was gay."

"Maybe, maybe not. She might also find comfort in meeting someone who loved her father as much as she did. I'm sure she knows her mother didn't love him."

"Look, it's almost three o'clock," Danny said. "You must be exhausted. Let's get some sleep, and I'll decide later if I tell her who I am. I don't want to think about it right now. I'm just glad you're okay."

"I'm sorry I didn't call you," Gideon said, pulling Danny to his side. "I guess I'm not used to having someone at home worrying about me." Gideon pressed his lips against Danny's and added, "I think I really like it. Come on. Let's get some sleep before she wakes up."

Chapter 11

Jasmine twisted fitfully on the couch in Gideon's living room. Her laced Giuseppe Zanotti sandals with six-inch heels rested on the cushions as she squirmed to find the most comfortable position in which to sleep off a night's worth of crystal meth and Cristal champagne. It was now just after three thirty in the morning, and the house was quiet except for the occasional muted blare of a siren reverberating off the canyon walls below.

Gideon fell into a deep sleep before his head fully rested on the pillow in his bedroom. Even the thought of Samantha Cleaveland's daughter sleeping in the other room was not enough to keep him awake. He had been too tired to remove his clothes after getting Jasmine settled in and kissing Danny good night at his bedroom door. He lay fully clothed on top of the comforter with his Gucci loafers still snugly on his feet.

Danny was already in his boxer shorts when Gideon and Jasmine arrived. He was now lying wide awake in bed in the guest room down the hall. Parker was curled in a furry ball at his feet, most likely dreaming of the rat in the hillside brush that got away earlier that day.

Danny sighed as he thought of Hezekiah's daughter sleeping in another part of the house. What would he say to her when she woke? Would he tell her about his relationship with her father? Would she fly into a rage and curse him if she knew of the affair? His instincts begged him to keep silent about his time with her father. *What good would it do to tell her? She would be devastated to learn her father was a homosexual,* he thought while staring at the ceiling. *The first person she'll tell is Samantha, which will make her even more desperate than she already is.*

His desire to share his love for her father battled his instincts. *She loved him, and I loved him too. We have something so beautiful in common,* he thought. He wanted desperately to speak to someone who understood how easy it was to fall in love with Hezekiah. He wanted to share some of the love they had created together. By doing so, he would somehow immortalize his feelings and elevate them beyond the fading memory he feared they would soon become.

Danny looked at the neon clock on the nightstand. It was 3:37. The city was asleep, and night had enveloped the house like a black cloak draped over a birdcage. He knew sleep would not come and resigned himself to spending the next few hours tossing and obsessing over the young woman in the other room.

What sounded like glass breaking somewhere in the house caused Danny to bolt upright in the bed. His eyes darted to the door, and his ears strained to hear whatever was next to come. The sound was followed by dead silence. He thought it must have been his imagination, and lay back down on the pillow.

"Get a grip on yourself. There's nothing out there," he said out loud. "She's not crazy enough to send someone to kill me here in Gideon's house. Or is she?"

He knew all too well the answer to that question, and it caused his heart to flutter. *She's crazy enough, and by now desperate enough, to do anything to get rid of me,* he thought.

Moments passed, and the house slowly drifted back into the night's abyss. The glowing green numbers on the clock served as a painful reminder that the night would soon come to an end and he would come face-to-face with his lover's troubled daughter. The question of whether to confess or not to confess again volleyed back and forth in his mind. *Don't be a fool,* he thought. *Why would she want to share anything with me? She's just an angry, troubled kid who lost her father and hates her mother. Why complicate her life any more?*

The numbers continued to tick, moving him closer to the inevitable. *She might find some comfort in knowing her father was loved by someone when he died. She must have known how much her mother hated him.*

As his mind whirled, Danny heard the distinct sound of a footstep on the hardwood floor in the hall outside his bedroom door. Again, he sat up in the bed. He looked at the door handle and saw it was unlocked. There had never been a need to lock the door. He had welcomed the times when Gideon had slipped quietly into the room and had curled up next to him in bed. It never felt intrusive and was always preceded by Gideon saying, "I was lonely in my room by myself. May I sleep in here with you tonight?" And his answer was always, "Yes, I was feeling a little lonely too."

He prayed it was Gideon this time too. But as the steps slowly passed his door, he knew it wasn't him. The steps were deliberate, as if the person was trying hard not to be heard. That person was walking in the direction of the master suite at the end of the hall. Danny did not move. His breath caught in his chest and refused to exit his body. He could hear his heart pounding in his ears as blood pulsed through his body.

Again, there was silence in the house. *Maybe it's Jasmine,* he thought with eyes focused keenly on the door. *But why would she be walking toward Gideon's room?*

His gut told him that it wasn't Jasmine and that something was terribly wrong in the house. Danny slowly hung his legs off the side of the bed and waited for another sound, but there was none. Seconds passed, and then he slowly made his way to the door and pressed his ear against the wood. Still there was no sound. Danny turned the handle and opened the door just enough to look out. His pounded double time in his chest. There was no one there. He stepped into the dark hallway and looked in both directions before lightly walking toward Gideon's bedroom.

When he turned the corner leading toward the master bedroom, he saw Gideon's door was open, which was nothing unusual for a man who lived alone. The door was always open. Danny walked slowly to the door and looked into the room. The view of Gideon's bed was almost completely blocked by a man wearing a black leather jacket and black pants. His arms were raised directly in front of him, and he was looking at Gideon's sleeping body on the bed.

Without thinking, Danny lunged forward and in a flash had his arms around the man's neck.

"Gideon!" Danny yelled. "Wake up!"

As he gripped the man's neck with his forearms and forced his body forward, Danny heard a gunshot. The large man and Danny landed on Gideon, the full weight of both their bodies bearing down on him.

"What the . . ." were the first words out of Gideon's mouth when he awoke and realized there were two men wrestling on top of him.

"Gideon, he's got a gun!" Danny yelled as the man hit him full force on the jaw with a fist that felt like a sledgehammer.

Gideon wiggled out from beneath the two of them and forcefully pulled the black-clad intruder away from

Danny. Both Gideon and the intruder landed with a thud on the dresser, sending a lamp, framed photographs of Gideon, and a crystal vase crashing to the floor. The nightstand was kicked over by Gideon's feet, causing another lamp and the clock radio to crash against the wall and tumble to the carpet. Books from shelves, a Bose sound system, and racks of CDs came cascading down on them as they thrashed, punched, and kicked.

Danny immediately regrouped and dashed toward the two of them, who were now wrestling violently on the carpet. Danny could see the man was still clutching the gun, and he took a flying leap at him.

"Watch out, Gideon!" Danny yelled in midair. "He's still got a gun."

When Danny landed on Gideon and the man, he heard a second gunshot. The sound echoed in his head and caused him to flash back to the night in Griffith Park when Samantha tried to have him killed. The muscular contours of the intruder's body and the smell of his musky cologne made Danny suddenly realize that the man lying motionless under him was the same dark figure he had wrestled with on that fateful night in the parking lot.

The three lay still. Danny could feel someone's chest beneath him rise and fall, but he couldn't tell who it belonged to. When he finally opened his eyes, he found himself looking over the shoulder of the black-clad man and into Gideon's panting face.

"Take the gun from his hand, Danny," Gideon said softly, as if not to wake the sleeping man lying on top of him.

Danny rolled off the two, who were stacked like dominos, and quickly snatch the gun from between their bodies. He tossed it across the room, to the opposite side the bed, as if it were burning the palm of his hand.

"Get him off me, Danny," Gideon gasped. "I can't breathe."

With one full-body tug Danny pulled the intruder off Gideon and onto his back in the midst of jumbled CDs, books, and shattered bric-a-brac.

Gideon struggled to Danny's side and let out a series of desperate coughs and gasps. "Are you all right, Danny?" he asked through frantic breaths.

Gideon's shirt was covered in blood. Danny rushed to him and said, "You've been shot! Oh God, he shot you!"

"No, I'm okay," Gideon said, pulling Danny to his heaving chest. "He shot himself. I think he's dead."

When he said the words, a bloodcurdling scream filled the room.

Jasmine was standing in the doorway, hysterical. She covered her mouth with trembling hands and screamed again and again.

Gideon and Danny immediately scrambled to their feet and darted toward the screaming girl. Gideon tripped over the man's body as he dashed toward Jasmine.

"Stay away from me!" she screamed and ran into the dark hallway. Gideon and Danny followed closely behind as she ran frantically through the living room and into the foyer to the front door.

"Jasmine, wait!" Gideon called out behind her. "Honey, please everything is all right. You're safe."

"Stay the fuck away from me!" she said, frantically groping for the front door handle. "I'm going to call the police."

Danny dashed into foyer just behind Gideon, and they each grabbed her thrashing shoulders and tried to hold her steady.

"Jasmine, you are safe," Danny said, holding her close. "Everything is all right now. Calm down. We have to call the police."

Jasmine was hysterical as she tried desperately to break free from the two men preventing her from leaving the strange house. "Let me go!" she demanded. "Who the fuck are you? Let me go!"

"Jasmine," Danny said, forcefully shaking her shoulders. "Listen to me, Jasmine. My name is Danny St. John. I was a very close friend of your father. Trust me. You are safe with me."

Morning had come much too soon for Hattie Williams. She could feel the sun rising over the horizon long before it made its presence known with the first ray of light. Sleep had not come easily to her since Hezekiah's death. In the odd moments when she was able to doze off, her dreams were filled to overflowing with images of the downfall of her beloved pastor.

She had become almost afraid to close her eyes for fear of what was to be revealed. Hattie didn't believe in ghosts, but she imagined this would be what it felt like to be haunted. She did, however, believe in her gift. She knew God wasn't simply trying to entertain her with the flood of images. "What do you want me to do, Lord?" she prayed each time she saw a vision of Hezekiah. "Please, Lord, tell me what it is you want me to do."

It was past 4:00 a.m., and Hattie had long since given up on the idea of sleep. The coffee was already brewing on the stove. Brown bubbles leapt up into the glass dome at the top of 1950s percolator, vying to become her morning's first sip of coffee. She could see the hints of day through the kitchen window.

Hattie busied herself with the morning rituals she had performed most of her adult life. She knew the key to living a long, happy life was to stay busy and stick to a schedule of activities planned for the week. Laundr was always done on Monday mornings. Monday was also occupied with roasting a chicken, or some other favorite meat, that would last the week. Tuesday mornings were for cleaning the already clean house, and Tuesday afternoons were reserved for signing checks at the church. Wednesday was Bible study with other seniors at church and polishing all the wood in the house with lemon wax. Thursday was the market. Friday was another Bible study at church. Saturdays were reserved for all the gardening that she was too busy to tend to during the week, and Sunday . . . The entire day on Sunday was dedicated to New Testament Cathedral. This was a routine that had begun years earlier, on the day after her husband was lowered into the ground, and it had kept her healthy and happy and her mind sharp.

Hattie was disappointed that she had had so little sleep the night before, but she was also grateful that she had not been subjected to another vision. Until she could understand what God was trying to tell her, she knew these visions would continue. Peace would come in the exact moment when she finally understood His divine plan. It always had, and once she knew her duties, she would act on them swiftly and decisively. There was no questioning and no doubt. If God wanted her to do something, both He and she knew it would be done. That was why He had made her Hattie Williams.

Hattie's fuzzy house slippers flapped against the linoleum as she puttered around the kitchen. The tea towels had been hung in their place, on hooks over the sink. The remnants of the dishes from the evening meal had been washed and placed in their exact spots on the shelves and in the drawers and cupboards. A bulging grapefruit had already been halved, placed squarely in the center of a saucer, and positioned in front of her seat at the dinette table. Every item in the kitchen had its place, and Hattie would not sit until each was where it should be.

The coffee finished brewing, and she poured it into her cup. Black, no cream and no sugar. Hattie settled into her seat and reached behind her to turn on the radio. The familiar crackling voice of her favorite radio preacher filled the room.

"God bless all you brothers and sisters out there in radio land," was the preacher's greeting, delivered with a thick Southern drawl. "Today's sermon is entitled 'God Doesn't Play by Our Rules.'"

Hattie reached for her Bible on the counter and read silently as the preacher preached on.

"Now, I know many of you think you know God's will for your life. Well, I'm here to tell you this morning that you are probably wrong. God's will and His plans are so far beyond our understanding that it is only an arrogant man who thinks he knows what God plans to do with his life. I'm encouraging you this morning not to be that man. Don't try to figure out what God wants you to do. You'll never figure it out. All we need to do as believers is do what we believe is the right thing. Never mind what others tell you to do. Ignore what we preachers tell you to do, because contrary to what we been telling you all these years, none of us ain't got no special pipeline to God.

"Stop being a fool and start listening to your own heart. Stop allowing these self-proclaimed prophets, preachers, and so-called men of God to tell you what God's plan is for your life. You know what the right thing to do is. Always listen to your heart and stop waiting for someone else to tell you. That's why black folk ain't much farther ahead today than we could be. We always waiting for Sunday morning to come for somebody else to tell us what to do, what to believe, and what to say. If you don't hear anything else I've said this morning, please hear this. If a preacher tells you they have a special message for you from God, pick up your purse and check your pocket to make sure your wallet is still there and tell him, 'No thank you, sir. If God has a message for me, He'll tell me Himself.' Believe me, if you will stop and be still for a moment and listen to your heart, you'll hear clearly what it is God wants you to do."

Hattie froze when she heard the words. They reverberated in her head like the toll of a bell in a church steeple. Hattie looked out her kitchen window. She was strangely comforted as she slowly came to the realization that what the old Southern preacher had said was true and that his words served as a reminder of truths that she already knew.

As she eased into a sense of peace and clarity, something that had eluded her for weeks, the kitchen window slowly filled with a thick fog. Hattie rested her hand on the open Bible and calmly waited for what was to come.

Her wait was brief. Gideon Truman appeared in a flash. He was standing on the edge of a cliff. She could see a tempestuous ocean slamming against a floor of jagged rocks below. The wind was blowing, and the sky was filled with ominous clouds that floated quickly by. Gideon had his back to her, and he was looking off into the distance. His jacket was billowing in the wind as he took a series of steps backward, away from the cliff.

Suddenly a hand appeared on his shoulder and stopped him from moving away from the cliff. Hattie could see that he was trying to move away from the dangerous edge, but the hand on his shoulder prevented him from moving farther. The wind seemed to double in strength, and his jacket flapped violently around his torso. The hand then began to guide him back toward the cliff.

Hattie craned her neck to see who the hand belonged to. The entity's feelings were so well camouflaged that she could not discern who it was or even if it was a man or a woman. Slowly, the owner of the hand came into view.

Hattie gasped slightly when she saw it was Samantha. In the past she could always feel Samantha long before she came into view, whether it was in a vision or in real life. Hattie knew this was a sign that Samantha was slowing evolving into an entity whose emotions even she would not be able to read.

The thought frightened Hattie as she continued to watch Samantha guide Gideon back to the cliff's edge. The waves below pounded the rocks and sent plumes of frothy sea mist into the air above their heads. Hattie could smell the ocean in her kitchen. She could hear the screeching cries of the seagulls that flew frantically overhead as the inevitable plunge of Gideon Truman drew near.

Hattie noted that Gideon put up little resistance as Samantha moved him forward. She could feel his fear, but it was not matched by any sign of struggle to save his own life.

Samantha was dressed in white. A white that seemed unearthly and deceptively pure. Her sandal-clad feet barely touched the earth as she glided behind Gideon. There was a comforting air emanating from her. Almost as if she was trying to convince Gideon that jumping was the right thing to do.

Hattie studied the scene more closely than she had ever studied one before. She searched the canvas for any detail that would provide a clue to what her role in it should be. The birds flying overhead, the waves crashing below. The clouds rushing by. Anything. Then, suddenly, she heard the old radio preacher's voice coming from the window. "You know what the right thing to do is. Always listen to your heart and stop waiting for someone else to tell you."

Hattie sat upright in her chair. She looked questioningly at the radio on the counter behind her and then back at the window. The radio preacher had long since ended his sermon. Now a ragtag choir was struggling through an old-time hymn on the radio.

Samantha moved Gideon steadily forward. By the time Hattie looked back at the window, Gideon's feet were slipping at the edge and he was struggling to remain on the cliff. Samantha was standing an arm's length away. Her raven-black hair was flapping wildly in the now tumultuous wind. The white color seemed to spill off her dress and slowly fill the window. The two figures were soon engulfed in white light from Samantha's dress, and gradually, they disappeared from Hattie's view.

Despite the troubling scene, Hattie was consumed by a sense of calm when it disappeared from her window. She looked down at her cup of black coffee, and the steam still rose up to meet her nose. It was as if time had stood still. Hattie took a sip, and the coffee was still as hot as when she first poured it. Daylight had come, and her vegetable garden was awash in the first muted rays of the morning sun. Stalks of collard greens, the lilting flowers of her foxgloves, the peach tree waiting for its second harvest of the season all seemed to yawn and stretch toward the sun as they readied themselves for a new day and a plentiful bounty.

"Thank you, Lord," Hattie said as she gently blew into the steaming cup of coffee. "Thank you, Lord, for showing me the answer was always right here in my heart."

Yellow crime-scene tape stretched across Gideon's front door. The body had been removed, and a police officer was posted on the porch. News crews lined the winding street that led to his home. Reporters, who had been told to stay off the property, stood in the street and in neighboring yards, feeding the story to their morning viewers.

"We are coming to you live from in front of the home of CNN reporter Gideon Truman in Hollywood Hills, host of the show *Truman Live,*" said a female field reporter, wearing a cheap blue blazer with running shorts and tennis shoes, as she looked directly into the camera hoisted on the shoulder of a burly cameraman.

"The Los Angeles County Department of the Coroner just removed the body of an unidentified man who, according to the police, was killed in the home of Mr. Truman. No additional details have been provided by the police, but we have been told that the body was not that of Gideon Truman, who we believe is currently in the house."

The cameraman was very careful to shoot her only from the waist up as she continued. "We also understand that in addition to Mr. Truman, there are apparently two other people in the house at this time. Here's what we know. Neighbors heard gunshots coming from the residence sometime between three o'clock and four o'clock this morning and called the Los Angeles Police Department. According to witnesses, the police arrived and surrounded the property with guns fully drawn.

"For those of you who aren't familiar with Gideon Truman, he is a nationally known reporter and the host of *Truman Live* on CNN. Truman is known for his high-profile stories. For instance, he was the first person to interview Bobby Kristina after the tragic death of her mother, Whitney Houston, and he interviewed Janet Jackson after the death of her brother Michael Jackson.

"As you can see behind me, this narrow street in this exclusive section of Hollywood Hills is filled with reporters from around the world." The cameraman shifted the lens to show the army of white vans clogging the street, the men and women toting cameras on tripods, and the reporters tripping over themselves to get the best shot of the house.

"I'm Trisha Montoya. We will keep you informed as the details of this shocking story unfold."

Jasmine sat curled on the couch, under a blanket, while Gideon and Danny escorted the last police officer to the door.

"Mr. Truman, you all might want to stay in the house for a while and not answer your door. There's a crowd of reporters out there, and you are going to be mobbed if you leave anytime soon."

"Thank you, Officer," Gideon said. "Is there any way you can ask them to leave?"

"I'm afraid they're not breaking any laws as long as they stay off your property and don't block the road. You're just going to have to wait them out."

"What's going to happen next?" Danny asked nervously.

"Since in your statements you both say you didn't know the man, we're treating this as a home invasion for now. You had every right to protect yourself in your home, and I seriously doubt the district attorney will pursue this as anything more than a burglary and a justifiable homicide. I know this has been very traumatic for you, so I suggest you maybe speak with a mental health professional to help you put all of this in perspective. If we have any other questions, we, of course, will be in contact with you, and we ask that you not leave the city for a few days, until the investigation is complete. Are you sure we can't give the young lady a ride home? I can arrange to have an officer take her."

"Thank you, but she said she prefers to stay here until the media has cleared out. We'll make sure she gets home safely. She'll be fine," Gideon replied.

When the officer left, Gideon and Danny walked side by side back into the living room, where Jasmine was still sitting on the couch.

"Jasmine," Gideon said in his most fatherly voice, "are you all right? I'll make us all some tea and give you two a few minutes alone."

As Gideon walked past Jasmine, he placed his hand gently on her shoulder and said, "I'm so sorry you had to go through this, but it's over now and everything will be back to normal for you soon." Then he left the room.

Danny sat at the opposite end of the couch. "How you doing over there?" he asked her gently. "You had a pretty rough night. Are you okay?"

"I'm fine," she said without looking at him. "How did you know my father?"

Danny had already decided that the best way to deal with Jasmine was to be direct and honest. He was prepared for her to hate him and call him a liar, but he was also prepared to take that risk.

"Jasmine, there's no easy way to explain this to you other than to tell you the truth. You're old enough to handle it."

"I'm not a child. I've seen more and done more than you'll probably see and do in a lifetime. I'm a Cleaveland, remember?"

"Yes, I remember."

"Then tell me what the fuck is going on."

"Your father and I were lovers." He paused for her reaction, but there was none, so he continued. "We were together for almost two years before he died. On the day he was killed, he was going to announce to the congregation that he was leaving the church so that he and I could be together."

"You're lying," she said calmly. "You're just another opportunist trying to capitalize on his death."

Danny was prepared for that reaction. He retrieved his laptop from the coffee table and logged into his e-mail account. The series of e-mails from her father was stored in a special file.

"I'm sorry, but I'm not lying to you, Jasmine. I'm also not trying to hurt you or capitalize on his death. I loved you father very much. If you'd like, I can show you some of the e-mails we sent each other."

Jasmine unfolded her arms from under the blanket, took the laptop, and read the first e-mail from her father to Danny.

> I love you, Danny. I told Samantha about you today, and her response was predictable. She threated to destroy me if I ever left her. I love you so much, I'm willing to risk everything. I can't wait to hold you in my arms again and make love to you. Trust me, I am going to do everything in my power to make you happy.
>
> Love you with all my heart,
> Hez

E-mail after e-mail spoke of the undeniable bond and love between the two men. As Jasmine read the glowing pages, silent tears fell from her eyes. After reading the fifth e-mail, she closed the laptop and handed it back to Danny. The tears continued to flow as she rested her head on the couch. Danny silently allowed her to process the startling revelation.

Moments passed before Jasmine spoke. "It sounds like he really loved you. Did you love him, or was it his money?"

"That's a fair question. I know a lot of people threw themselves at your father for his money, but I assure you I loved him deeply. He was the most important person in my life. I miss him more than anyone could ever understand."

"That's where you're wrong," Jasmine said, wiping a tear from her cheek. "I miss him so much sometimes, I wish I were dead."

"I know that feeling," Danny said as his own tears began to flow. "In the days and weeks after it happened, I didn't think I was going to be able to make it. I stayed locked up in my apartment for weeks. I almost lost my job."

"I tried to commit suicide when I heard about it," Jasmine said, matching his pain. "They had to pump my stomach. I wish they had let me die."

"I understand, but I'm very glad you didn't. You are a beautiful young woman, and I know your father loved you deeply. It means so much to me to share with you my love for your father. You're taking this much better than I imagined you would. How do you feel?"

"I'm not sure how I feel right now," Jasmine said, curling into a tighter ball on the couch. "Part of me is happy he found love before he died. My mother didn't love him. She just ordered him around and used him, like she uses me and everyone else in her life."

Danny was surprised when he heard the words. "Thank you, Jasmine. I did love him, and I believe he loved me."

"I can tell. I wish he had lived so that he could be with you. He deserved to be happy."

"How are you two doing?" Gideon asked, walking into the room with a tray holding two steaming mugs of tea, lemon wedges, sugar cubes, honey, and cream. "I didn't know how you like your tea, Jasmine, so I brought a little bit of everything."

Gideon placed the tray on the coffee table in front of the two. "I'll be in the kitchen. Let me know if you need anything else," he said gently. "The police said we should stay put for a while. I can take you home when things settled down outside. Are you hungry? I can make us breakfast if you'd like."

"Don't leave, Gideon," Danny said. "I told her everything. She's doing okay."

"Did you know my father too?" Jasmine asked, looking up at Gideon.

Gideon sat down in a chair near Jasmine. "No, I never met him."

"Then why were you following me last night? Why did you bring me here?"

"I'm doing a story on your father's life and death, and I wanted to talk to you. When you left the club, you were so out of it, I was worried about you. You were leaving with some man who was almost old enough to be your . . ." Gideon did not complete the sentence. "Anyway, I brought you here to let you sleep it off. Now I wish I hadn't gotten involved. You might have been better off going home with that guy."

"I don't even remember who he was," Jasmine said, reaching for one of the mugs. "Thank you for stepping in. Are you two lovers now?"

Danny did not respond.

"I love Danny very much, Jasmine," Gideon said shyly. "But I also know he loved your father very deeply, and it will take him some time to get over the loss." He looked at Danny and continued. "But I'm willing to wait."

"Have you met my mother?"

Danny immediately stood and walked to the kitchen. "Would you excuse me a minute?" he said nervously. "I'm going to get a cup for you, Gideon."

"I've met your mother," Gideon said boldly. "I'm sure she's worried about you. Maybe you should call her."

Jasmine released a pained scoff. "She probably hasn't even noticed I'm not in the house. What did you think of her?"

Gideon was not accustomed to being on the receiving end of such a pointed question. "She's a lovely woman," he replied diplomatically. “One of the most beautiful women I’ve ever met.”

“You know that’s not what I meant. What did you think of her as a person?”

“I’ll be honest with you, Jasmine,” Gideon said, silently bracing himself. “She frightened me.”

“That’s not unusual. She frightens everyone,” Jasmine replied coldly. “She frightens me too, and I’ve known her my entire life.”

“I didn’t mean it in a scary way. I meant I’m usually a good judge of a person’s character,” Gideon said, proceeding with caution. “I couldn’t get a read on just what exactly she is capable of or willing to do to get whatever it is she might want.”

“I know what she’s capable of, “Jasmine said with a distant look in her eyes. “I think she killed my father.”

“What makes you say that?” he asked casually.

“She hated him. I saw her with a gun the other day.”

“Did you ask her about it?”

“Yes. She denied everything and told me to never mention it again. She must have freaked out when Daddy told her about Danny. Now I know she thinks she had a good reason to kill him.”

Danny returned to the room and quietly sat back down on the couch. He had heard their entire conversation from the kitchen.

“There’s something I didn’t tell the police,” Jasmine said, ignoring his return. “I know the man who was here. He goes to the church, and I’ve seen him at the house a few times since my father died. I think my mother sent him here to kill you, Danny.”

“Do you actually think your mother is capable of murder?” Gideon asked, casting caution aside.

“Do you think it’s a coincidence that he broke into your house with a gun?” she asked.

“I knew him too,” Danny finally said.

“From where?” both Jasmine and Gideon asked simultaneously.

Danny fumbled with the now tepid mug of tea. “He tried to kill me before. Gideon, he was the man who attacked me.”

“Why didn’t you tell the police?” Gideon asked angrily.

“I couldn’t, and you already know why—”

“I don’t know why,” Jasmine interrupted.

Danny stood again and began to pace the floor.

“Tell her, Danny. She’s been honest with us. We have to be honest with her.”

“Jasmine, I very embarrassed to say this, but I tried to blackmail you mother. I was afraid and confused after your father was killed, and I thought she would try to do something to me next,” Danny said in a nervous rant. “I was going to use the money to leave the country and disappear. It was stupid and wrong, but I didn’t know what else to do at the time.”

“It looks like you were right,” Jasmine said, pulling the blanket tighter around her. “And if she thinks you know about any of this, Gideon, then you are in as much danger as Danny. I don’t think she’s done with you. When my mother starts something, she sticks with it until it’s finished to her satisfaction. She never backs down—”

The conversation was interrupted by Gideon’s telephone ringing in his pocket. “This is Gideon Truman,” he answered.

“Mr. Truman, This is Pastor Samantha Cleaveland. I’m watching the news. You are on every channel. Are you okay?”

“Sorry to disappoint you, Pastor Cleaveland,” Gideon said, looking at Jasmine and then at Danny, “but I’m fine, and so is Danny St. John, no thanks to you.”

Both Jasmine and Danny sat erect on the couch. Jasmine gestured to Gideon not to say she was in the house.

"I'm not sure what you mean, Mr. Truman. I'm just calling to tell you I'm praying for you."

Gideon decided all bets were off at that point. Jasmine was in his home, Danny's life and his own life had almost been taken away, and the woman responsible for it was on his phone.

"Did you notice that the man you sent here was taken out in a body bag?" Gideon pressed the speaker button on the phone and placed it on the coffee table in front of Jasmine and Danny.

"I doesn't matter that this one failed," Samantha said, her voice filling the room. "Trust me, there'll be another one coming for you soon, and another and another, until the job is complete."

Jasmine cupped her trembling hand over her mouth to muffle her cries.

"What do you mean?" Gideon asked, goading her.

"It means that I took care of my husband, so you must know I now have to take care of you and his handsome young lover. Hello, Danny. I assume you are listening to this conversation."

"You can't believe you can get away with killing us without anyone knowing," Danny said timidly.

"You'd be surprised at just how much I've gotten away with over the years, Danny. Eliminating you will be easy compared to some of the things I've had to do in my life."

Danny took the now trembling Jasmine into his arms. She buried her face in his chest to muffle her sobbing.

"What makes you think we won't go to the police with what we know?" Gideon asked calmly.

"Oh, I know you won't," she replied smugly. "Because if it comes out that Danny was Hezekiah's jilted lover, he becomes the prime suspect in his murder. Danny, I forget to mention to you that I have a recording of you blackmailing me. If the police learn that you actually met David Shackelford before tonight, and under such incriminating circumstances, they'll easily come to the conclusion that you killed him to cover up the fact that you were trying to blackmail me. If they put me on the stand as a witness for the prosecution, my performance will be so convincing, you will most likely get the death penalty. When it all comes down to it, it will be your word against mine. Who do you think they'll believe, Danny? You or me?"

"Mother, how could you do this!" Jasmine finally blurted out uncontrollably. "You'll never get away with this."

"Jasmine?" Samantha said in shock. "Is that you? What are *you* doing there? Leave that house immediately. You are in danger. Those men killed your father. Leave there now."

"I heard everything, Mother," Jasmine shrieked. "I know you killed Daddy, and I know you sent David Shackelford here to kill them."

"Jasmine, I was just saying those things to scare them into leaving us alone. They've been threatening me since the day they killed your father. Danny claims he was having an affair with your father. He's defiling the memory of your father. He's nothing more than a deadly opportunist. Did he tell you he tried to extort two million dollars from me? They're cold-blooded killers and thieves. I want you to get out of there now. If you two harm my daughter in any way, I'll kill you both myself."

"Stop it, Mother!" Jasmine yelled and lunged at the telephone on the table. "I can't take your lies anymore." She disconnected the line and threw the cell phone across the room.

The phone rang immediately as Gideon and Danny sat on the couch, Jasmine crying hysterically in their arms. The three stayed huddled together for as long as it took for Jasmine's tears to fade into gentle sobs and the sobs to melt into painful contemplation, the telephone continuing to ring the entire time.

Chapter 12

The day that had cost millions of dollars, four lives, public humiliation for many in Samantha's orbit, lost love, emotional meltdowns, divorce, and destroyed reputations was now only two days away. The eyes of the world were preparing to focus on the first Sunday morning service in the new sanctuary. Samantha and an army of A-list entertainment industry publicists had successfully spun the completion of construction into a worldwide event.

News networks across the country featured it as their opening story for the entire week. Samantha was interviewed on *The View, Ellen, The Steve Harvey Show, Jimmy Kimmel Live!, Conan, Good Morning America,* and *The Today Show*. A flock of helicopters buzzed the campus daily for the perfect aerial images of the cathedral, and a steady flow of news vans clogged the streets.

A month of events, which included black-tie dinners, prayer breakfasts, VIP tours of the campus, and a series of live broadcasts of the finishing touches being put on the cathedral, was scheduled to culminate with a star-studded black-tie affair at the Cleaveland estate. Samantha's gown for the evening had already been flown in from Paris, and the shoes were on a private jet from Rome and were scheduled to arrive at any minute. The jewelry to be worn that evening had been delivered in an armored car directly from Cartier on Rodeo Drive.

The estate had been filled the entire week with caterers and waitstaff crews rehearsing every choreographed step and the placement of every champagne glass and utensil. Groundskeepers had laid fresh grass, planted fields of flowers, and pruned trees to perfection. Security teams had combed the grounds for any possible breaches and had placed cameras discreetly in bushes, in chandeliers, behind paintings, and in other undetectable locations in every room of the mansion. No chances were to be taken with the security of Pastor Cleaveland and her guests.

Samantha paced the floor of her office, repeatedly pressing REDIAL on her cell phone.

"This is Gideon Truman," said the recorded message over and over. "Please leave your name, number, and a detailed message, and I'll return your call as soon as possible."

"Damn it, Gideon," Samantha snapped into the phone after the fifth try. "You're fucking with the wrong person. You better get my daughter out of your house, or I'll come there myself to get her. And believe me, you don't want to see me at your door."

"Jasmine, have you left the house yet?" Samantha said after dialing her daughter and hearing the recorded message. "Call me as soon as you get this message. I'm worried about you. Mommy loves you, honey. Come home so we can talk about this."

Samantha slammed the phone down on her desk and walked to the window. For the first time since her husband's death, something had not gone as planned. *Fucking idiot,* she thought while looking scornfully down at the scrambling ants on her property below. *I should have never trusted him with a job this important. He probably had a goddamned panic attack and shot his own bumbling ass by accident. Now what am I going to do?*

Even Samantha could see this had all the elements of a disaster. Her bravado earlier, during the call to Gideon, was only a cover for the fear that was steadily rising from her core. She had committed the perfect murder and had driven her unwitting accomplice, the Reverend Willie Mitchell, to suicide, thereby eliminating any link between her and Hezekiah's assassination. *Everything was perfect until that little shit, Danny, got greedy,* she thought. *I've got to keep them at bay at least until after Sunday. I'll take care of them myself once and for all after that.*

Her thoughts were abruptly interrupted by her assistant's voice on the intercom. "I'm sorry to disturb you, Pastor . . . ," she said.

"Didn't I tell you I don't want to be disturbed?" Samantha yelled from the window.

"Yes, Pastor Cleaveland," came the apologetic reply. "But I thought you would want to take this call. It's the White House. The president would like to speak to you."

Samantha darted to the desk, snatched up the receiver, and snapped, "Put him through."

"Samantha dear, how are you holding up? Every time I turn on the television, I see your beautiful face. I wish my spin doctors were as good as yours."

"Hello, Mr. President. How nice of you to call. It's been a busy week, but everything seems to be falling into place."

"With you in charge I never had any doubt. How is Jasmine? We heard she completed the rehab program a few weeks ago. I hope she's doing better."

"Thank you, Mr. President. She's doing much better now. With the help of God, I'm praying all that is behind us now."

"Look, my dear, I'm afraid Carol and I won't be able to make the opening this Sunday, after all, and I wanted to let you know myself. This damn fiscal crisis is making my life a living hell, and I have to stay close to Washington these days. I hope you understand."

"I'm so sorry to hear that, but of course, I understand."

"I promise Carol and I will come out as soon as things settle down here, and we'll spend some quality time together."

"I would enjoy that, and of course, I expect you to stay at the estate. Whenever you have time, just have your people call and we'll make all the necessary arrangements."

"I would love that. Even if Carol isn't able to make it, I . . ." The commander in chief's voice shifted to a whisper. "I would love to see you again. I've thought about you a lot since our last time together."

"I've thought about you as well," Samantha replied coyly. "I always enjoy spending time with you . . . with or without Carol."

"Good. Then it's settled," he said, returning to his presidential tone. "I'll get the folks here working on it right now. Please give my love to Jasmine, and best of luck on Sunday. We'll be praying for you and watching it all live here at the White House."

"Thank you, Mr. President, and please send Carol my love."

Samantha hung up the phone and returned to the window. The call vanished from her mind in the time it took to walk back to the crystal pane.

The gawkers were still milling around, the helicopters were still whirling overhead, and the cameras were still rolling. "You're not going to ruin this for me, Danny St. John," she said out loud. "I'll spit on your grave before I let that happen."

"This just in. The man killed in the home of newscaster Gideon Truman has been identified as Los Angeles attorney David Shackelford," said the anchor on the evening news. "We're going to take you live to our field reporter Kevin Spencer, who is at the scene now."

A picture of Gideon's home flashed on the television screen. "Kevin, what else have we learned about David Shackelford and the circumstances surrounding his death?" inquired the anchor.

"Well, as you just said, the police have confirmed the identity of the victim as being David Shackelford of Los Angeles," said the reporter, who was standing on the sidewalk in front of Gideon's house. "Mr. Shackelford was forty-five years old and a partner with the law firm of Shwartz, Nichols, and Pincus in Century City. Shackelford is survived by his wife and a five-year-old daughter. We've tried to reach Mrs. Shackelford at her home, but no one is answering the telephone or the door. We spoke earlier with a representative from Shackelford's law firm, and he had this to say."

The screen cut to a distinguished man with gray temples who was standing at a reception counter, in front of a bronze sign that read SHWARTZ, NICHOLS, AND PINCUS, ATTORNEYS AT LAW. "We are shocked and saddened by the news of our colleague's death. At this time we have no details concerning the circumstances under which he was killed, and are cooperating with the police as they investigate the cause of his death."

"Have you spoken with his wife?" asked the reporter, standing next to him.

"Unfortunately, all our efforts to reach Mrs. Shackelford have been unsuccessful. We will, of course, continue to reach out to her and her daughter and do all that we can to assist her through this difficult time."

Kevin Spencer appeared on the screen again, in front of Gideon's home. "We understand from the police that Mr. Truman is currently in the home, along with possibly two others, whose identity we do not know at this time. All attempts to speak with Mr. Truman have been unsuccessful. Just to recap, the body of Attorney David Shackelford was found in the home of CNN reporter Gideon Truman in the early morning hours. Neighbors reported hearing a gunshot and called the police. The police are not providing a lot of information at this time, but they have told us that it appears to be a home invasion that went horribly, horribly wrong and resulted in the death of one man. There is an ironic twist to this story. Mr. Shackelford was a member of New Testament Cathedral here in Los Angeles, which has been in the news a lot this past month. They are celebrating the opening of a new twenty-five-thousand-seat church this Sunday. Truly a sad way to mark what should have been a joyous occasion for Pastor Samantha Cleaveland and the members of that congregation. I'm Kevin Spencer. Back to you in the studio."

"Kevin," said the studio anchor, "before you go, do we have any idea what Mr. Shackelford was doing in the house at that hour?"

"The police aren't saying much. The only thing we know is all signs point to a home invasion."

Scarlett sat alone in her dark bedroom as the news about the death of her husband played on the wall directly in front of her bed. She had screamed uncontrollably for almost thirty minutes after the police arrived that morning to inform her that David had been killed. She could provide them with no clues as to why her husband would break into Gideon Truman's home other than to say, "I know it had something to do with her."

"*Her* who, ma'am?" had been the question from the female constable.

"Samantha Cleaveland. She killed him."

"I'm sorry, Mrs. Shackelford, but what reason would Samantha Cleaveland have for killing your husband?"

"I don't know, but I know she did it."

"Ma'am," came the officer's gentle reply, "Pastor Cleaveland was not in the home at the time of your husband's death. Also, he brought the gun into the house, and the only prints on the gun were his and those of one of the intended victims. I'm afraid all the evidence leads us to conclude that your husband broke into the home with the intent of killing Gideon Truman."

"I don't care what the evidence points to!" Scarlett screamed hysterically. "She did it. She killed my husband!"

The officer gently touched Scarlett's shoulder in an attempt to calm her down, but Scarlett was inconsolable.

"Mrs. Shackelford, I know this is difficult, but I'm going to have to ask you to come with me to identify the body. Is there someone you can call to come with you? A family member, friend, or a neighbor?"

"No, I don't have anyone. I told him something terrible was going to happen," Scarlett said, rambling. "But he wouldn't listen. He just wouldn't listen to me."

It was now after six o'clock in the evening. Scarlett had not left the house the entire day, other than for the brief moments she had spent at the morgue, standing over the lifeless body of her husband. He'd been wearing the same clothes he had on the day before. He hadn't come home that evening, and now she knew why. He was in the process of being murdered by Samantha. Scarlett had leaned over his body, stretched out on the cold silver slab, and had gently kissed his cheek. She'd whispered, "I won't let her get away with this. I promise you, darling. I won't let her get away with it." Her tear-drenched hand had covered his as the police officer gently pulled her away and escorted her, quivering, from the room.

Now in the quiet of her bedroom Scarlett watched her life unravel on the six o'clock news as Natalie slept quietly in the next room. Back-to-back Valiums had provided just enough fog to allow her to tuck Natalie in bed and make her way back to her room to curl up into a tight ball on the bed. The pills were the only things that allowed her to continue breathing.

Before Scarlett was aware of what her hands were doing, she found herself dialing the phone on the nightstand.

"Hello," said the voice on line.

"She killed him," were the first words from Scarlett's mouth.

"Scarlett, I've been trying to reach you all day," Cynthia said after immediately recognizing the voice. "Honey, I'm so sorry. Are you all right?"

"No, I'm not."

"Is there anything I can do? Do you need me to come over? I can be there in thirty minutes. You shouldn't be alone."

"There's nothing anyone can do now."

"This is so horrible. Do you know what he was doing at Gideon Truman's house?"

"No, but I know she had something to do with it."

"*She* who?"

"Samantha. She killed him."

"But the police said it was a home invasion. He had the gun. He was killed in self-defense."

"I don't care what the police are saying. I know she killed him. Gideon was working on a story about her. I told him Hezekiah was Natalie's father. David must have confronted her about it, and she sent him to Gideon's house."

"But how on earth could Samantha have that much influence over David? Did she know him that well?"

Scarlett wiped her cheek with the sleeve of her sweatshirt and said, "I didn't tell you before, Cynthia, I was too embarrassed, but . . . David was having an affair with Samantha."

A gasp could be heard on the line. Then there was silence.

"He told me he was going to leave me for her," Scarlett added, breaking the silence.

"When?" Cynthia asked, unable to conceal her shock.

"Two weeks ago. He said he was in love with her. I tried to convince him that she's not capable of loving anyone but herself, but he wouldn't listen. I told him, Cynthia," Scarlett said, crying again. "I told him she would destroy him, and now she has. Why couldn't he listen to me? He would still be alive if only he had listened. She destroys everything she touches."

"This is unbelievable, Scarlett. I'm so sorry you have to go through this. Are you sure you don't want me to come over?"

"No. I'll be fine."

For moments the only sound was the news playing in the background. Cynthia could not find adequate words to offer as comfort. At that moment silence seemed to be the most appropriate condolence.

Then Scarlett spoke. "Do you remember what you said to me the other day?"

"What?"

"That the only way to stop her would be to do something that is irreversible, quick, and permanent."

"Yes, I remember," Cynthia replied cautiously.

"Well . . . I want to stop her now."

Samantha studied the wall of monitors in front of her desk. At her direction, the studio control room crew had programmed each monitor feed to tune automatically to television stations whenever they mentioned her name.

Of the twenty monitors now on, seventeen featured programs where the most recent tragedy to befall New Testament Cathedral was being discussed.

Samantha focused on one of the monitors. “Only two days before the inaugural service,” said a news reporter, speaking live from the steps of the cathedral just below Samantha’s office window, “in what many architects are calling one of the most beautiful churches built anywhere in the world in the last five hundred years, another tragic death has touched the lives of Pastor Samantha Cleaveland and the members of New Testament Cathedral.”

Viewers could see the glass skin of the church behind the reporter.

“David Shackelford, longtime member of New Testament Cathedral and husband of board member Scarlett Shackelford, was found dead in the home of veteran CNN reporter Gideon Truman. Many are now speculating on the possible connection between this murder and the very popular recently installed pastor of this international ministry.”

A talking head on another monitor had this to say. “The religious community is being rocked for the second time in three months, and the pastor of New Testament Cathedral is once again at the center of it all. Only months earlier her husband, the Reverend Hezekiah Cleaveland, was brutally gunned down in the pulpit of their church.”

The reporter continued as snippets of the day’s top stories scrolled beneath him. “Only hours later Reverend Willie Mitchell, a high-ranking New Testament Cathedral minister, was found dead in his home from a self-inflicted gunshot wound to the head. Now, weeks later, David Shackelford, attorney, church member, and husband of Scarlett Shackelford, who herself is a longtime member of this church, the former secretary to the late Hezekiah Cleaveland, and a board member, was found dead by police in the home of CNN reporter Gideon Truman.”

On yet another monitor the Entertainment Network offered the most sensational spin of them all. "We're standing live on the newly built campus of New Testament Cathedral in Los Angeles, California. If the occurrences of the last few months are any indication, it would be safe to say there appears to be a curse on this magnificent building. First, the death of their pastor Hezekiah Cleaveland, then the suicide of a top minister and a key financial donor to the church, and now, today, the baffling murder of an attorney who has in the past provided legal services to the Cleaveland family and is the husband of Hezekiah's former secretary."

As the reporter, a Hollywood blonde, spoke, a steady stream of tourists filed behind her. "Only two days before the grand opening," she continued, "the campus is filled with people who have come from all over the world to witness this event. I talked to some of them earlier, and here's what they had to say." A middle-aged housewife with obvious Midwestern roots appeared on the screen. The handbag hoisted on her hip hung from her neck, the strap lying diagonally across her ample bosom.

"Ma'am, what do you think of the latest tragedy that has happened to the folks here at New Testament?" the blond reporter asked from off screen. Her perfectly manicured fingernails holding a mic to the woman's mouth were all that could be seen of her.

"This is all just so sad," the Midwestern mom said, dabbing one eye with her sleeve. "My heart goes out to the poor man's family, but especially to Pastor Cleaveland. She is such a brave woman, and I just hate that she has to go through something like this again."

"What would you say to Pastor Cleaveland if you could speak with her now?" the reporter asked, pressing on.

"I would tell her that we're all praying for her and that she's a strong woman and we believe God is going to see her through this."

"Sir, is this your wife?" the blond reporter said to an attentive man who was standing next to the weeping Midwestern mom. "What did you think when you first heard of this third death involving New Testament Cathedral?"

"We drove here from Michigan to see the church and to maybe see Pastor Cleaveland in person," he said with a digital camera in one hand and a bulging gift bag from the New Testament Cathedral souvenir shop in the other. "The first thing I thought was the devil must be really mad about this beautiful church being built and he's just testing her. But we know that Pastor Cleaveland is stronger than the devil and that she's gonna come out of all this victorious and stronger than ever."

On another monitor a nondescript guy with a perfect haircut and a tan was much less generous with his sympathy and praise. "Is it just me, or does anyone else out there think it's awfully strange that there have been three deaths, all of which have some connection to this televangelist? That's right. I said it. *Televangelist.* Even though Samantha Cleaveland doesn't look like your typical polyester suit–wearing Bible-thumper, she is. If you look past that face, and I must admit she is a knockout, and past the expensive clothes, her message is the same as that of all the other shysters and snake-oil salesmen on television. 'God wants you to send me your money.'"

Samantha recoiled in her leather chair when she heard the words.

"In my humble opinion," the guy with the haircut continued, "the police ought to take a closer look at the lovely Pastor Samantha Cleaveland. If they do, I suspect they'll find a snake in this crystal Garden of Eden."

A picture of Samantha and Jasmine standing in the pulpit flashed on another monitor. Samantha pressed the buttons on her control panel to increase the volume and to transfer the story to the largest monitor on the wall.

"We are interrupting our regularly scheduled programming to bring you this breaking news. This has yet to be confirmed, but a neighbor of CNN reporter Gideon Truman has reportedly told police he saw Jasmine Cleaveland, the daughter of Pastor Samantha Cleaveland and the late Hezekiah Cleaveland, going into the Truman house between two and three o'clock in the morning."

"I was just getting home from a night out," said a man who was standing in the front yard of a house across the street from Gideon's. "I was sitting in my driveway, trying to sober up a bit before I went in. I was there for maybe five minutes when I saw Gideon Truman pull into his driveway. He got out of his car and went to the passenger side and let out this girl."

The man seemed to be talking to no one in particular as he continued his account. "A car drove by and pointed their headlights right at them. I immediately recognized the girl. It was Jasmine Cleaveland. I've seen her before on television. My wife watches their TV show, and I sometimes watch it with her. The girl was obviously very drunk, and Gideon had to help her out of the car and up the stairs to his house. I'm positive it was her."

Samantha immediately dialed Jasmine's cell phone and was greeted with "I hate you."

"Jasmine, are you still in that house?"

"Yes."

"Is there any way you can get out without being seen?"

"No," came the curt reply.

"Then stay put," Samantha said firmly. "I'm going to send a car for you. His instructions will be to wait near the house until all the media have left the street. He will then come into that house and remove you forcefully if you resist. Is that clear?"

"If I see any of your cars on this street," Jasmine said coldly, "I promise you I will walk out the front door and hold a press conference right here on the steps and tell the world that you killed my father. Do you understand?"

"I did not kill Daddy!" Samantha yelled.

"Don't call him Daddy!" Jasmine yelled back into the phone. "He was the only person who ever loved me, and you took him away from me. You gave up the right to call him Daddy when you had him killed."

Samantha bolted to her feet and fought to contain her rage. After a deep breath, she said calmly, "I wish you would stop saying that. You are going to find yourself in more trouble than you can handle if you continue with this fantasy. You're confused right now. I promise things will get better. When you come home, we'll go away together. Would you like to go to the house in Spain for a few days? Or maybe the flat in London? We can do some mother-daughter bonding and get in some serious shopping, like we used to. I underestimated the impact this all would have on you. I should have paid more attention. I'm sorry."

"I know what I heard. You admitted killing him and trying to kill Gideon and Danny," Jasmine replied, ignoring her mother's obvious attempt to remove her from the reach of prying reporters. "The only other person in the world who loved Daddy besides me," she added as a dig.

As Jasmine spoke, it became clear to Samantha that the days of authoritative mother and obedient child were over. She quickly recalibrated her approach, speaking woman to woman.

"I guess you're old enough to hear this now, Jasmine," she said. "Yes, your father was a homosexual. He never really loved me. He married me to further his career. He thought he would take over your grandfather's church after he died." Samantha paused to gauge the effectiveness of this new approach.

There was silence, so she continued. "He hurt me, darling. I was devastated and afraid for our future, for your future. I admit I was embarrassed, but that is it. I never did anything to hurt your father. I dedicated my entire life to him. Everything I did, I did for him. I loved him. You have to believe me."

There was still no response.

"Are you alone now?" Samantha asked, lowering her voice.

"Yes, I'm alone," Jasmine answered with a hint of exasperation.

"Good. Honey, Danny killed your father. I can't prove it, but your father told me the day before he died that he was being stalked by Danny. He threatened to kill your father if he didn't leave me."

Jasmine was standing near the pool in Gideon's backyard, looking into the water. Parker scampered at her feet. Danny was in the kitchen, preparing a light snack for their lunch, and Gideon was in his study, closely following as his life was being dissected on the news.

The events of the evening before were still buzzing in Jasmine's head. As her mother spoke, she could remember only her father's large hand holding hers as they walked in the mall. She thought of all the times he had held her in his arms and kissed her good night on the forehead and said "I love you, princess."

"Then why didn't you tell that to the police?" Jasmine finally asked.

"Don't be so stupid," Samantha said cruelly. "I can't admit that your father was gay. His memory would be ruined. He would become a national joke. Would you want that to happen?"

"I don't believe a word you're saying," Jasmine finally said to her mother. "You hated him, and now you're trying to blame Daddy's death on Danny. Danny loved him, and I believe Daddy loved Danny too. I saw how you treated Daddy all those years. You only used him and me to make yourself look better than you really are. It's always been about you."

"That's not true, darling. I've done everything for you. I have bought you everything you've ever wanted. I built a beautiful home for us—"

"Daddy hated that house, and so do I. It's hideous, and I'm embarrassed every time I walk in the front door."

"Darling, you're just upset and confused," Samantha said, barely containing her rage. "As soon as the media leaves, the car will bring you home. Everything will be fine soon. You'll see."

"Nothing will ever be fine again." Jasmine began to cry. "I'm not sure what I will do if I see you again."

"Are you threatening me?"

There was silence on the line. Jasmine sobbed into the phone and sat down, trembling, on a wicker chaise near the edge of the pool. Parker quickly leapt to her side and snuggled at her hip.

"I hate you," Jasmine whimpered and dropped the phone onto the cushion, next to Parker.

"Jasmine," Samantha said to the sound of Parker's purr. "Jasmine Camille Cleaveland, answer me." Still there was nothing but Parker's steady purr. "Jasmine!" she finally shouted in the phone, causing Parker to jump when he heard her voice.

The next thing Samantha heard was the sound of Parker hissing at her screaming voice as he clawed at the glowing cell phone screen. Parker disconnected the call with the third tap of his paw as Samantha screamed, "Jasmi—"

It was now Saturday morning, the day before the inaugural morning service. A month of frantic preparations coordinated by a squadron of celebrity party planners, publicists, and security experts was approaching a climactic ending on the campus of New Testament Cathedral and at the Cleaveland estate.

The elaborate lighting installed in the sanctuary was designed to enhance the natural light that would pour through the five hundred thousand rectangular panes of glass. Samantha had commissioned the twenty handblown chandeliers that now dangled from the ceiling. The waterfalls flanking the pulpit sent dramatic sheets of water cascading into reservoirs that doubled as the baptismal pools.

Fresh perennials had been spread over the entire campus and looked like red, yellow, magenta, and lavender snow, and the French light fixtures that lined the pathways had been polished to resemble brand-new pennies. The cobblestone walkways appeared to have never been trod on by leather soles. Nothing could be considered perfect and complete until Samantha deemed it to be so. It was showtime, and New Testament Cathedral was ready for its close-up.

The only way to get on the guest list for the party that was to be held that evening at the estate was to be placed on it by Samantha herself and then to purchase a ticket that required a minimum one-hundred-thousand-dollar donation to the ministry. The list had been full for months. The guests had all written their six-figure checks months in advance for fear of being bumped by someone with deeper pockets or a sexier name than their own. It was no secret to anyone who could afford to attend the party that the more money you gave, the closer you were allowed to stand to Samantha Cleaveland, and those who had the wherewithal eagerly paid the price of admission to her inner circle.

Samantha had sequestered herself in her bedroom suite Saturday morning and had no intention of coming out until she made her grand entrance at the party that evening. Stylists, secretaries, personal assistants, and her make-up artist were allowed in the inner sanctum upon demand.

The master suite was a series of six rooms, each more elaborate than the other. Samantha held court in the entrance, which was the size of a living room in a normal home.

"I need to see my dress," was one of her commands. "Please bring it in. And send for the designer and seamstress, in case I need it altered again."

"I need to be assured the valet service has everything under control," she said to one of three personal assistants in her bedroom suite. "Send for the man in charge and tell him I want a detailed description of the operations. I don't want any mistakes."

Samantha dictated every detail of the evening from the suite. The cooks were summoned three times for last-minute menu adjustments. The sound engineer had to make an appearance to allay her fears of a technical glitch during her speech. The head waiter spent an hour describing the finely choreographed routine of the platoon of servers.

"I need to go over the guest list again," she said to another assistant.

"Yes, Pastor," the highly efficient young woman said, rushing to Samantha's side with an iPad in one hand and an iPhone in the other.

"Bill and Camille confirmed yesterday. Their plane arrives at three o'clock, and a driver will pick them up and bring them directly here. They've requested their usual room."

"Have Camille's favorite flowers in the room."

"Already taken care of, Pastor."

"Janet, Jennifer, and Chaka will be doing their sound checks this afternoon," the assistant reported, proceeding efficiently. "Cars will be picking up the senator and her husband, the Richards, Diamond and Jerry Getty, Ms. Winfrey, Barry, and Anderson Vanderbilt at their hotels at exactly seven o'clock. The governor will arrive at seven thirty. His wife will arrive separately at seven forty-five. His security team has been fully briefed and arrived on the premises this morning. The mayor and his wife will arrive at seven. He has asked if he can say a few words at the party."

"Tell him no."

"Yes, Pastor," she responded without question. "The delegation from Dubai arrived at the Beverly Hilton yesterday. They've requested ten private minutes with you this evening."

"Tell them yes. Make sure the library is set up for it."

"Yes, Pastor."

"The prince and princess of Thailand's private jet arrived as scheduled at LAX last evening. They have also requested a private audience."

The assistant rattled off the list of three hundred guests and provided Samantha with the details of their individual care and handling. Samantha reacted with her usual dismissive tone as the names of the world's richest and most famous inhabitants were read.

Throughout the day, Samantha left numerous messages on Jasmine's cell phone.

"I've respected your wishes and did not send the car to pick you up," was one such message. "Now I hope you will respect mine. Tonight is very important to me, and I expect you to be here. Everyone is going to be looking for you, so please do not disappoint me."

There was no response.

"Are you all right, honey? I'm worried about you," was another message. "Please don't believe any of the lies I'm sure those two are telling you. Danny hated your father for not leaving me, and now he only wants to get even. He will do anything to destroy me."

"Jasmine, honey, your gown just arrived," was another of Samantha's messages between party preparations. "It's lovely, darling. You are going to look like a movie star. I picked out a few pieces for you that Tiffany sent over this morning. I think you'll like them. Call me please."

Gideon, Danny, and Jasmine each awoke that morning within minutes of each other. Gideon emerged from the master suite, Danny from one of the guest bedrooms, and Jasmine from another. They converged in the kitchen, where the only sounds were the gurgling of the coffee-maker and the clanging of mugs being removed from the rack.

"How did you sleep last night, Jasmine?" Danny finally asked, placing a steaming mug of coffee in front of her at the table. "I checked on you a few times, and you looked very peaceful."

"I kept dreaming about Daddy," she said groggily after a long sip of coffee. "He was standing in a stream, with water flowing around his ankles. It was sunny, and butterflies were everywhere. I was sitting on the bank, watching him. Then, suddenly, the water began to rise up to his waist, and it started moving faster and faster. The butterflies began to circle around his head, and the water began to carry him away.

"He kept calling my name and reaching out for me so that I could pull him out, but by then he was moving too fast down the stream. I ran as fast as I could and tried to grab his hand, but he . . . he just floated away, with the butterflies fluttering around him the entire way down the stream. He was looking directly at me the whole time and calling my name. . . ." Jasmine's voice trailed off as she said those final words.

Gideon came over to her, placed his arm around her shoulder, and kissed the top of her head.

"I'm so sorry, Jasmine," he said. "I can't begin to imagine how difficult this has been for you."

"I can," Danny said, reaching across the table and cupping her hand. "Remember, I loved him too."

"I know you did, Danny," she said, looking in his eyes. "That's the only good thing that has come out of this. At least I know he had love in his life before he died. I just feel so horrible. I wasn't there when he needed me. I was too busy partying. He needed me, and I wasn't there."

"You were a kid, Jasmine, and you still are. It wasn't your responsibility to save your father," Gideon said gently.

"I know, but I can't help but wonder if there was something I could have done."

"Did you ever tell him you loved him?" Gideon asked.

"All the time," Jasmine said as a tear fell from her eye. "Every time I saw him. He would kiss me on the forehead and say, 'I love you, princess' and I'd say, 'I love you, Daddy.'"

"What more could anyone ask for than to know that they were loved? If we're honest with ourselves, deep down, that's all anyone really wants in life. And he was loved by you and Danny. He was a very lucky man, and I think he knew that."

The three sat at the table in silence and nursed the mugs of coffee.

"I looked out the window earlier," Gideon said, breaking the silence. "There are no reporters out there. Have you thought about what you're going to do next? At some point you are going to have to speak to your mother."

Jasmine released a long sigh. "She's been calling me nonstop. She wants me there tonight, at the party."

"I read about that," Gideon said, retrieving the morning paper from the counter. "It's here on the front page of the Style section."

The headline jumped from the pages as Gideon sat the paper in front of her.

STAR-STUDDED BLACK-TIE EVENT MARKS OPENING OF GLASS CATHEDRAL.

"Are you planning on going?" Danny asked cautiously.

"I can't. I'm afraid of what I might do when I see her," was her painful reply.

"At some point you know you are going to have to see her face-to-face. Maybe with all those people around it will be less painful," Danny said.

"Maybe," she said hesitantly. "I can't go alone, though. Will you come with me?"

Danny laughed until he saw the serious expression on her face. "You're joking, right? I can't go to your house. She'll have me arrested."

"I guess," she said grudgingly. She then turned to Gideon. "Come with me, Gideon. I can't face her alone. You're the press. No one will question you being there, and even if they do, you'll be with me."

Gideon was cautious about appearing too eager to accept the invitation. His reporter's skin tingled at the idea of being in the room with a killer, surrounded by some of the most wealthy people in the world. At the same time he was concerned about Jasmine's well-being. He had seen how fragile she was over the past few days, and he was worried that she might do something she would later regret.

"Please, Gideon," she said, interrupting his internal thought process. "I can't stay here forever, and I can't face her without someone I trust with me. I know it's too dangerous for Danny. I think she actually would have him arrested, if she didn't have her security kill him first. She's less likely to do anything to you because you're almost as famous as she is."

"She's right, Gideon," Danny said, chiming in.

"What are you planning on doing when you get there?" Gideon asked.

"I don't know. I just want to make sure she gets exactly what she deserves," Jasmine responded as she carefully avoided eye contact with either of the men. "I won't know until I actually see her standing in front of me."

Jasmine remembered where her mother had placed the gun that day. It was in the back of the top desk drawer in her office. The sight of her mother placing the gun there was seared in her brain. That would be the first place she would go when she returned home.

First, I'll get the gun, she thought as Gideon and Danny hovered nearby. *Then I'll decide what I'm going to do to her.*

Cynthia Pryce sat at her dining room table with the awakening city at her back. Her morning coffee grew tepid as she read the Style section of the *Los Angeles Chronicle.*

Reverend Samantha Cleaveland, pastor of New Testament Cathedral in Los Angeles, will host a star-studded gala at her Bel Air estate this evening. The event is to celebrate the completion of the new twenty-five-thousand-seat mega church.

The guest list includes many of the top names in entertainment, politics, business, and religion. For the past three days invitees have been arriving from around the world to celebrate this momentous occasion with Pastor Cleaveland and the members of her congregation.

Cynthia was uncharacteristically calm as she read the article. In the past, whenever she ready Samantha's name in the newspaper or saw her face on television, her anger would get the best of her and cause her hands to shake and her eyes to twitch. Not this morning. She read quietly and with a steady hand as she turned the page.

The church has been rocked by a series of tragic deaths that began with the assassination of the founding pastor, Hezekiah Cleaveland. The church also lost Reverend Willie Mitchell, who committed suicide the day after Cleaveland was killed. Most recently the church's attorney, David Shackelford, was killed in the home of noted CNN reporter Gideon Truman.

"The tragic deaths of my husband and these two anointed men of God has brought the members of our church closer to each other and closer to God," Pastor Cleaveland said.

"I will not be deterred. These events have only served to make me stronger," she said.

Percy entered the room and saw Cynthia reading the paper at the table. As he approached, he quickly gauged her mood.

"Good morning, darling," he said, gently kissing her forehead. "What's in the news today?"

"The usual," she said, sipping her coffee. "War, mayhem, murder, and Samantha," she added calmly. "There's an entire article about the party tonight."

"We don't have to go if you don't feel up to it," Percy said carefully. "We can spend a quiet evening at home. They won't even know we're not there."

"Don't be ridiculous," she said, looking up at him. "I wouldn't miss it for the world. Besides, you're the assistant pastor. What would it look like if you didn't show up?"

"I don't care about that. I care about you."

"Don't worry about me, darling. I'll be fine."

Percy gave her another kiss and said, "I'll understand if you change your mind. I have to go to the church and give the lieutenant governor a private tour of the facility. He wasn't important enough for Samantha, so they assigned him to me. I won't be gone long."

"Take your time. I'll be fine," she replied casually.

After Percy left the penthouse, Cynthia went to the bedroom and took her plastic-covered gown from the closet. It was an off-the-shoulder, formfitting red velvet dress by Elie Saab that cost Percy a large portion of his most recent paycheck. Dazzling red Venetian crystals outlined the plunging neckline. Cynthia draped her body with the dress and surveyed herself from head to toe in the mirror on the closet door.

"Gorgeous," she said out loud and hung the dress on a hook in front of the mirror. She removed a beaded red clutch from a Louis Vuitton box on a closet shelf and placed it on the bed. She then reached for another box in the closet, on the top shelf, tucked behind a row of her colorful Sunday hats. The box was metal, and the handle clanked as she placed it next to the purse on the bed. She opened the box and removed an object that was wrapped in one of her silk scarves.

Cynthia slowly unraveled the scarf, and the Smith & Wesson 422 fell onto the bed, next to the clutch. Cynthia stood and stared at the gun, as if waiting for it to levitate and come to her hand. The flat, satiny steel finish deflected the light in the room, causing the gun to almost fade into the gray duvet.

"Cynthia!" Percy called suddenly as he approached the bedroom.

She quickly grabbed the revolver and placed it in the beaded clutch.

"I though you left. Why are you back?" she said when he entered the bedroom.

"I forgot my Bible," he said, rushing to the nightstand. "I was reading last night and left it in here. Is that what you're wearing tonight?" he said, pointing at the gown. "Do you think the neckline is a little . . . revealing?"

Cynthia ignored his question and took him by the arm. "You don't want to keep the lieutenant governor waiting, darling," she said, guiding him back to the door.

"Are you okay? You seem . . . preoccupied."

"I'm fine, darling. Just thinking about how lovely the party will be this evening."

Every time Scarlett thought of David lying on the silver slab, she doubled over from the pain in her stomach. The only thing that kept her from floating away in despair was the little pills, which reduced the grief to a low and persistent throbbing through her entire body.

Natalie was now on a flight to Detroit to spend a month with her godmother. Scarlett couldn't find the words or the strength to tell her about the state of the man she called Daddy. She couldn't find the strength to accept it herself.

Next week you can fall apart, she thought over and over again. *After this is all over.*

For now, she had unfinished business that had to be attended to if her world was ever to be tolerable again. She had accepted that she would never be fully alive again. The thought of happiness lay slowly rotting with David in the sterile room downtown. But there was one thing she could do to ease the torment. There was only one act that would, at the very least, give her the strength to take her next breath. And tonight was as good a time as any to do it.

Her dress was already laid out on the bed. It was an aqua Dolce & Gabbana floral lace gown that traced her figure to perfection. Each elegant twist and turn of her torso would be highlighted by the formfitting fabric, which flared at the knee, leaving a trail around the heels of her T-strap Fendi sandals. The dress cost more than she had ever paid for a garment, but David had insisted months earlier that she look her most radiant at the party at the Cleaveland estate.

Scarlett sat on the bed, next to the dress, and rested her hand on the delicate lace. *I have to do this for . . . ,* she thought. *For Hezekiah and for David.*

She picked up the telephone and dialed.

"Do you have it?" she asked Cynthia.

"I do," came Cynthia's response. "What time are you arriving?"

"Seven thirty."

"Are you sure you'll be able to go through with it?"

"I . . . I'm . . ."

"You don't sound sure. Honey, it's the only way," Cynthia said. "Someone has to do it. We don't have a choice."

"I'm just afraid I won't be able to do it when the time comes," Scarlett said. "I want to do it. I know it has to be done. I just don't know if I'll have the nerve once it's time."

Cynthia took a deep breath to contain the panic that was rising in her chest.

"Scarlett, just remember what she's done to you. Think about how she killed Hezekiah. I know you loved him, and she took him away from you. Think about poor David, lying dead, cold, and lifeless in that morgue. You'll never be able to hear his voice again, thanks to her. You and Natalie are alone in the world with no one to love you, and it's all because of her."

Cynthia took another breath. *Don't overdo it,* she thought. *I don't want to push her too far over the edge.*

"If we don't do this," Cynthia continued, "who is she going to kill next? Scarlett, just think of the lives you'll be saving. We're doing God's work."

"I know you're right. I want her dead more than anything in the world right now. Nothing gives me more pleasure than the idea that she will get exactly what she deserves, but I don't know if I'm the person to do it."

"What about your poor little beautiful daughter, Natalie?" Cynthia said, desperately playing her last card. "Samantha took both her fathers away. That woman has not only destroyed your life, but she has also destroyed Natalie's. Did you ever think she might try to kill Natalie next? I personally think she would do anything to make sure that story never got out."

An image of Natalie lying on that cold slab flashed into Scarlett's mind. The picture served to buoy her resolve.

"I'll be there with you the whole—" Cynthia continued, not realizing there was no further need for convincing.

"You are right," Scarlett interrupted. "It has to be done."

"Good girl," Cynthia said. "I believe in you. Everything will go just fine. There's nothing to worry about. By this time tomorrow the world will be a better place, because Samantha Cleaveland won't be in it."

Cynthia breathed a sigh of relief and continued. "When it's done, come straight to me, and I'll cover for you. Just act distraught, and I'll run interference to give you time to compose yourself without raising any suspicions. I'll show you the perfect spot to do it from. No one will see you, and you'll be able to blend easily back in with the rest of the guests after it's done. I'll be waiting for you when you arrive. There's a bathroom on the second floor, at the end of the hall. Meet me there at exactly eight o'clock, and I'll give it to you."

"Are you sure it can't be traced back to you?"

"I'm positive. I used fake identification."

"Where did you buy it?"

"Scarlett, the less you know about it, the better. Just give it back to me when it's over. Someone in the house is going to hide the gun in the house. No one will ever find it, and, if they do, it will lead them to a dead end."

"Who's in the house?" Scarlett asked, jolting upright on the bed. "Who else knows about this?"

"Don't worry. It's someone we can trust. They told me the best place for you to shoot from to have a clear shot and give you enough time to blend back into the crowd."

"I don't like this, Cynthia. You never said anyone else would be involved."

"It was the only way. We've both been in the house, but neither of us would know where to hide a gun, and you can be sure everyone will be searched before they're allowed to leave."

"How do you know they can be trusted?" Scarlett asked.

"I know because they hate her as much, if not more, than we do."

"Are you sure we're doing the right thing?"

"I know we are. It's God's will," Cynthia said firmly. "I've prayed about this for weeks. I've never been more sure of anything in my life."

"I'm too afraid to pray about it. I don't want God to tell me not to do it," Scarlett said, lying back on the bed, next to the dress.

"There's absolutely no reason to be afraid," Cynthia said confidently. "I truly believe God wants us to do it."

Hattie had spent most of Saturday in her garden. The gentle summer breeze and the smell of freshly tilled soil had helped to calm her nerves and clear her head. She prayed that no more visions would make their way down from heaven to her doorstep. Since Hezekiah's death, the visions had come through clearly and frequently, but they had left her with more questions than answers.

The tips of her gardening gloves were covered in soil mixed with her favorite fertilizer and Miracle-Gro. The earthly brew had served her well over the years. Not only did it make her garden grow, but it also fed her family and the families of so many others.

Hattie looked at her watch. It was 3:35 p.m. The driver would be there at exactly 6:30 p.m. to take her to the estate. This offered her just enough time to bathe, prepare her hair, dress, and pray. The evening called for her to be in a spiritual state that would block the feelings and emotions of everyone in the room. She could not be distracted by the concerns of the rich and famous. The channels had to be kept clear, and her heart pure.

As a trustee and founding member of New Testament Cathedral, Hattie would be paraded around the room like Rosa Parks during Black History Month. She represented all that was left of the early struggles and the difficult days of New Testament Cathedral. A time that Samantha would prefer to forget. But Hattie would soon be dead, or removed from the board, so putting her on display like a relic of bygone days seemed innocuous enough to Samantha.

Hattie stood over the foxglove plant near the pink brick wall. Her knees trembled slightly as she sensed the beginning of another vision. She planted her feet firmly in the soil and braced her spirit for the revelation to come.

In an instant she saw Samantha standing in her garden. She wasn't alone. The troubled spirit of Scarlett Shackelford appeared next to her. There was desperation in her face. The pain that Hattie had grown accustomed to seeing around her was even more intense than ever.

Poor child, Hattie thought as she scanned her tormented face. *Lord, don't let her do something she's gonna regret. That little girl needs her now more than ever.*

Hattie quickly returned to the role of passive observer. Samantha began to wander through her garden, between the rows of collards and the bushes of zucchini. She aimlessly made her way around the trellises of tomatoes and into the rows of okra and peppers. She was oblivious to Scarlett, who followed only a few steps behind her.

Suddenly Cynthia Pryce appeared in the garden, at the end of the path that Samantha was walking down. Scarlett was at one end of the row, Samantha was in the middle, and Cynthia was at the opposite end. The three women paused. Samantha studied Cynthia closely, still unaware that Scarlett was only a few feet behind her.

Hattie was abruptly aware of the heat of the afternoon sun on her brow. Her knees began to ache from standing in the moist soil. She had lost track of time since the vision began, but the pangs in her knees indicated it had been much longer than she had imagined. *No time for that,* she thought. *Lord, give me the strength to stand here as long as need be.*

The three women remained suspended in time amid Hattie's squash, tomatoes, and snap peas. Hattie noted it was the first time she had ever seen a vision integrated with the tangible. Two white butterflies executed a well-choreographed dance between the plants. Bumblebees performed their duties, and electric-red ladybugs continued with their afternoon meal while the three women stood above and beyond the reach of time.

Then Samantha took a step toward Cynthia. Cynthia matched her with a step forward. Scarlett followed from behind. The three women were now one step closer. The movement caused Hattie to shudder slightly. She quickly covered her mouth with one gloved hand, as if to prevent a gasp from disturbing the three visitors in her garden.

Samantha turned around quickly and was now aware of Scarlett standing behind her. She looked back and forth between the two women who blocked her path and to the right and left. She reacted as if she were trapped between the two women and the bounty of Hattie's vegetable garden.

Hattie stopped short of taking a step forward and removing Cynthia from the path. She raised her hand and then quickly tucked it into her apron pocket.

The three women were on a collision course, and Hattie was helpless to stop the crash. Cynthia and Scarlett began to glide toward Samantha without moving their feet. At first they glided slowly, but then their pace steadily accelerated to an alarming speed. Samantha stood firm between the two women as they rushed toward her. Then, suddenly, the three spirits collided. There was an explosion that sounded like two trains crashing head-on at top speed. Hattie closed her eyes tight on impact.

When she opened her eyes, the only thing remaining of the three women or the vision was a plume of smoke that wafted above the garden and faded into the heavens. Hattie surveyed the garden for damage, but there was none. The butterflies fluttered, the ladybugs munched, and the bumblebees darted from flower to flower as if all were well in the world.

Hattie removed the soiled gardening gloves from her trembling hands and dabbed her brow with a wrinkled handkerchief that was always kept in one of the apron pockets.

The foxgloves were in full bloom next to her and drooped from the weight of so many pink blossoms. She pulled a pair of gardening sheers from one of the apron pockets, expertly cut the tips from four stems, and placed them in her pocket along with the knife.

On her way to the back door, Hattie stopped and plucked three tomatoes and eight leaves from a bulging collard green stalk for tomorrow's Sunday dinner. It was the day that the first service in the new sanctuary was to be held, but somehow Hattie knew there would be plenty of time to cook her greens.

Chapter 13

It was a starlit night at the estate. A full moon hung in the heavens, as if by design, just above the glowing main entrance. The grounds and the mansion were lit especially for the evening, giving the home a luminescent amusement park glow. Limousines, Rolls-Royces, Bentleys, Mercedes, and every other imaginable top-of-the-line driving experience lined the road, waiting for their turn with the army of red-vested valets.

Each car had been briefly detained at the gate by armed security personnel to verify the occupants' names on the guest list. The instructions were clear. If a name was not on the iPad and accompanied by a photograph, the license plate number of the vehicle was to be written down, a photograph of the passengers was to be taken by the camera concealed in the tree just above, and the car was then to be discreetly directed from the property.

Helicopters whirled overhead, with spotlights and zoom lenses aimed at the partygoers as they exited their cars and entered the house. Once again, Samantha had garnered the world's attention, and everyone who was not on the guest list watched the aerial coverage on the evening news, wishing they had been invited.

Guests were welcomed by name by a member of the ministerial staff in the foyer. "Good evening, Ambassador and Mrs. Buchannan," came one such greeting. "On behalf of Pastor Cleaveland and New Testament Cathedral, welcome to the Cleaveland estate. Pastor Cleaveland will be down shortly. Please enjoy your evening."

The parade of celebrities, domestic and foreign dignitaries, millionaires, and billionaires seemed unending. By 7:30 p.m. more than two thirds of the three hundred guests had arrived, and the cars continued to flow through the gates.

The mansion was flawless, thanks to the creative hand of one of the country's most sought-after party planners, known only as François. His flamboyant manner, his earrings in both ears, his rubber wrist, and the ever-present "hiss" weren't enough for Samantha not to hire him. She winced every time he extended his hand to her with his palm turned down, revealing a ring on every finger, but he was the best, and the evening required no less.

Exotic floral arrangements, which were on nearly every surface, had been flown in from Italy. Candles designed in the shape of the glass cathedral glowed in every room. Stations serving up the most delicate and exotic hors d'oeuvres were positioned throughout. The centerpiece of each station was a four-foot glass cathedral carved in ice. Red bow-tied waiters pirouetted unobtrusively through the crowd, carrying silver trays of black beluga caviar, pâtés, truffled quail eggs, and other exotic delicacies selected by Samantha.

The oil painting of Hezekiah and Samantha that had once hung over the fireplace in the living room had been replaced by a portrait of Samantha standing alone. She didn't want him at the party.

The buzz of a hundred animated conversations in the living room was accompanied by the melodic chords of a string chamber ensemble in front of the grand piano. Flowing gowns and black tuxedos filled every inch of the living room and the adjoining rooms. The world of people with over fifty million dollars was very small, so most of the guests in the room were either old acquaintances or were familiar with everyone else in the room.

Cynthia Pryce dutifully followed behind Percy as he meandered from circle to circle. His instructions from Samantha had been to personally greet every person in the room and introduce himself as "the assistant to Pastor Cleaveland," which he obediently did. Cynthia gritted her teeth and smiled every time she heard the words.

Just a little while longer, girl, she said silently, girding herself. *Just a little longer and he'll no longer have to say that.*

Her bloodred dress garnered disapproving glances from most of the women and admiring glances from the men. Her overflowing almond breasts were the first thing seen as she approached, and her snugly encased behind was the last thing viewed as she walked away. Whenever someone entered the room, she craned her neck to see if it was Scarlett. It was already 7:45 p.m., and she had not arrived.

Please don't screw this up for me, Scarlett, she thought between extolling the architectural wonder of the new cathedral to pampered faces. *I need you, Scarlett. I can't do this without you.*

At 7:47 p.m. Scarlett entered the room alone. The exquisite tailoring of her aqua-blue lace gown coupled with her perfect feminine silhouette turned heads as she walked through the crowd, directly toward Cynthia.

"Would you excuse me for a moment, darling?" Cynthia said to Percy as he regaled a group of three with stories of Samantha's bravery. "Scarlett just came in. I want to extend my condolences."

"Why is she here?" he said in a whisper, turning his head slightly away from the three guests. "David hasn't even been buried yet."

"I don't know, darling," she responded through a gritted smile. "Maybe she didn't want to be alone tonight."

"Please give her my condolences as well," he said, grabbing her arm before she could walk away. "Tell her I'll speak with her later tonight."

"I will, darling. Just keep making your rounds. I'm sure Samantha is watching," she said condescendingly.

The two women wove their way through the crowd and met in the center of the room. Cynthia extended her arms in an exaggerated motion and embraced Scarlett. The half smile on Scarlett's face told of the recent loss and the troubled plans ahead.

"Where have you been?" Cynthia said through her painted smile. "You're late. I was worried you had changed your mind."

"I almost did," Scarlett said, unable to conceal her nervousness. "But I'm here. I'm ready. Do you have it?"

"Yes. Right here," Cynthia said, slightly raising the red beaded clutch. "We don't have much time. Samantha is making her entrance at exactly eight o'clock. Meet me in the bathroom on the second floor, at the end of the hall."

With that, the two women parted. Cynthia returned to Percy's side, and Scarlett made her way to the foyer and up the staircase, and then vanished down the hall.

Hattie Williams sat alone in a chair near the fireplace with her black patent leather purse resting on her lap. The comfortable chair offered little relief for her throbbing knee. Guests were periodically introduced to her and addressed her with the respect due a senior statesman.

"Mr. Governor, may I introduce you to Mrs. Hattie Williams," was one such introduction. "Mrs. Williams is one of the founding members of New Testament Cathedral. Pastor Hezekiah Cleaveland often referred to her from the pulpit as one of his most trusted confidants."

"It is an honor to meet you, Mrs. Williams," said the governor, bending down to take her hand. "My condolences on the loss of your pastor. He was a very good man, and we all were saddened by his untimely death."

After a few moments of obligatory banter, the conversations typically ended with, “It was a pleasure meeting you, Mrs. Williams. I can see why Pastor Cleaveland trusted you so deeply. He was a lucky man to have a friend and counselor like you.”

Hattie graciously accepted the compliments and gentle touches on her hand, but she never took the corner of her eye off Cynthia and Scarlett when they spoke in the center of the room. *I can’t let them do it, Lord,* she thought. *I can’t sit by and watch two more lives being ruined.*

“I’m sorry, Ms. Cleaveland, but your guest’s name is not on the list,” said the apologetic security guard.

“I don’t care if his name isn’t on the list,” Jasmine said from the passenger seat of Gideon’s car at the gate. “If you don’t open my gate immediately, I will call my mother,” she snarled, “and ask her to come here personally and tell you to let him in. And trust me, she will not be pleased.”

The guard took a step away from the car and spoke into a receiver on his wrist. “She said he’s her guest,” he said softly. “Gideon Truman.” There was a pause then. “Yes, sir, *the* Gideon Truman. Yes, sir.”

The guard returned to the window and said, “I’m so sorry for the misunderstanding, Mr. Truman. Please enjoy the evening.”

With that the gate glided open, and Gideon entered the property. “You really can be a bitch when you want to be,” he said with a nervous smile.

“I learned from the best,” was her reply.

“Have you decided what you’re going to say to her?”

“Not yet,” she said, looking directly ahead at the glowing house. “I won’t know until I’m looking her in the eye.”

“One word of advice,” Gideon said as the car rolled to a stop in front of the house. “This is a private family matter. There’s no need to make a scene.”

The valet stood patiently at the car door.

"After all you've been through with my family, you still don't understand the Cleavelands, do you?" she said, opening her door. "Scenes are what we do best."

As they walked up the front stairs, Jasmine took Gideon's hand and said, "I'm going to my room to change. I'll meet you back here in a few minutes." She then clenched his hand tighter and said, "Gideon?"

"Yes?"

"Thank you for coming with me. I couldn't do what I have to do tonight without you."

The haunting words caused Gideon to pause in the foyer as Jasmine walked up the stairs and disappeared into the hallway.

Jasmine went straight to her mother's office and closed the door. It was dark. She could hear the music from downstairs through the vents. As she walked to the desk, she prayed that it would be unlocked.

The desk drawer slid open with ease. Jasmine rifled through the contents until her hand touched the cold metal at the back of the drawer. She slowly removed the gun and stared at it in her hand. She instinctively knew it was the gun that had killed her father. She could almost feel the pain it had caused him burning into her palm. The first tear that fell from her eye was followed by a stream as she placed the gun in her pocket and left the room as quietly as she had come.

At 8:00 p.m. exactly, Samantha appeared alone at the top of the foyer staircase. She wore a Christian Dior mocha-toned gown created especially for her body and for that night. The A-line bodice was sleeveless and was covered in Austrian Swarovski crystals. The heart-shaped neckline dipped suggestively to reveal the top of her securely braced bosom. A 69.42 carat Cartier diamond dangled casually just above the V of her breasts. The lower portion of the gown billowed with each step from layers of sheer organza in hues of cream, mocha, and brown over a formfitting satin skirt.

Dolce & Gabbana strap sandals barely touched the marble as she glided down the stairs. At the halfway point, she was greeted with applause from the guests, who steadily streamed into the foyer to witness her entrance.

"Good evening, my very special friends," she called out, gently waving her diamond-wrapped wrists as she continued her descent. "Welcome to my home. Thank you, everyone, for coming. How lovely you all look tonight."

At the foot of the stairs she was greeted with air kisses from everyone who had assembled at the base. As she worked her way through the crowd and into the living room, she received a flurry of comments.

"You look fabulous, Pastor Cleaveland."

"Thank you so much for inviting us."

"The cathedral is magnificent."

"We are honored to be in your lovely home."

"Hezekiah would be so proud."

"Darling, who are you wearing?" several guests asked.

"Dior," was her modest reply each time.

Victoria greeted her with an air kiss from one foot away. "Bitch, you look fierce," she whispered into Samantha's ear. "You should have killed that bastard years ago if this is how fabulous you look as a widow."

"Thank you, darling," Samantha replied, with every available tooth showing for the curious eyes around her. "Who are you wearing?"

"Versace, darling. That old queen might be dead, but he can still make me look like a diva."

The two women exchanged a muted party laugh.

"You sure got a house full of rich motherfuckers here tonight," Victoria said through a clenched smile, without moving her lips.

"And you better believe I'm going to squeeze every dollar I can out of every one of them," Samantha said, leaning in close.

"Mr. Governor," Samantha said, touching his arm as he walked past. "Have you met my dearest friend in the world, Victoria Johnson, the wife of Pastor Sylvester Johnson?"

"Yes, I'm very familiar with Mrs. Johnson and her husband. I don't see him here. I hope he's all right. He owes me a golf game. The last time we played, he cleaned up the course with me."

"He's just fine, Governor. He's in Augusta this weekend. He hated missing this evening, but it couldn't be avoided," Victoria replied.

"Can I get you a drink, Mrs. Johnson?" the governor said as Samantha was pulled into an adjoining conversation.

"I thought you'd never ask, Governor," Victoria said suggestively, taking his arm. "Are you alone tonight? I haven't seen your wife."

It was a glorious evening. The rich and beautiful were assembled under Samantha's roof, and their wallets were within her grasp. Every flower was in a perfect state of bloom. Every champagne glass was in the right hand, and every morsel of food was prepared to perfection.

At 8:05 p.m. Cynthia made her way up the stairs and into the bathroom where Scarlett was waiting nervously.

"Where have you been?" Scarlett asked urgently. "It feels like I've been in here forever."

"I had to wait until she came downstairs. I couldn't risk running into her in the hallway. Now, listen closely.

We only have a few minutes until she gives a toast at the top of the staircase in the foyer. Here's the gun." Cynthia handed Scarlett the revolver. "It's very easy to use. Just take a deep breath, steady yourself, aim, and pull the trigger. Can you do that?"

"Yes."

"There's a flight of stairs halfway down this hall on the left that leads back down into the room just off the living room. Stand at the top of those stairs when you shoot."

"Yes, I saw them," Scarlett said intently.

"Samantha will be standing a few yards away from you at the top of the foyer staircase. Everyone will be below, in the foyer, so they won't be able to see you. This is the important part. As soon as you shoot her, go down the stairs to the living room and then come to the foyer and stand with everyone else. I'll be waiting for you at the entrance between the living room and foyer."

"What do I do with the gun?"

"Sit the gun on the second landing of the stairs as you're coming down. I've arranged for someone to pick it up and dispose of it for us."

"Who?" Scarlett asked in a panic.

"I told you not to worry about that. They can be trusted. Now, as soon as you hear her speaking from the steps, come out of the bathroom, get into position, and do it. Do not wait. Understand?"

"Yes, I understand. Cynthia, are you sure this will work? Are you sure we can get away with it?"

"I'm positive. Nothing will go wrong. Trust me."

With a champagne flute in one hand, Samantha made her way through the crowd, giving everyone no more than three minutes of face time.

At 8:10 p.m. she walked over to Hattie Williams, who was still sitting by the fireplace. She placed her glass on the table next to Hattie, bent down, and said, "Mother Williams, I'm so glad you came. You look lovely."

"Thank you, Samantha," was Hattie's brief reply.

"I'm about to invite everyone into the foyer for a toast. I'm going to acknowledge you as a founding member."

"That's not necessary," Hattie said coldly.

"I thought it appropriate since you are about to leave the board of trustees."

"What do you mean? I'm not leaving the board."

"Yes, you are, dear," Samantha said, looking her directly in the eye. "Now that Hezekiah is no longer with us, there's no reason for you to continue as a trustee. We need someone younger and with more business experience. I'm recommending that you be removed immediately. For your health. Are you able to stand long enough to join us for the toast?"

"No, Pastor, my knees won't allow me to stand for that long tonight," Hattie said calmly. "I'm going to stay here. I'll be able to hear you just fine from here."

"Very well, then, Mother." Samantha stood and turned her back to Hattie. She raised her hand, a signal to stop the music.

"May I have everyone's attention please," she said over the multiple conversations. "Would you all be kind enough to join me in the foyer for a toast?"

Samantha retrieved her glass of champagne from the table next to Hattie and proceeded to the foyer, with the crowd following close behind.

When everyone was assembled, she walked to the top of the stairs and looked down on the sea of diamonds, bow ties, and face-lifts.

"Tonight is the culmination of five years of work to build one of the most beautiful churches in the world."

The crowd applauded.

"None of this could have been accomplished without the love, support, and prayers of everyone in this room. You all made it a reality, and for this I thank you. The evening is a mix of joy and sorrow for me. Tomorrow we will hold the first morning service in the new cathedral."

Again the audience applauded.

"The joy comes from knowing that twenty-five thousand people will be assembled to hear the word of God preached and millions more will be watching around the world on television. My sorrow comes from knowing that my dear departed husband will not be standing by my side in the pulpit. I know his spirit is with me, though, and he's looking down from heaven right now and seeing that something he had dreamed of for years has come to fruition."

Samantha raised her glass above her head and said, "Would you all please raise your glasses with me in a toast to my husband, the late, great Pastor Hezekiah Cleaveland."

Crystal glasses were hoisted throughout the foyer. "To Pastor Hezekiah Cleaveland!" came the loud chorus as Samantha took a sip from her champagne glass.

Scarlett stood in position, with the gun aimed directly at the back of Samantha's head. She closed her eyes and, with a trembling hand, slowly applied pressure to the trigger.

Suddenly a bang echoed through the room. Samantha froze in place and looked down on the crowd with bulging eyes. She released the crystal flute sending it crashing into pieces down the marble stairs. The crowd was filled with stunned and confused faces. Samantha stumbled forward onto the first step, then the second. She grabbed her chest and began to desperately gasp for air. On the third step, she collapsed onto the stairs and, as if in slow motion, tumbled head over foot the entire length of the staircase, until she crashed on the marble floor at the feet of her well-heeled guests. She landed in a jumbled pile of organza, satin, and diamonds. Her eyes were wide open and pointing directly at her prized Picasso.

The first loud shriek was then heard. It was followed by screams from every corner of the room. Scarlett ran immediately down the hallway stairs. She dropped the gun on the first landing and continued down to the main floor, racing into a small room off the living room. As she turned the corner, she found herself standing face-to-face with Etta Washington.

Scarlett froze like a deer caught in headlights as their eyes met.

"Don't stop, Mrs. Shackelford," Etta whispered urgently. "Go through the living room there and get to the foyer. You don't have much time. I'll take care of the gun."

Scarlett thanked Etta with her eyes and darted through the door and into the living room. She ran so fast through the room, she didn't notice Hattie Williams watching her from the chair near the fireplace.

By the time she reached the foyer, the room was in full panic mode. People were running out the front door to their limousines. Women were crying hysterically, and seven security guards had surrounded Samantha's body, their guns fully cocked and pointing into the frantic crowd.

Trembling, Scarlett clutched Cynthia's hand. "I did it. It's over," she whispered, crying into her shoulder. "It's over. She can't hurt me or my baby anymore."

Cynthia placed her hand over Scarlett's quivering mouth and quickly walked her back into the living room. Hattie sat calmly by the fireplace, watching the two women as they huddled, whispering, in the corner. She clutched her purse in her lap. When they finally noticed

Hattie, Cynthia sat Scarlett in a chair and quickly walked the length of the room to her.

"Are you all right, Mother?" Cynthia asked, kneeling in front of her. "I'm afraid something terrible has happened. Samantha has been killed."

"I know, baby. I saw the whole thing."

Cynthia looked puzzled. "But how . . . how could you have seen it from here?" she asked suspiciously.

"I see more than you could ever imagine. Now, go back to Scarlett, Mrs. Pryce. She needs you now more than I do," was Hattie's simple reply.

Gideon spotted Jasmine standing near the front door in the foyer. She was staring blankly across the room at the lifeless body of her mother at the foot of the stairs. He quickly made his way to her, hurdling over a woman who had fainted in the melee and around men shielding their crying companions in their arms. Two security guns followed him as he dashed across the room.

"Jasmine," he said, clutching her and gathering her into in his arms. "My God, honey, please tell me you didn't do this."

She collapsed, crying hysterically, into his arms, unable to speak. As she pressed her body against his, he felt the heavy weight of metal against his hip. He reached into her jacket pocket and traced the outline of the gun.

"Oh, Jasmine, no!" he cried.

Suddenly he felt a firm hand on his shoulder. "Mr. Truman, we have to get her out of here quickly."

When Gideon turned around, he found himself standing eye to eye with a security guard whose gun was raised at face level.

"Please follow me," the guard said.

Gideon bundled Jasmine under his arm and pressed the gun between them with his body. They followed the guard out the front door to the steps.

"I'll take her to my home," Gideon said to the man. "She'll be safe there."

"I'm afraid that's not possible, sir. She will have to come with me. A secure location was set up two blocks away in the event of an emergency such as this."

"No!" Jasmine screamed, clutching Gideon's body. "I'm going to Gideon's. Gideon, please take me with you. I don't want to be anywhere near this place."

"Miss Cleaveland, you'll be much safer if you come with me," the security guard said authoritatively.

"No!" she screamed again. "Let's go, Gideon. I want to leave now."

"Sir, my car is right over there," Gideon said, pointing to his vehicle. "You can send someone to my home and station them outside. My address is five-forty-three Hollow Point Road. Now, please call the gate and tell them to let us out. Thank you."

With that Gideon whisked Jasmine to his car, carefully securing the gun between their bodies. He quickly helped her into the passenger seat and sped toward the gate. The iron bars slide open as he approached. Gideon swerved the car onto the road and sped down the dark hill.

"Give me the gun," he said, firmly extending his hand.

Jasmine did not move or respond.

"Give me the gun!" he yelled.

Jasmine removed the gun from her jacket pocket with a trembling hand and placed it in his open palm. Gideon rolled down his window and hurled the warm gun into the dense trees and foliage of the canyon thousands of feet below, where it would never be seen again.

Chapter 14

The police car blocked the gate at New Testament Cathedral on Sunday morning. Thousands of mourners stood weeping at the eight-foot fences and along the streets surrounding the campus. A carpet of flowers covered the sidewalks, and reporters scrambled for sound bites among the crowds.

"The world is in shock this morning over the death of Pastor Samantha Cleaveland," announced a news anchor on one of the major networks. "Police have not released the cause of death, but witnesses at the star-studded party she hosted at her estate in Bel Air are saying she was shot."

The camera cut to a visibly shaken woman who had been interviewed the evening before. "She was giving a lovely toast to her husband when all of a sudden I heard a loud pop. She started to gasp for air and grab her chest. The next thing I knew, she was rolling down the steps and landed right at my feet." The woman dabbed her eye with a silk handkerchief. "It was just horrible."

The camera cut back to the anchor. "The evening was to mark the opening of her new church in Los Angeles. But today the sanctuary doors are locked, and the members of New Testament Cathedral are in mourning."

Cynthia Pryce watched the news from her bed. Percy sat at the foot, staring at the screen in disbelief.

"Are you okay, honey?" Cynthia asked, placing her hand on his shoulder.

He did not respond.

"I suppose this means you'll have to step in as pastor until the trustees decide what to do."

Percy turned to her sharply. "How can you even be thinking about that right now? Are you that unfeeling? Did you really hate her that much that you can't even pretend to be upset by this?"

"You know exactly how I felt about her," she replied coldly.

"You hated her." He looked directly in her eyes. "Did you hate her enough to kill her?"

Cynthia sat back dismissively. "What are you talking about? I was standing next to you when it happened."

"You know exactly what I mean. Were you in any way involved in her death?"

"They kept us there until three in the morning," Cynthia said, standing abruptly from the bed. "I'm too tired to have this conversation with you."

Percy grabbed her arm and yanked her back to the bed. "Answer me, Cynthia. Did you have anything to do with this?"

"No!" she yelled, jerking her arm free. "You know I could have, but I didn't. We should thank whoever did it, though. She got exactly what she deserved."

"You disgust me," Percy said, standing. "I don't know who you are anymore, Cynthia. Jealousy has turned you into a heartless woman, and I can't stand it anymore."

Percy stood and walked out of the room. Cynthia followed close behind him.

"It's over now, Percy. Don't you see? Now we can have everything we've ever wanted. They'll have to install you as pastor."

"You mean, everything *you* have ever wanted," he said, walking through the hall into the living room. "I've never wanted to be pastor, and even if they did ask me, I would turn it down."

Cynthia froze when she heard those words. By now Percy was in the kitchen, filling a coffee decanter with water from the sink. "Don't be ridiculous," she blurted, bursting into the room. "Do you know what I had to do to make you pastor?"

Percy slammed the decanter to the floor, sending glass and water splashing in every direction. "I know you tried to destroy Hezekiah with those e-mails. I know you fucked Lance Savage in the backseat of my fucking Mercedes to get him to run the story. What else did you do?" he asked, sprinting across the kitchen and grabbing her shoulders violently. "Tell me! Did you kill her?"

"No!" she shrieked. "I told you I didn't have anything to do with it."

"You're lying." Percy raised his hand and slapped her hard on the cheek. Cynthia's body slammed against the marble island and fell to the floor. "You're lying, you horrible bitch! You killed her! I know you did!" Percy shouted as he continued to level a series of powerful slaps at her while she tried in vain to shield her face.

Percy raised his hand one last time and froze. He watched as she scampered for safety under the island. He looked up at his hand and saw trickles of her blood running down his wrist. Percy stood still and looked down on her bloody face. "If you did it, then you did it for nothing. I will never be pastor, and you will never be first lady."

"You're no better, you fucking murderer!" she screamed as he walked out of the kitchen. "You killed Lance Savage, but you didn't have the brains to handle Samantha. I did it all for you! I swear, Percy, if you don't accept the pastorship, I'll tell the police everything!" she howled. "I'll tell them you killed Lance Savage! I mean it!"

Her final words were pounding in his head when he slammed the bedroom door. The horrible reality of his life battered his body even harder than the blows he had delivered moments earlier. Percy frantically paced the length and width of the room like a caged animal desperate to escape. Moments passed, and his pace gradually slowed as he found it more and more difficult to propel his body through the room.

Finally exhausted, he dropped the full weight of his body onto the bed, breathless and covered in perspiration. His chest heaved as he gasped for air. Percy struggled to free himself from the reality that their lives would be forever bound together by the blood of Lance Savage. But he was too tired to fight. His future was no longer his own. It now belonged to the woman cowering in the kitchen, under the marble island.

"The streak of bad luck that many are now calling the Cleaveland Curse has struck again. Pastor Samantha Cleaveland, the wife of the late Hezekiah Cleaveland, was brutally murdered last night in her home, in front of hundreds of horrified guests."

Scarlett sat quietly in a chair in her bedroom, cradling a picture of Natalie in her arms. The curtains were drawn, and the only light in the room came from the television hanging on the wall in front of her bed. After the police allowed her to leave the estate, she'd driven home in a daze. She still had on the gown.

The night had brought her a steely resolve. I had to do it, she thought over and over again until she believed it herself. I had to stop her before she killed again. Before she killed me or my little girl. She found comfort and absolution in the words. *Forgive me, God, but I had to do it.*

"Police are now distancing themselves from their original theory that Pastor Cleaveland died from a gunshot wound," the news anchor continued. "Here's what Los Angeles Police Department chief Anthony Cordova had to say at a press conference held earlier this morning about their latest findings."

A grave-looking Chief Cordova, standing at a podium flanked by his top brass, appeared on the TV screen.

"Contrary to what witnesses originally told police, we have just been told by the coroner's office that Pastor Cleaveland did not die as a result of a gunshot," he said.

There was a collective gasp from the crowd of reporters that filled the room.

The police chief continued. "There were no signs of trauma to her body other than those sustained when she fell down the stairs in her foyer. We are waiting for autopsy results before we announce the official cause of death."

Scarlett bolted upright in the chair, sending the picture frame flying to the floor. "That can't be," she said out loud. "I shot her. I know I did."

"There was no blood?" someone in the crowd called out.

"That is correct," the chief said. "No blood was found at or near the crime scene."

"Chief Cordova, Chief Cordova," the reporters called out in unison.

"What are they saying was the cause of death if it wasn't from gunshot wounds?" one reporter yelled above all the others vying for the chief's attention.

"We're not speculating at this time. We are going to wait for the results from the autopsy, which we're expecting later today."

"Was anyone else hurt?" asked another reporter. "Numerous witnesses said they heard a single gunshot just before she collapsed."

"No one else was injured. We are still investigating to determine if it was in fact a gunshot that was heard or possibly something like a champagne bottle being opened by one of the waitstaff."

"Do you have anyone in custody, and if not, have you identified any possible suspects?"

"No one has been arrested at this time, and we have not identified any suspects," the chief said, bowing his head slightly. "As soon as we are sure of the cause of death, we hope that will lead us to possible suspects."

"We understand her daughter was present. Did she witness the murder, and where is she now?"

"Yes, the daughter of Pastor Cleaveland was present. She was immediately removed from the scene and taken to an undisclosed secure location. She is safe and under twenty-four-hour protection."

"Do you suspect the killer is the same person or persons who assassinated her husband? Has any progress been made in that investigation?" a reporter called out from the back of the crowd.

"We haven't ruled out the possibility that the killer is the same in both murders. That, obviously, is the first theory we are investigating at this time." The chief then raised his hand to the crowd. "That's all I am able to say at this time. We will hold another briefing as soon as we hear from the coroner's office. Thank you."

"Danny!" Gideon called out from the living room. "Danny, did you hear that?"

Gideon was sitting in the living room, watching the morning news closely as the chief of police announced the new details. He ran to the kitchen, where Danny was cradling a cup of coffee at the table.

Gideon burst into the room. "She wasn't shot," he said with a puzzled expression.

"What do you mean? I thought you said you heard a gunshot," Danny said, equally puzzled.

"They think it might have been a champagne cork. They don't know what killed her, but there was no blood and no gunshot wounds. Do you know what that means?"

"What?"

"It means Jasmine didn't kill her mother."

"Thank God," Danny said with a sigh of relief. "I was so worried about her. She would have never been able to live with herself if she had killed her."

"Where is she?"

"She's still sleeping. Should we wake her and tell her the news?"

After Gideon and Jasmine had arrived home from the party, he'd whisked her into the house. Two police cars and one private security car arrived only minutes after he had closed the front door.

Jasmine was silent the entire ride. When they entered the house, Danny was waiting at the front door. Jasmine ran into his arms and wept into his chest.

"Are you all right, Jasmine? I heard everything on the news." He then looked at Gideon and mouthed the words, "Is she dead?"

Gideon simply nodded his head yes.

Jasmine did not speak. They took her into the guest bedroom and put her under the covers. The tears were flowing, but there was no expression of remorse, grief, or pain on her face. It was simply blank. Gideon and Danny sat on the bed next to her until she drifted off to sleep.

The police officers and the security guard tapped on the door only once.

"Hello, Mr. Truman. I'm Officer Bryant, and this is Officer Kantor. This is Scot Wilkins with Pastor Cleaveland's private security," said one of the officers, pointing to a plain-clothed man standing behind him. "We just want to let you know we will be posted in the front and back of your home this evening. You all are safe tonight."

"Thank you, Officers," Gideon replied nervously and closed the door.

He and Danny had been awake the entire night, tormented by the thought that the girl sleeping in the next room had killed her mother and they were the only people who knew it.

"No, let her sleep," Gideon said after hearing the morning news. "She may not have killed her, but her mother is dead nonetheless," he added, sitting down at the kitchen table next to Danny. "Now both her parents are dead."

"But at least she doesn't have blood on her hands."

"It also means we're safe now, Danny. She can't hurt us anymore."

"Poor kid. No parents. What is she going to do now?"

Gideon was silent for a moment, then said, "I hope you don't mind, but I told her she could stay here with us as long as she liked."

"You're a very special man, Gideon Truman, and that's why I love you. Of course I don't mind. It's the right thing to do."

Danny rested his head on Gideon's shoulder. There were moments of silence between them before Danny finally asked the question that was now on both their minds.

"Then I wonder who killed her?"

At 7:23 p.m., Sunday evening's regularly scheduled programming was stopped suddenly to provide viewers with the latest on the death of Samantha Cleaveland.

"We are interrupting this program," reporters across the country said in unison, "to bring you live coverage of the press conference that is just about to start at the Los Angeles Police Department, where police chief Anthony Cordova is said to be announcing the cause of death of Pastor Samantha Cleaveland."

"We've received the toxicology reports from the coroner's office," the chief announced, reading from a prepared statement, to the sea of cameras. "Pastor Samantha Cleaveland died of a massive coronary brought on by the introduction of the substance known as digitalis into the glass of champagne she drank after giving a toast to her late husband. Traces of the drug were found in her system, on shreds of glass from a champagne flute, and in the liquid that was spilled on the steps when she dropped the glass.

"Digitalis, also known as digitalin, is typically prescribed to patients suffering from congestive heart failure. It has been determined that a lethal dose was placed in her glass, which led to a fatal increase in her heart rate. Digitalis is derived from the common garden plant known as fox . . ."

Hattie Williams turned off the television in her living room. The house was now quiet. The only sounds were the *tick, tick, tick* from a clock that sat proudly over the fireplace, in the center of the mantelpiece.

Hattie had undressed and gone straight to bed after being driven home from the party. It was the first night in months that her sleep was not interrupted by the haunting dreams. There were no visions and no visitors from the other side. She slept deeply and woke to the sound of a sparrow singing just outside her bedroom window. Somehow the world seemed more peaceful than the day before. The coffee that morning was more satisfying than usual, the sun seemed brighter through her windows, and her spirit was at peace.

The first words she spoke when she woke that morning was, "Lord, forgive me for not listening to what you were trying to tell me all this time."

At 11:00 that morning, she cleaned and prepared the collard leaves she had picked from her garden on Saturday. Just as she had predicted, there was plenty of time to cook them, because the glistening cathedral in the center of downtown Los Angeles was locked tight.

This was the first Sunday she had not gone to church in years. The last time she had missed a Sunday morning service was ten years earlier, on the day after her husband died.

That afternoon Hattie picked up her purse from the couch in the living room and walked into the kitchen. The smell of collard greens filled the house, even though she had already eaten an early dinner and the leftovers were neatly tucked away in the refrigerator. Hattie sat her purse on the counter next to the sink and slowly removed the contents.

A crumpled wad of clean Kleenex was first, followed by her wallet, a powder compact, three peppermint candies wrapped in cellophane, and a small tube of her favorite lavender-scented hand lotion. The last thing she removed was another Kleenex, this one neatly folded. She carefully unfolded the fragile white paper and held it over the side of the sink that contained the garbage disposal. When she turned the Kleenex upside down, two green stems, each less than half an inch long, fell into the sink. The paper was still slightly damp from the liquid that had oozed from the stems.

Hattie used the Kleenex to scoot the stems down the drain. She stuffed the Kleenex down behind them, turned on the water, and pressed the garbage disposal switch on the wall just above the sink. Hattie washed her hands under the warm running water. *Lord, I'm sorry I waited so long,* she thought as she applied an extra squirt of dish washing liquid to her palm. *Hezekiah might still be alive if I had listened to you sooner.*

As she dried her hands, she heard the chimes of her doorbell. "Lord, who could that be?" she said as she made her way to the front door. "Hold on," she called out. "I'll be right there."

When she opened the door, she saw Gideon's silhouette through the metal screen door.

"Hello, Mrs. Williams. It's Gideon Truman. I didn't get a chance to speak to you last night. I wanted to make sure you were all right. May I come in?"

"Of course, baby," she said. "That is very sweet of you. Please come in. Would you like something to drink? I made a fresh pitcher of lemonade for my dinner. Are you hungry? I could warm something up for you. There's plenty greens left. I always make enough just in case someone drops by unexpectedly."

"That is very kind. But no thank you, Mrs. Williams. I've already eaten. Have you been listening to the news? The police are saying Samantha was poisoned with digitalis." Gideon watched her face closely for the slightest reaction, but there was none.

"Yes, I heard that," Hattie said as she made her way slowly down into her favorite chair. "Sit down, baby."

"Thank you," he said, sitting on the couch directly in front of her. "I can't stay long, but as I said, I wanted to check on you. This is all so tragic."

"Yes, it is," she agreed.

"It's unbelievable that they were both killed only months apart and in such similar ways."

"How do you mean?" Hattie asked.

"Well, you know. Hezekiah was killed in front of the entire congregation, and then Samantha was killed in front of all her guests."

"I never thought of it in those terms."

"If it weren't so sad, it would be almost . . . poetic," he said, studying her face. "I mean, it's as if it were orchestrated by some higher power."

"Everything in this world is orchestrated by a higher power, baby," she replied. "Even death."

"Yes, ma'am."

"Are you sure I can't get you some of those greens? I picked them fresh yesterday."

"No thank you, ma'am. Mrs. Williams, do you know where digitalis comes from?"

"No, baby, I don't."

"From foxgloves. Don't you have a foxglove plant in your garden?" he asked coyly. "I remember you showed it to me the last time I was here."

"That's right, Gideon," she replied, looking him directly in the eye. "Is there something you want to ask me? If there is, you should go on and get it off your chest before you explode."

"Well, as a m-matter of f-fact, there is," he stuttered. "I don't know how to say this, but . . ."

"The only way to say it is to say it," she said boldly.

"All right. Mrs. Williams. Did you poison Samantha Cleaveland?"

Hattie flashed the gentle smile of grandmothers throughout the ages. "Now, why would I do something like that?"

"I've been wondering the same thing ever since I heard the cause of death. I didn't make the connection at first. But I did a little research on the Internet, and then it hit me. The flowers in your garden contain one of the deadliest poisons in the world and have been used for centuries to commit . . . murder."

"I know that, honey. I told you they were poison, but you still haven't said why you would think I killed Samantha."

"Ma'am, I also remembered how personally you took Hezekiah's death. Almost as if you blamed yourself. Like there was something you could have done to prevent it."

As he spoke, a tear rolled down Hattie's cheek.

"You always knew she killed him. As a matter of fact, I suspect you knew it even before she did it. Am I correct?"

"Yes, I knew it," she said, lifting a handkerchief to her mouth. "I should have warned him, but I didn't. He would still be alive if I had listened to what God had been trying to tell me."

"I saw Samantha put her drink down next to you just before she invited everyone into the foyer."

"She was the devil," Hattie said gently, sobbing into the handkerchief. "If I hadn't done it, a troubled woman would have done it and ruined her and her baby's life. I couldn't let that happen."

"What woman?" he asked gently. "What bab—"

Before he finished the question, the picture of the little girl sitting on the mantel in Scarlett's living room flashed in his head.

"You did it for his child."

"Yes," Hattie said resolutely. "I couldn't protect him, but it wasn't too late to protect his daughter. Her mother was going to do something that would ruin their lives. I couldn't let her do that."

The two sat in silence. Hattie stared out the window as the summer sun slowly set. The ticking clock on the mantelpiece chimed 8:00 p.m.

Gideon finally stood and walked over to Hattie. He kneeled down beside her and took her hand in his.

"Mother Williams," he said softly. "Let's never speak of this again. I'm going to go out back now and dig up those flowers. I'll destroy them for you."

Hattie looked into his eyes. Another tear rolled down her cheek.

"Thank you, baby," she said, gently squeezing his hand. "You do that. I won't be needing them anymore."

Gideon stood and began to walk toward the back door.

"Gideon," Hattie called out to him.

"Yes, ma'am?"

"Take care of Danny and Jasmine," she said. "They need you."

"Yes, ma'am. I will."

The joy in the Sunday morning church service at New Testament Cathedral was palpable. Brass instruments, drums, violins, guitars, and pianos caused the sanctuary to pulsate with rhythmic music. The two twenty-five-foot-high JumboTron screens alternated rapidly between various sweeping images of the twenty-five-thousand-member congregation standing, clapping, and singing in the glass cathedral.

Four months had passed since the death of Pastor Samantha Cleaveland. On cue, the pace of the music gradually shifted to a more melodic and reverent tone. A soprano sang a hypnotic tune, and the audience obediently chimed in. A billowing hum from the crowd rolled from the front of the church to the top row and filled the room as congregants softly sang in unison and looked upward to heaven.

The camera followed Percy Pryce from the front row as he walked up the steps to the center of the stage. To his left and right at the pulpit were the waterfalls that poured ribbons of water into the pools below. Then a booming disembodied voice filled the sanctuary and announced to the congregation, "Ladies and gentlemen, Brothers and Sisters, please stand with me and welcome our pastor, Reverend Percy Pryce, and his lovely wife, First Lady Cynthia Pryce!"

Cynthia stood on the front row and turned to wave to the crowd as they rose to their feet and erupted into thunderous applause.

Scarlett sat quietly on the forth row and straightened Natalie's crinoline dress as Percy approached the podium. Gideon, Jasmine, and Danny remained seated on the third row, directly behind Hattie Williams. Hattie sat on the second row with her cane resting on her knee and the patent leather purse at her feet. She closed her eyes and prayed silently, *Lord, bless New Testament Cathedral this Sunday morning*.

ORDER FORM
URBAN BOOKS, LLC
97 N18th Street
Wyandanch, NY 11798

Name: (please print):_______________________________

Address: _______________________________

City/State: _______________________________

Zip: _______________________________

QTY	TITLES	PRICE
	16 On The Block	$14.95
	A Girl From Flint	$14.95
	A Pimp's Life	$14.95
	Baltimore Chronicles	$14.95
	Baltimore Chronicles 2	$14.95
	Betrayal	$14.95
	Black Diamond	$14.95
	Black Diamond 2	$14.95
	Black Friday	$14.95
	Both Sides Of The Fence	$14.95
	Both Sides Of The Fence 2	$14.95
	California Connection	$14.95

Shipping and handling-add $3.50 for 1st book, then $1.75 for each additional book.
Please send a check payable to:

Urban Books, LLC

Please allow 4-6 weeks for delivery

ORDER FORM
URBAN BOOKS, LLC
97 N18th Street
Wyandanch, NY 11798

Name:(please print):_______________________________

Address: _______________________________

City/State: _______________________________

Zip: _______________________________

QTY	TITLES	PRICE
	California Connection 2	$14.95
	Cheesecake And Teardrops	$14.95
	Congratulations	$14.95
	Crazy In Love	$14.95
	Cyber Case	$14.95
	Denim Diaries	$14.95
	Diary Of A Mad First Lady	$14.95
	Diary Of A Stalker	$14.95
	Diary Of A Street Diva	$14.95
	Diary Of A Young Girl	$14.95
	Dirty Money	$14.95
	Dirty To The Grave	$14.95

Shipping and handling-add $3.50 for 1st book, then $1.75 for each additional book.

Please send a check payable to:

Urban Books, LLC

Please allow 4-6 weeks for delivery

ORDER FORM
URBAN BOOKS, LLC
97 N18th Street
Wyandanch, NY 11798

Name: (please print): ___________________________________

Address: ___________________________________

City/State: ___________________________________

Zip: ___________________________________

QTY	TITLES	PRICE
	Gunz And Roses	$14.95
	Happily Ever Now	$14.95
	Hell Has No Fury	$14.95
	Hush	$14.95
	If It Isn't love	$14.95
	Kiss Kiss Bang Bang	$14.95
	Last Breath	$14.95
	Little Black Girl Lost	$14.95
	Little Black Girl Lost 2	$14.95
	Little Black Girl Lost 3	$14.95
	Little Black Girl Lost 4	$14.95
	Little Black Girl Lost 5	$14.95

Shipping and handling-add $3.50 for 1st book, then $1.75 for each additional book.
Please send a check payable to:

Urban Books, LLC

Please allow 4-6 weeks for delivery

ORDER FORM
URBAN BOOKS, LLC
97 N18th Street
Wyandanch, NY 11798

Name: (please print): ___________________________

Address: ___________________________

City/State: ___________________________

Zip: ___________________________

QTY	TITLES	PRICE
	Loving Dasia	$14.95
	Material Girl	$14.95
	Moth To A Flame	$14.95
	Mr. High Maintenance	$14.95
	My Little Secret	$14.95
	Naughty	$14.95
	Naughty 2	$14.95
	Naughty 3	$14.95
	Queen Bee	$14.95
	Say It Ain't So	$14.95
	Snapped	$14.95
	Snow White	$14.95

Shipping and handling-add $3.50 for 1st book, then $1.75 for each additional book.
Please send a check payable to:
Urban Books, LLC
Please allow 4-6 weeks for delivery

ORDER FORM
URBAN BOOKS, LLC
97 N18th Street
Wyandanch, NY 11798

Name: (please print):_______________________________

Address: _______________________________

City/State: _______________________________

Zip: _______________________________

QTY	TITLES	PRICE
	Spoil Rotten	$14.95
	Supreme Clientele	$14.95
	The Cartel	$14.95
	The Cartel 2	$14.95
	The Cartel 3	$14.95
	The Dopefiend	$14.95
	The Dopeman Wife	$14.95
	The Prada Plan	$14.95
	The Prada Plan 2	$14.95
	Where There Is Smoke	$14.95
	Where There Is Smoke 2	$14.95

Shipping and handling-add $3.50 for 1st book, then $1.75 for each additional book.

Please send a check payable to:

Urban Books, LLC

Please allow 4-6 weeks for delivery

Notes

Notes